KU-124-078

Acknowledgements

The author and publisher are grateful to the estate of T.S Eliot, through Faber and Faber, for permission to reproduce an extract from 'The Wasteland'.

Scriptures sourced from the Good News Bible published by the Bible Societies, Harper Collins Publisher Ltd U.K. and the American Bible Society 1966, 1971, 1974 and 1992.

We are further grateful to Denise Dodkin for all her hard work on the editing and formatting of this book.

To: Dareshia

Fond Regards to Ray & Louise,
Whose combined efforts at D.I.Y
always left my drum DAMAGE
RENDERED!

L.O.L.

Jonathan E. Richards

Happy are those who reject the advice of evil people
But evil people are not like this at all;
Do not follow the example of sinners
They are like straw that the wind blows away
The righteous are guided and protected by the Lord
But the evil are on the way to their doom.

(Psalm 1)

Chapter I

The mountain was looking its best, sharp against the blue sky. A few buzzards winged their saturnine way around in the foreground, foraging aerially for their breakfast. There in the stand of pines by the fort a foal skipped playfully watched with pride by her mare. It was one of those cool, crisp, invigorating, Montana scenes, barely witnessed by any human this day but the town's newest resident, Bryan Creet.

Creet drank from a glass with a petroleum corporation logo, enjoying the daily first of his many bourbon interludes. He lit a cigarette and sat down on the wooden bench which ran the length of the frontage of his shack. It was seven a.m. He would go down into town soon and order up a flurry of pancakes with maple syrup and strong coffee to wash them down.

It was only the fourth week Creet had been in Moonstone and yet he had settled into an unbending routine. He enjoyed the last gulp of his rich libation then trod out his cigarette butt on the decking. He put his hip-flask into his pocket and walked towards town. As he strolled down the rather disingenuously named *Main Street*, hands gently linked in the small of his back, he felt happy – perhaps for the first time truly in ten long, terrible years.

"Hiya man," acknowledged the sheriff thru an iridescent fug of cheroot smoke.

"Nice mornin', ain't it?" replied Creet, taking his customary seat by the window.

"Sure as hell is!" exclaimed Baker, smiling his gap-toothed grin.

Creet took the proffered coffee, absent-mindedly warming his fingers on the white cup.

"How ya doin'. There're ya pancakes, Bryan."

"Thanks. I sure need these today," said Creet politely.

He had the same thing every day, requiring minimal verbal contact now in order to maintain the proprieties with his new acquaintances.

Kim, a brunette, returned from the bathroom and poured herself a milky coffee. Creet's eyes casually met hers and she smiled. He wolfed down the second of his pancakes and tuned into the radio station that was currently playing a Beach Boys song. Fleetingly it occurred to him how incongruous the epitome of sixties West Coast cool seemed in the environs of down-home Moonstone.

"Whatdya think o' this business then, sheriff?" asked Baker, pointing to the front page of yesterday's newspaper showing the cataclysmic scenes at the World Trade Center.

"Gotta nuke 'em back – that's the only goddamn language these terrorists understand," he replied. "Things will never be the same again!" he added, shaking his head.

"Sure. Right you are, sheriff," averred Baker bashing the page.

Creet was sure too that the retired lawman was speaking the truth. He had watched the whole unbelievable event unfold on television. He and billions of others could not believe that this assault on the citadels would not be comprehensively answered by Bush and the Pentagon. If anything in the history of the last fifty years demanded nuclear action then positively this heinous crime did.

He finished the last of his breakfast, bade everyone farewell in his usual understated way and made for the door. Creet looked up at the frosted alp and smiled. With beauty like that what right had he to feel anything but joyful at his new life. He halted outside the general store and got himself some cigarettes and a loaf of bread. He went home, his mind full of the vastness of the evil just perpetrated against his country, yet still a semblance of individual contentment channeling thru the endorphin process centers in his brain. It was hardly inexplicable considering the fact that the natural world, which he had so craved whilst in jail, was now liberally all around him.

Creet walked up the dirt track to his ramshackle abode, the home that (for all its domestic privations) he had dreamed of, to the point of obsession. No one locked their doors in the magnificent wilderness around here except of course for the Yuppies who frequented the weekend cabins on the southern edge of town.

He went in and, as was his wont, went to the bathroom and the chemical toilet that due to the isolation of the shack had been deemed too costly to upgrade by his predecessor. There would be no way he either would be able to link up to the town's system in the foreseeable future, but the inconvenience of the arrangements was to his mind not a burning issue after a decade of penal insanitation.

Having completed his ablutions Creet went out onto the veranda and took a slug of liquor. He lit a cigarette and, looking at the awesome view of the mountain, he started ruminating on what he was to do with the day. He had spent the time since he had arrived on the bus doing nothing in particular. 'Acclimatizing to the freedom' he called it when catching himself yet again wasting his days reading his Raymond Chandler collection, supine on his divan.

Thus the weeks since liberating his lungs from the fetid atmosphere in his cell had passed in a hazy blur of whisky, smokes, hardboiled P.I.'s and natural beauty. Whenever a translucent moment of perspicacity dawned on him between books or when a bottle prematurely was exhausted at night, Creet did question himself thru a miasma of guilt about what he was to do next with his life – guilt which not only reflected his short-term self-indulgence but deep regret in regard to his whole life.

All of a sudden his peaceful reverie on the rickety decking was interrupted by the footfall of another person approaching. He had received no visitors until now – either because of his demeanor or by local custom, his solitude had not thus far been intruded upon.

"How're you doing," she said, her voice a blend of Midwest and possibly metropolitan influences.

"How're you," he answered noncommittally, not even a trace of a smile lighting his granite-set features – the safe straightjacket of routine that he had acquired in prison and persevered with since his release now compromised.

"I've been camping in these woods for the last three days," she went on by way of introduction, sensing that his lack of hospitableness might be the instinctive reaction of a preternaturally cautious man.

"Hhhum," Creet mouthed softly, his eyes taking in the woman's backpack and dirty jeans, her khaki cap and hiking boots.

"Thing is — I had a kinda accident with my car about five miles back."

She pointed in the vague direction of the road that ran thru the forest.

"I was driving along fine and then a mink or a stoat or something suddenly ran out into the road and I automatically slammed on my brakes. I must have skidded on the wet leaves and I ended up wrapped around a tree."

"I get ya okay," commiserated Creet in his singular way. "You're all right though?"

"Yeah, thanks. I think so," she said. "I was lucky I was wearing my seatbelt."

She un-strapped her rucksack and settled down unbidden on the steps. Creet saw that she was slightly older than he had first appraised and also far better looking. She took her headgear off and shook her hair, which fell in lovely mahogany tresses over her shapely shoulders.

"I'll make some coffee," he offered, retreating into the cabin and flicking the switch on the electric kettle.

"I sure could do with a cup," she responded smiling, fidgeting in her flak jacket for her cigarettes and a lighter. She shouted thru the semi-open door, "Do you smoke?"

Creet demurred and went about getting the coffee things together. She seems friendly he thought, peeking a look at her in profile, sitting there on his stoop, taking in the sharp line of her cheekbones, the almost architectural ski-slope nose. She had obviously had quite a shock, an adventure, which he somehow deduced, was totally alien to her normal existence. Not so much the accident, he mused – although, patently, she had been fortunate – no, the story of her sojourn in the woods he felt sure, with some intuition which all human beings possess when surmising other people, had not yet yielded up to him all of its transforming detail.

"There you go – a nice hot coffee for you. You look like you need it," he said, handing her the cup.

"Thanks," she replied, Creet noticing for the first time her fine ivory-varnished fingertips, ladylike and sophisticated, reminding him with an internal jolt of a lover he had once had in San Diego.

"My name's Desdemona," she said after a couple of sips. "But mostly people call me Desi."

She downed the beverage insatiably.

"Bryan Creet. Pleased to meet you, Miss," he responded, allowing himself a smile as he held out his hand.

He suddenly realized that it was the first woman's skin he had consciously touched in ten years.

Silence took its insidious toll for the next twenty seconds whilst she devoured the reviving dose of caffeine. Creet could see that she felt uncomfortable, as he himself did, neither knowing what to say next to fill the void.

"Are you hungry?" he enquired at length. "I've got eggs and beans and it'll only take me a minute to fix you something."

"That's really kinda sweet of you," she replied, her face visibly relaxing at the way the situation had suddenly lost its slightly sinister air – real or imagined.

"Well, in that case, I'll go and start up."

He ambled into the kitchen and began busying himself with the can-opener.

"Thanks again, but I couldn't use your bathroom could I?" she called after him. "I haven't had a proper wash for days!"

Creet invited her in and led her there, explaining the inadequacies of the toilet but also that there was copious hot water and soap.

"I'll leave you to it and I'll go fetch those towels," he said, having shown her lastly the idiosyncrasies of the faucet above the tub.

Creet presently returned and gave two cotton squares to her. He went back to his cooking, wondering at this turn of events when only twenty minutes previously he had been debating with himself how he was going to fill his day. This was more excitement than he had had since moving in: a highly desirable lady naked in his bathroom.

Soon he completed the basic cuisine and lowered the gas. He strained to hear the state of progress in the bathroom and could just make out some watery sounds thru the wall. He would have a cigarette outside, he thought. It was by now nine-twenty a.m. and the lumberjacks with their chain saws were dimly audible. The air had a keen edge and he could see an osprey rising above a fir-covered knoll on a warm air column. He drew deep on his tobacco, inhaling the rich Virginian notes. Creet felt that he could do with a slug and as he savored the heat of the bourbon, there was the click of the bathroom lock.

She had dressed in fresh clothes. Her hair was damp and covered partially by an informal turban of white terry-cotton, her face flushed like a ripening apple. She looked beautiful, pristine like no woman had looked to him in probably two decades. He went inside and started doling out her meal.

"Why don't you sit down over there," he instructed kindly, motioning with his left hand.

There was a table that had seen better days on which he put down the plate.

"This is damn good," she complimented him. "Any ketchup?"

"No, sorry."

"Don't worry. I think I kinda prefer to taste my eggs plain anyhow."

While she ate her fill, Creet eyed her up surreptitiously from his vantage in the kitchen. She sure was a very attractive woman. Her eyes were almond in shape, cobalt blue in color, her facial skin a newly moisturized porcelain peach of feminine grace. She was wearing black leggings now and blue kitten heels, her white blouse not quite buttoned-up revealing a "V" of glowing skin.

"Do you want a bourbon to finish with?" Creet asked at length.

He had enjoyed watching the spectacle of her eating, was pleased that she had consumed his humble offering so ravenously.

She nodded her assent and he poured a finger of whisky into a glass.

"Cheers!" she ventured and downed the ochre liquid in one hit.

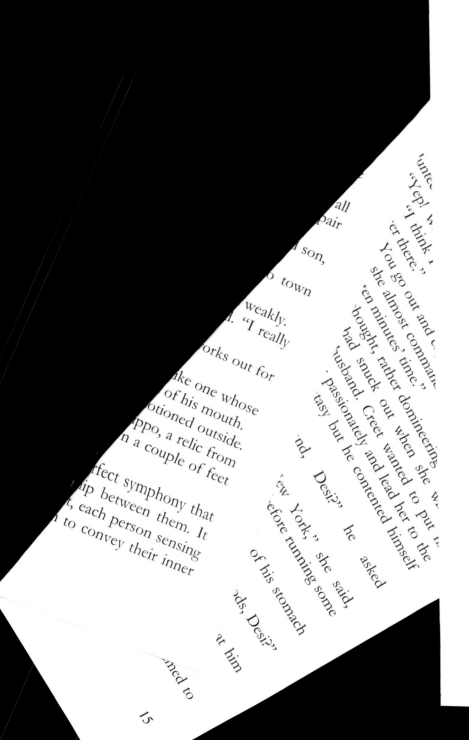

"I must ring my husband," she said. "I coul et a
signal from the woods. He'll be really worried ab
just go outside."

"I'll wash the dishes," announced Creet,
elegant legs stride onto the veranda.

She had stirred a long-latent sexual
All those years in jail he had dreamt i
woman like Desi, but now that she
could hardly bear it. The theoretical l
had been a fictive device only to get
and night. Desi here, sexy and
proposition altogether. He could
her presence welling up within
that they had given him had p
interregnum which he was nc
he had had a woman must
His eyes narrowed against
to admire the gorgeous
against the backdrop of

"That's mighty str
perplexity. "There's
off, not ever."

"Maybe he's in
pondered Creet, although,
the 1990's, had been left comple
in telephonic technology.

"No, I think something's wrong. I ca
responded, striding inside once more.

"There's no point getting all worked up at this sta
Creet advised. "Give him fifteen minutes and try again."

14

Creet put his unlikely, pessimistic thoughts to the
back of his mind and accepted the coffee newly served. He
reached for the half-full bottle of Kentucky and offered her
a tot as if by way of apology for giving her what he could
only discern were the heebie-jeebies.

In silence he poured the liquor, smiling that lopsided
rictus of his as he did so, eloquent testament to his anxiety
and sorrow at upsetting her.

"What's happening with the car?" he asked as he
fortified his own drink with the spirit.

"Oh yeah," she responded, as if she had forgotten
about it. "I suppose I had better ring a local auto re
shop. Do you know of any?"

"Sure there's one in town. It's run by a father an
the Dempseys. I ain't got the number though."

"That's okay," she said. "I'll take a walk int
when I've finished this."

She raised her cup slightly and smiled at him
"Thanks for all your help," she commented
appreciate it, you know."

"No problem. I sure do hope everything
you."

Creet spoke the words in a distant way
mind is not really connected to the autopilo
He lit her up à la Bogart with his trusty Z
his old days in Tucson, and they sat dow
apart.

Sometimes people are in such pe
words merely befuddle the relationsh
happens sometimes merely by defaul
the inadequacy of their own lexico

16

voice and thereby at risk of despoiling the moment by ill-considered words. Symmetry of silence is thus the prevailing result. It was so here. Totally without the tension of the previous silence between the protagonists, for an elegiac seven minutes the mood was set fair, the only sounds a woodpecker and the distant spluttering of the chain saws. They saw a bald eagle swoop across the superb vista and a flock of Canada geese fly above the sphagnum moss-like treetops to and fro the lake.

At last she rose, shook his hand and, nodding to Creet, picked up her backpack and walked off in the direction of the town. Neither party felt a requirement to verbalize a 'farewell' – it was as if they both somehow inexplicably knew that they would meet anon.

I pursue my enemies and catch them;
I do not stop until I destroy them.
I strike them down, and they cannot rise;
They lie defeated before me.

(Psalm 18)

Chapter II

"I'll have pastrami on rye to go. Hold the mustard," the bespectacled man instructed.

"Three bucks, thanks," said the deli-boy at length, handing over the sandwich. "Have a nice day, now."

The man walked across the street and into a sixties-build office block. At the entry phone grid a brass plate proclaimed 'Montana Probation Service'. He went up in the elevator to the third level and used his key card.

"Hiya, Marv," said a girl self-consciously.

She was not unattractive, but at only nineteen she was still displaying the puppy fat which when it receded would enhance her looks tenfold. Recently she had been told by her line manager to stop calling her superiors by their surnames — it was allegedly an informal working environment.

Marvin Pentavsky went to the office percolator and poured himself a large cup in a Styrofoam, before entering his glass-encased office.

He picked up the phone and dialed 552.

"Hello Dunk," he said to the security guard on reception, the man whom he had just passed, unacknowledged, when he had come into the building.

"Yeah, Marv. You gotten them ponies?" he replied conspiratorially, drawing the pad on his desk closer.

"Sure do. You ready?"

"All set. Fire away."

"Okay. The first one is in the second at Columbine, Transco Gal, No. 6. The second is Mantra Ray in the fourth at Prairie Meadows – No. 2. Got that?"

"Sure. Yeaaaa."

"And the third is Salt Lake City Boy in the first at Arlington, okay – lucky No. 7."

"Huh, um yeah."

They put their receivers down in synchronicity; the important deed of the day done for both and it was still not quite nine-fifteen a.m.

Pentavsky slurped his coffee, realized that he had forgotten his Sweet 'N' Low and picked up the phone again.

"Krystal, hi! Um... have you, er... have you got any sugar substitute. Yeah. Thanks."

He watched her size fourteen figure beat a path to the box of sachets by the coffee machine, retract a few and then sashay over. He watched her black skirt billow as she meandered thru the office.

"That's real kind of you, Krystal," he thanked her, putting on his best serious, professional face and shifting some papers on his desk to make it appear he was extremely weighed under already.

"No problem, Mr. Pent....I mean, um, er... no problem, Marv," she stammered, retreating from the goldfish bowl office of the senior official.

Marv stirred his newly sweetened beverage and unwrapped his sandwich. He could never understand why people wanted mustard smothering the authentic taste of the sausage-meat. He set about wolfing his breakfast with a relish however, eyes focused on the card at Arlington in the newspaper spread before him.

Before too long the office started to fill up. There, Chuck and Ben, Grade 3 officers both, occupying the window seats across from each other, twenty years' service between them. More central in the office, Candy and the rather stunning Amy, administrators, who had started in the same week, not six months previously. It went on and on until the whole wide expanse of desk-strewn floor space had become a bureaucratic nirvana of pen-pushing, typing, filing and computer activity.

He looked up at the tap on the door. There was Dirk Niemeyer, his long-suffering lieutenant, punctual for the morning debrief session.

"Morning Dirk! How the hell are you? Siddown," Marv said jovially, screwing up the brown paper from the sandwich and aiming and firing, with aplomb, at the steel trash can eight feet away.

"Yeah, fine," he said in his slow Louisiana drawl. "I lost a couple of heavy dudes yesterday though. Could be a problem. One of them was in for six for aggravated burglarizing and the other, a Murder 1, had just done a fifteen stretch."

"What the hell's going on?" Marv snapped.

He took a sip of coffee, a grim expression now deepening the furrows on his forehead.

"Well, seems they've both taken off – one on a Greyhound it seems. That's the Murder 1. The other was last seen at the railroad station."

Niemeyer spoke matter-of-factly, maintaining eye contact all the while. He would have Marv's job one day – they both knew that – but in the meantime, until the powers-that-be, in their infinite wisdom, decided to deal with Marv's lackadaisical approach to both management and paperwork, he had to be professionally courteous to the boss.

"So do you reckon they're OTLD," Marvin Pentavsky asked of his deputy. "Should we notify the F.B.I.?"

Niemeyer could not reconcile his superior's question with the prevailing situation. It was a statement of the obvious that these two violent men had to be treated with the utmost caution on the assumption that neither surely would jeopardize his parole to attend a convention on motherhood and apple pie. The enquiry was one more borne out of concern for saving his own skin career-wise rather than that for any members of the public who may fall foul of the fugitives.

This brought to seventeen the number of parolees who had absconded during the year to date. Of these, thirteen had had to be referred to the Feds, as on all known information they could be dangerous, and the others had been kept in-house, so to speak, as there was no known violent background in their files.

"We have to notify," Niemeyer replied.

"Yup. We've no choice, but it's damn bad news just before the autumn review....?"

Marv trailed off, shaking his head so hard that his spectacles vibrated on the bridge of his aquiline nose.

"They are the very definition of 'On The Loose and Dangerous'," stated Niemeyer. "If one of them does do something we've got to have covered our asses."

He had elucidated the main reason dancing in Marv's mind as to why it was essential, now that the formal sixteen hours had elapsed, to bring in the G-men. Niemeyer was political enough to know that a leavening of empathy with the boss, on occasion, was no bad thing and definitely greased the wheels on their often-fraught professional relationship.

"Anything else to report?" asked Marv, exasperatedly.

"Nope, nothing else. Shall I fax Seattle Feds with the description of this Sholtz charac…."

"What," Marv interrupted sharply. "What's his name?"

"Robert Sholtz," said Niemeyer, enunciating the name, this time, with a definite second syllable 'Tze'.

"Why didn't you mention this before," the boss, leaning forward now, quizzed him, eyes ablaze.

"What! You know this guy?" said Niemeyer, his gaze drawn to the peculiarly pressurized vein palpitating below Marv's hairline.

"Know him! That's like asking if Hoover knows Al Capone or if the Pope knows Ali Agca. Of course I fucking know him!"

Marvin Pentavsky stood up. A few employees who had him in their sightline reacted instinctively to the movement and optically homed in on the sight of Marv abruptly raising his shirt and tie to his chest, revealing a horribly gnarled abdomen like a relief map of Colorado, blood red and ravined, a skin topography free of normal, unblemished, unpuckered flesh.

"Oh my God," exclaimed his No.2, clutching his palm to his mouth and involuntarily retching.

Niemeyer scooped his handkerchief out of his pants with his other hand.

"Yep! I know him! I should remember the fucking son of a bitch!" cried Marv, reclaiming his seat, still unbuttoned. "Fax Seattle, call Smithson, call O'Hara, call Colin Powell if you have to. This guy is one badass with a capital B."

"Okay. I'm onto it straight away. No problem," reacted Niemeyer, swallowing down the remnants of milky cornflakes that had recently made a surprise reappearance in his throat.

The rest of the floor had now been alerted to the strange scene which had been unfolding in the office and there was a general low-level hubbub as colleagues discussed in hushed tones what had been occurring between the two most senior personnel in the regional operation.

Niemeyer disengaged himself from his meeting with the boss and made immediately for the water cooler. He took a plastic cup and filled it up with cold still water, then drank it down in one draught.

Chuck, a career probation officer, who it was thought in the office had missed his true vocation as a Klu Klux Klan wizard, looked up from his work-station and spoke solicitously.

"You okay, Dirk?" he asked, watching the man's ashen face gradually trying to resume its normal hue.

"Yep. I'm fine thanks," he replied, leaning forward onto the plastic barrel in a fashion that belied his words.

"You don't look so fine to me, no siree! What the hell was all that about with the main Marv?"

He shot a look across at his colleague Ben as if to bring him into the nascent conversation, knowing that his own limited powers of diplomacy alone may not elicit the necessary information.

Niemeyer swallowed hard and pushed himself up to his full stature.

"It's nothing. Gotta press on," he said. "I've a very full day ahead."

He nodded at Ben, took his leave and went back to his own desk, sitting down with a heavy sigh.

He picked up his phone and made the requisite calls. For nigh on three years he had worked alongside Marvin and been rewarded with less insight into his past than, on all known criteria, was normal. For all his bravado and temper tantrums, he knew now that the man had been thru something devastating in his life, and he felt strangely drawn to him for all of his previous antipathy. Nevertheless, his ignorance of the full horror of what had happened all those years ago gnawed at his inquisitive mind.

It was a non-smoking building and Niemeyer needed a smoke. He went down in the elevator, past Dunk, who raised his eyes and gave a half-smile, and out into the sunny freshness of the still demure city. A cigarette was lit and he put one foot against the outer wall of the lobby, breathing in the nicotine and wondering what exactly the next few hours would bring.

A parole officer's work is never done, he idly mused, always something new to make the stomach heave or the heart to skip a beat. He knew that the department had a good record on finding and catching absconders and that the co-operation of the F.B.I. was often critical. Something however prevented him from being complacent in this singular case, an inner voice seemingly at pains to warn him of the dangers that lurked around the corner – threats not only to his and his staff's personal safety, it seemed, or to the civilian populace, but also to his thus far unsullied career record. He could not rationalize whence this clairvoyance emanated however – he just sensed it with his every electrical connection.

He watched the lights change at the intersection and the traffic roar off. He stubbed out his cigarette and re-entered the office block. It was going to be a long day, a day that he would long remember but it was to be a week that he would long try to forget, that he would wish to obliterate from his cerebellum if he, in truth, could. Niemeyer did not know this at this point. How could he? Yet here was a man of silent strangeness and festering internalizations who did not disavow the psychic dimension of life, as nor indeed did he actively believe in it. Nevertheless he now felt the imprimatur of fate in his soul, felt that his life had, in some peculiar way, been leading up to this juncture in space and time and that there was nothing he could now do about it except stay strapped into the rollercoaster for the ride.

"Dirk, I've got Special Agent O'Hara of the Seattle Feds on the line. Do you wanna take it here?" Chuck asked, holding the phone out to him as Niemeyer hurried to his desk.

"No, transfer it," he instructed. "Extension 221. Yup. Thanks. Hello Mr. O'Hara. Any news on Sholtz yet?" he enquired coolly, yet feeling anything but.

"Well, Mr. Niemeyer. We've had a sighting of him in Bozeman. Fortunately the Greyhound was delayed. One of our agents was able to interview the driver and it seems the guy did alight at the depot. We're working now with the police to find him. We've notified Amtrak, Hertz, Avis and the airport and are interviewing people from the passenger list just in case he let something slip. He's only had a ten minute start on us because of the delay. Lucky break we've had here...."

O'Hara paused for breath.

"Thanks. What else are you doing?" Niemeyer asked.

"Well I've got every cop in the region watching out for him and I've got our own guys checking out hotels and showing his mug shot on the street. He can't get far. We'll get the bastard. You can bank on it."

"Yes. Thank you," reiterated the probation man. "Thanks for acting so quickly. This guy's a real piece of work. We've gotta get him fast."

"Yeah, well. We're well aware of that," responded O'Hara archly, not reacting well to Niemeyer's statement of the blatantly obvious. "I'll call you when there's any more news."

"Thanks," said Niemeyer for the fourth time in a minute, replacing the receiver.

He looked up and his gaze was met full-on by Marv, one dark raised eyebrow commanding him sonorously to fill him in with the update on his old and, still to Niemeyer, mysterious nemesis. He walked into the glass cubicle and told him exactly what had transpired.

"This guy's gotta be caught for all our sakes," said Pentavsky, his expression blanker and yet somehow more intense than Niemeyer had ever previously seen.

"What exactly did this motherfucker do to you?" he asked softly. "I mean I think I should know, so that I can tell O'Hara. It may have a bearing on how they run the search. You never..."

"I can't tell you more than I can show you," Marv snapped back.

"I can understand your reluctance to go over it in detail after all these years, Marv, but it might be relevant and important to the ongoing search and investigation," he went on, feeling his superior officer's eyes searing into his own, as if oxyacetylene torches trained on living tissue.

At length Marv adjusted his stare and began to speak in little more than a whisper, a sotto voce monotone suffused with a long suppressed pain.

"A long time ago I was married with a kid, a little girl. I came home early one night. I let myself in quietly – I had flowers, blue irises, Holly's favorite. Holly… was my wife. I wanted to surprise her and not finding her anywhere else in the apartment I went into the bedroom…. There was my wife in bed with Shhhh…."

He stopped, tears welling up, not able to say the name that was now almost as detrimental to his physiognomy as any battlefield biological weapon.

"He had been a housepainter I'd hired to decorate the apartment, our apartment," he continued, distressed, Niemeyer helplessly listening with a sympathetic frown.

"I stood there, the blooms in my hand, looking on, completely stunned… mute, I s'pose. And then he came at me with a knife, a bowie. No warning, just flailing, naked, ripping the blade into my midriff, screwing it in, gouging the flesh. I tried to stop him with all my might but I couldn't. He was too strong. He held me with his left hand and cut me and…all the while Holly was screaming 'Stop! Stop!'. I fainted – only to come around in hospital six hours later."

He took a tissue from a box on the desk and blew his nose, then palmed it and hurled it across the room wide of target.

Niemeyer could hardly believe his ears. The bestiality of the scene conjured up could hardly have been more shocking. He insinuated himself into the chair, his legs suddenly feeling weak as Jell-O, tears trickling down his cheek. He too took a tissue and dabbed, vaguely conscious that people were starting again to look.

Marv's eyes, it seemed, were all wept out long since, the moistness shining forth not translating into an actual cascade. His body had become too accustomed to the exterior symptoms of his agony and had learnt to compensate. Niemeyer could hardly however guess at the depths of the interior agony that he was now experiencing in reliving the episode after so many years of mentally concreting it over.

"I'll never forget the moment I came round. There was a nurse adjusting the drips in my nose. She had a gold crucifix around her neck, with a silver Christ appliquéd to the cross. I'd lost half the blood in my body, had tubes in my arm. I couldn't move an inch because of the stitches and the bandages. I would lie like that for ten days – my consciousness bludgeoned by morphine."

He paused again. Niemeyer, maintaining a grimace of vicarious anguish, waited for the denouement of the story though not certain that he could physically cope with it, barely repressing, as he was, a spasm of lung fluid in his throat.

Pentavsky was, whatever his faults, a man who once he started something did not flinch from finishing it. And so it was to be here. However, given the sheer mental torture of retelling these terrible events from almost seventeen years ago, he could have been forgiven for breaking down. He wiped one solitary tear away with his finger and forged on, eyes focused intently on the shooting star screensaver in front of him.

He recommenced his brutal statement.

"Finally I was conscious," he held forth once more. "I asked the nurse about my darling little girl, Sabrina, who had been sleeping in her cot in the next room. She was fifteen months old, the most gorgeous..."

Again he broke off, double-swallowed and recomposed himself for the final descent into that hellish emotional crevice from which it was increasingly obvious he could never – except in some pale pastiche of living – extricate his perma-frosted heart.

"The nurse said she would go get someone. Minutes, maybe hours, I don't know, went by and then a detective came into the room. He introduced himself and said that he was really sorry. That there had been an incident – an incident!"

Marv spat out the word, a term so obviously flawed and underweighted for the gravity of the events that he was about to describe. His head was oscillating now.

"There had been a fire at the apartment. 'Your wife and daughter died before the Fire Service had reached the scene,' the officer told me. Those were his precise words. They had been strangled. Sholtz on the other hand had left me for dead in his haste at getting out. Another twenty minutes to the paramedics arriving and I would have bled to death – if only!"

Niemeyer handed his boss his own carefully laundered handkerchief from his breast pocket. He stood up and touched the shoulder of the man now finally letting go of his taut, reined-in grief. As he shut the door behind him, he could hear a sobbing which tone was unlike any that he had ever heard before or since, a sound so awful, the final dam-burst expression of years of unimaginably pent-up mourning.

Dirk felt not a little guilty at having been the catalyst for such volumes of distress but as he returned to his desk and glanced thru the glass viewing Pentavsky's rocking form, handkerchief covering his face, he realized that this was something inexorable that would have had to come out eventually anyway were this man ever somehow to start to live once more in any meaningful way.

His first priority was to oversee the capture of the madman before he could destroy any more lives. He clicked on the mouse by his computer terminal and went into 'Criminal Histories'. Finding Sholtz's biographical details, he scrolled down to the period of the mid-eighties. Nothing was there in detail about Marv's family at all, other than allegations of two murders and one attempted murder by a Mr. Marvin Pentavsky of Newton Asprill, Washington State, thus far uncorroborated. Then in 1986 there was an alleged murder in Bozeman, in '87 an alleged murder in Glacier Park, Montana, and finally in '87 also a conviction for the murders of two women in Billings, Montana. It seemed that all the other cases had been dropped by the State Prosecutor for lack of evidence once they had finally caught him and having accumulated enough forensic evidence from the final case to launch a pharmacological corporation.

Niemeyer watched as Candy ventured hesitantly into Marv's office amid much curious inter-desk chitchat and placed a soothing hand on his arched shoulder. This merest frisson of human contact seemed to stem the tide somewhat and within a minute he was red-eyed but otherwise back to a seemingly normal level of operational efficiency.

The phone rang on Niemeyer's desk. It was a routine call from the state penitentiary. The working day seemed to be returning to the mundane and that was in truth how he liked it. He rose, walked over and poured himself a milky coffee, with two saccharine tablets, side-stepping or stone-walling the fervent and well-meaning inquisitions of his colleagues as he did so. He said a silent prayer to God in thanks at the Teflon-coated life that he had thus far led.

Life with a capital L was for him however only now nosing into the starting stalls. He had always suspected that he was less a quarter horse than a mile and a half specialist. Now at the age of thirty-seven he somehow felt that he may soon be given the opportunity to prove it.

But I am no longer a human being;
I am a worm,
Despised and scorned by everyone!
All who see me jeer at me.

(Psalm 22)

Chapter III

Desi found the repair shop and lingered outside; there seemed no one there. The street was deserted. The sparseness of the little town, the solitude she suddenly felt, all alone as she was, acted on her to call her husband again.

She pressed the buttons. There was no response, only the unilluminating message from the telecom company stating the obvious. She really wanted to hear his voice, that special timbre he reserved for her; to regale him with her adventures and to sense the unspoken love in the gaps between his words – like a code that only she possessed the key to. Now she was starting to become more concerned; it was the first time in eleven years of marriage that she had not been able to dial him up whenever she wished. It was probably nothing she told herself with renewed effort – most likely a technical problem.

The sun glistened on the red BMW above the inspection pit. Desi noticed the Californian number plate; another holidaymaker with an auto problem, she thought, like herself holed up in this godforsaken place for the duration. Still there was no sign of a mechanic. Desi glanced at her watch – it was almost eleven. There was nothing for it but to wait for one of the Dempseys to appear.

She took out her packet of cigarettes and placed one between her lips. She could not find her matches immediately, however. Presently she heard the click of an electronic lighter and, looking up, saw a man offering his cupped hands protecting a flame. She accepted the light and inhaled, looking the fellow up and down.

"Thank you," she said having taken in the Native American complexion and cheekbones, the suede tasseled waistcoat and baggy hide pantaloons.

"You looking for a mechanic, lady?" he asked, putting his accessory artfully into an inside pocket.

"Yes. Do you know where they are?" she came back at him.

She offered him her last cigarette, knowing that she had cartons in the trunk of her car.

"Sure do, Miss," he answered, his tone rich and wearing the overlay of many years of strong tobacco use. "They're over there in the café."

"Thanks," she said, watching him light his reward with consummate care.

He shuffled off down the dusty sidewalk and Desi crossed the road. The sooner her car was back on the road the better, she thought, as she galvanized herself before pushing open the door. She had sampled enough small town color for the moment. She wanted her all mod-cons apartment, her state-of-the-art quadraphonic music system, a fine Merlot over dinner with Trip, before curling up together and re-affirming their wedding vows to the strains of Rachmaninov. In short she could not wait to take repo of her life – the same metropolitan glossiness of which had palled over recent times to the extent of instigating her journey westwards and which now she coveted anew with all the craving which had stirred her to take off ten days previously.

"I'm looking for Mr. Dempsey," she stated simply, to nobody in particular, her nostrils filling with the odour of steak and eggs.

"You've found him, Miss," responded a late middle-aged man with greasy overalls and a Teamsters Cap.

"My car needs repairing urgently, Mr. Dempsey. I need you to pick it up from the woods about five miles back and fix it up for me."

"Have you had an accident, Miss?" he asked, raising a chocolate brownie to his mouth.

"Yeah. I sure did. I went off the road and straight into a tree," she answered. "The engine's all mangled up."

Desi looked at the mechanic imploringly even as she heard her own sentence and the realization dawned on her that the prognosis was, in all probability, not good.

Dempsey wiped his mouth and swallowed; his Adam's apple swelled and then resumed its rightful place. He took a swig of soda from the can and shook his leonine, gray-haired head.

"Don't think I can cure that in a hurry, Miss," he said sagely. "Sounds like the vehicle's a write-off."

"Can't you do anything?" she pleaded, her stature, so braced on entering the door, now listless.

"All depends of course," Dempsey replied, working out options in his mechanic's brain.

"Money's no problem," she ventured, smiling at him and moving nearer to his table. "I just want to get back east. If there is some way to patch it up I…"

"Sure. There may be a way. It's not gonna look pretty and I might have to send away for parts," he interrupted, rubbing his stubbly chin with his hand, unbeknown to him smearing chocolate over his jowls. "If that's the case it may take a long time. Most probably not worth it."

"I see, Mr. Dempsey. Whatever you can do I'd really appreciate it," she said, taking out her credit card wallet from her money-belt and letting the subtle glint of gold and platinum plastic recount its own testimonial.

"First thing we do – I gotta see the auto," he said rising to his feet. "If it ain't worth fixing I'll tell you straight, Miss." He grinned at her. "I can go now if you're amenable", he offered, draining the last of his drink.

"Okay. Let's go then, Mr. Dempsey," Desi responded and the two of them meandered between the tables and exited.

The pick-up was battered yet solid and as they drove off down the country lane and along by the lake, Desi finally felt she was getting somewhere – hopefully a little closer to home. Dempsey himself, taciturn yet friendly, buoyed her up in this new sense of progress; he seemed to know his business well. It had taken her six days of hard driving to arrive at her destination, sleeping in the car at night, and although she did not relish the return journey, she did not want to give her husband the satisfaction of his being right all along. He had said for months that she was a city girl now, overly pampered and soft and that the vast landscape of the North West was no place for her to be traveling and camping alone. Desi wanted to be able to return triumphantly with the jeep or at the very least to be able to drive back in another car the two and a half thousand miles – to prove that she could do it. He would be so very proud of her and now she lived and breathed the anticipation of that moment of reunion with Trip. If nothing else this whole adventure had brought home to her the depths of her love for him.

"So you were camping out here were you?" Dempsey asked at length.

"Yeah. Suree was," answered his passenger with a little wry laugh at her own colloquialism and at the simultaneous image of Betty Hutton in Annie Get Your Gun that flashed thru her mind.

"No place for a woman out in these woods alone," he mooted with chauvinistic gravitas.

"It was all right…until I crashed the car," she returned. "I needed some space to be myself for a while."

"Nope. I'd never let no daughter of mine camp out in these woods," he reiterated, offering Desi a cigarette.

He ignited it with the lighter in the dash and she thanked him.

She looked out the windshield and saw the magnificent vista of the Rockies in the distance, a wisp of cloud obscuring the saw-teeth ridge, and the ever-present wildfowl swirling in formation above the clear blue water of Deadman's Basin. She sucked in the smoke and blew out fluently, the more flavorsome tobacco of Dempsey's brand agitating her throat. The scenery up in these parts was incredible, she thought. She would not have missed her sojourn here in Montana for the world.

A small outboard motor launch was making its way across the two hundred yard wide expanse of shiny meniscus and she could just hear the twentieth century noise above the antediluvian screeching of the gulls. A mother swan and her three adolescent progeny alighted on the timber-framed foreshore bumbling along to sip at the lapping edge. Everything was becalmed – the major part of

36

the bio-diversity of these virtually untouched environs neatly hidden by the millpond mirrored surface which glinted and dazzled with the reflections of the huge blue skies and the mountains.

Soon the pick-up rounded a bend, leaving the lake behind and entering a densely spruced canopy above the road. She remembered now that the skid of twelve hours before had been caused by a sudden jink in the road just ahead, as much as by the jaywalking wildlife.

"It's coming up. Slow down!" she instructed Dempsey, revisiting the moment when due to fatigue and prolonged self-absorption she had jammed her foot on the brake too precipitately and floundered into a fir tree.

"There it is, just where you left it," grinned Dempsey, pulling gently off the road and stopping. "Sure don't look too good from here though."

The two of them left the truck and walked over to examine the wreckage. It was indeed a sight; the bonnet had sprung up at impact and hugged the peeling bark of the tree. In despair at the newfound day-lit presentation of her beloved trans-continental vehicle Desi let out a scream of frustration.

Her mechanic eyed the debacle of the crushed engine, one half of its former length and stooped to see the axle that seemed prima facie to be intact. It had been a headlong crash and no lateral forces had impinged on the wheels. The engine had however taken the full brunt and was beyond saving. That much seemed self-evident, even for a laywoman like Desi.

She waited for the expert's verdict. She could not believe that she had not realized the extent of the damage when she had awoken, but it had still been partially dark and, if she were being honest with herself, she had not really checked it out, was still in fact suffering shock at her narrow escape. If she had not been wearing the safety belt then she would now be in pieces like the fractured windshield. After a night on the backseat she had not really been concentrating on anything other than finding a hot coffee and some human sympathy for her recent travails. How close she had come to being another anonymous statistic she only now was coming to apprehend and she became suddenly visibly upset.

"You sit down, Miss," coaxed Dempsey, leading her over to the open passenger door of the 4 x 4, his hand flat and comforting in the small of her throbbing back.

"I never knew it was this bad," Desi cried out. "I'm lucky to be, lucky to be…."

"Yup, I know," said the mechanic, chivalrously helping her into the seat, watching the mascara run down her cheeks and onto her blouse.

"Let's go," he said. "There ain't nothing we can do here."

Desi dug in her pocket and jangled a key fob in front of his nose.

"I've got to get my stuff from the trunk," she insisted thru the sobs.

"No problem. I'll get it all out and put it in the back."

Dempsey spoke with a nice manner, his words soothing Desi, and as a consequence her inner strength reaffirmed itself, the physical expression of relief of the uncondemned woman began to subside.

Soon they were on their back to Moonstone. The fact that Desi had stopped crying only mitigated a little in favor of her leaving on the great trek home to New York in her present state of mind. Although she could hire a car, she would, she realized, perhaps be more sensible to book a flight and get home in one day rather than six.

"You feeling any better?" enquired Dempsey after a couple of miles during which time they had not seen another vehicle, so isolated was this piece of God's own country.

"Yep. I think my tears are all used up now," she said quietly, sneaking a look in the rear-view mirror and dabbing a moist wipe over her besmirched eyes.

"So what do you want to do now?" he asked casually.

"I think I owe you some money, don't I," she confided in a cod-conspiratorial tone, fishing in her purse for a fifty.

"Thanks. I appreciate that," said Dempsey, tucking the bill securely into his work jeans where the IRS would never find it.

"I suppose I can't just leave the car where it is, can I?" she asked. "I better sort things out properly with you and the insurance company."

"Don't worry 'bout all of that. That's easy. We can sort out the details any time. I know a scrap yard where they'll come out and pick up the car if I give 'em a call."

He spoke loudly against the droning of chain saws.

"Fine. That's fine. Do you mind if I leave all of that to you," she said touching up her eyes. "I just want to get to the airport and get on home to my husband."

"Like I say I'll handle that, Miss. And I'll get my son to drive you to Seattle if you like. You go ahead and call your airline. See if they've got a flight this afternoon…"

His voice trailed off at the end, remembering the news that he had heard over breakfast on the radio: that many flights had been suspended and that there was general disruption to timetables because of the huge increase in security.

They pulled into the small town, a place seemingly untouched by the terrible news from the East Coast, and Dempsey got out of the pick-up.

His son had been upstairs where he and his father lived in comfortable bachelor accommodation above the shop. Now he had resumed his duties in the inspection pit, a ghetto blaster blaring out the latest songs.

Dempsey senior called out to him above the music and after a decent interval, monkey wrench in hand, he emerged, looking surly.

"Todd, can you give this lady a ride into Seattle?" he said.

"Why's that, Pa?" he asked.

Dempsey explained the circumstances of how the lady had pitched up in their neck of the woods and how Todd could combine doing her this favor with picking up a carburetor from the General Motors dealership in the city.

Desi had felt the patronizing chauvinism in Dempsey junior's face as her story had been related and now turned to the younger man.

"I'll pay you two hundred bucks, Todd, of course," she volunteered, sensing amused detachment merge into newfound interest.

"Sure. No problem," Todd agreed. "We'll leave in an hour. I wanna get myself cleaned up proper first and have something to eat."

He went out back and Desi could hear his footfalls on the stairs.

"I'm sorry about my son, Miss," Dempsey apologized, when sure that he was out of earshot. "He's got a difficult edge on him sometimes. He's had a bad run lately – but he's a good boy."

"No, that's okay. I should have offered to pay you a proper fee earlier," she replied. "I wouldn't expect a free ride."

"Well it's almost midday, now. How about you go for a coffee across the road and come back here for one O'clock."

Dempsey studied the dial on his left wrist as if he were planning a bullion job and was at the synchronizing watches stage.

"Yes, that sounds fine," she averred with a smile. "I can't thank you enough."

"I just hope that you can get a flight okay," Dempsey stated half-distractedly, hearing as he spoke the familiar jingle of the radio station transport segment which always augured in the news bulletin.

Desi had for the past few hours attempted to banish all pessimistic thoughts of her non-responsive husband from her mind. Because this had never happened previously it did not mean anything in itself. It could be that the model of cell phone which he had had for some time now had at last given up the technical ghost. The battery possibly could not be replaced being of defunct issue, that Trip perhaps had dropped it in the bath or perhaps numerous other perfectly benign explanations.

What she had not done, as yet, was to call home or to call the office or to have begun to wonder why she had not received a call from her doting husband for days now. She had however only been trying him for a few hours and he had been primed in no uncertain terms not to call her incessantly and devotedly but to allow her the space that

41

she had requested and required from him as much as from Montana itself.

She pressed the redial button and heard the now familiar refrain in computerized robot-speak: – 'The cell phone you have called is unavailable. Please call again later.'

She rang home now – no answer was forthcoming.

Desi sat in the café spooning white sugar into a cappuccino. She cursed herself mildly – it was a Thursday. He would most likely still be at work. Pressing the auto-dial, she could feel the reflexive pulse in her index finger; it was a sure sign, she thought, that her heart was palpitating beyond the norm.

There was no tone however from the phone, no ungracious switchboard operator or overly ingratiating receptionist, no voicemail service for Trip as per usual if he were not in the office or was in the men's room. Nothing. No Trip. She could not understand; the phone number of one of the most prestigious stock broking companies in New York was simply dead. There was no obvious rational reason for this that she could compute in a hurry in her mind. Why would the company's phone be so out of order on a weekday, costing thousands upon thousands of dollars in commission for every missed deal? Desi paused and took a lipful of froth off of her hot coffee. Now she was seriously concerned as well as not a little nonplussed. 'What the hell is going on?' she mentally exclaimed.

She espied a Danish in the chill cabinet and called out to effect her purchase.

"There you are," the proprietor said. "That's a buck, thank you."

He placed the gleaming pastry on the table in front of her, next to her phone. A necessity for comfort eating was freshly upon her.

The whole episode of running thru the gamut of abortive calls had taken merely a couple of minutes, such are the time-saving propensities of twenty-first century technology, yet it seemed more like hours, such was the total change of mindset orchestrated in Desi by the whole business. A feeling of deflation and intuitive metamorphosis had somehow taken over her, shrouding her mind in a black depression.

As long as she did not use the home and work numbers she had been able to retain some composure about Trip's uncommunicative cell phone. He often worked from the study in the apartment and that was the reason that she called at four O'clock in the afternoon Atlantic Seaboard Time. Calling the office and receiving no ringing tone was completely impossible to fathom and, needless to say, extremely disturbing.

'What the hell is going on?'

She again posed the question internally to herself. Her finger once more found its way onto No. 3 on her speed-dial. Again there was no normal ringing tone, merely an aural void coming back down the line. If it had been a fire alarm test then surely the voicemail on Trip's direct line would have been activated. Anyway it was not relevant because there was no ringing tone, no nothing. She now called the reception desk once more – again there was a telecommunications black hole. Deep concern instantly transmogrified into the vice-like grip of sheer panic.

Desi raised the Danish to her trembling lips and took a dainty bite out of one crumbly corner. She had come all this way to the back of beyond to find her spiritual and emotional identity. This, ironically, had been proved over the last week to be bound up inextricably with that of her husband. She was all set to go back and confidently reinvigorate their married life together, knowing now, as she did, that she loved him more than she loved herself – that nebulous creature who did not ever know solidly what she wanted in life... until now. That was the meaning of Montana for her; this self-knowledge could only be good – to ably empower her to enjoy their joint lives again, secure in the belief that there was no other life for her that she would ever covet, that she could not, would not desire to live without her husband by her side for the rest of her natural span.

She lit a cigarette and ruminated over just what could be up with Trip's workplace telephone system. She attempted to approach the conundrum rationally and with a cold logic like she did sometimes to problem areas of her life, albeit with scant reward for she was an emotional woman at base. It was the surging tides of her feelings that she was ever in thrall to and which varied consistently, making her sometimes unknown even to herself, and yet eminently knowable for this same paradox by the man who loved her beyond reason.

She was on the point of calling his cell-phone again when on the radio the news broadcast commenced, and life for Mrs. Desdemona Montifort it seemed was effectively neutralized as an effective fighting force forever. If she was the last adult person of sound mind to hear of the Twin Towers disaster then she was also surely one of the most hysterically affected in that moment of truth dawning. Before the first sentence of the broadcast was complete a projectile vomit of pastry and apricot in their semi-digested state had taken up temporary squatters' rights on the Coca-Cola branded icebox.

A deranged caterwauling emanated from her larynx like a lunatic she-wolf, before she psychologically collapsed in on herself amidst a monsoon of hysterical tears.

It was to be minutes before she came round in the café, yet years before she could ever look at a Danish pastry again. In those few seconds of frequency modulation her life had changed completely and utterly.

Little did she know what else lay in store for her just around the temporal corner.

And certainly it was a blessing that she did not.

Don't be worried on account of the wicked;
Don't be jealous of those who do wrong.
They will soon disappear like grass that dries up;
They will die like plants that wither

(Psalm 37)

Chapter IV

Bozeman's top hotel was how it was billed. The place had become the trendy haunt of weekending young Hollywood bucks and their sleekly long-thighed, inordinately blonde escorts. The turn of the last century architecture owed much to Old Orleans riverboats in its emphasis on curlicues and cladding, stucco and gilt. Deep-pile carpet enveloped the guests in its colorful repeating motif of a stylized eagle over a craggy peak.

The hubbub of the bar was palpably less than normal for a Thursday night, yet still people had flown up from Southern California for the weekend in their Lears and were up for showing themselves a good time – in the vernacular of those dark days, to carry on as normal lest the terrorists should think that they had won. Although the atmosphere was muted the bartender was having a little trouble with one particular new customer who was behaving in a way that could be conservatively described as rumbustious.

He was dressed not in the expensive casual gear favored by the majority of the other customers, but rather in an ill-fitting, polyester suit and a stained white shirt. His inky black hair was unkempt and two days growth of beard completed the look. He had arrived a couple of hours previously and been drinking heavily – neat bourbon. Having ordered and partaken of a club sandwich, with buffalo wings on the side, he continued plying the bartender with drinks and insisted on talking to every client, mostly in vulgarities. The bartender was loath to put an end to the spending spree however as he was surreptitiously saving up his 'tips'. The man was nonetheless as out of place in that lounge as it was possible to be, a relic from another age, another class, a throwback to the old gold prospecting times when the Grand would have been full of men like him: men newly pitched up in town after long railroad and stage journeys from Chicago or Philadelphia or Virginia, desperate for a drink, a meal, a woman and a bed for the night – preferably in that order. Robert Sholtz was adhering to the same litany, ogling every female in the hotel and making ill-mannered remarks. Ever since entering he had seemed desperate to have his own singular version of fun to make up for all the abstemious years.

"Give me another, bartender," he shouted. "And have one yourself."

"I'm afraid I can't serve you anymore sir," the youth told him with all the feigned confidence that he could muster.

He had just seen the hotel manager coming on duty.

"Give me a drink!" Sholtz bombasted. "After all the drinks I've bought you. You no good, pathetic son of a bitch! If I don't get my drink in this glass right now I'll pick up your scrawny body and throw you outta that door. Do you get me son!"

Everyone looked deep into the mysteries of their glasses, as if trying by psychic means to divine the alcohol by weight percentage. All conversation came to a sudden halt. There were at least two former cinematic heroes in the bar and one stuntman but no one intervened, no one fancied coming up against this intimidating six foot three rascal.

Silently the young man, feeling the lack of moral support behind his long overdue stand, reluctantly placed the whisky tumbler under the optic.

"Thanks boy," the man shouted, leaning forward into the bartender's face so that his halitosis could be savored. "That could be the wisest decision you'll ever make, son. Cheers!"

With that he downed it in one, slamming down a twenty-dollar bill.

For a while the general chitchat resumed, the fugitive ordering another drink, receiving now no contradiction from the callow youth, who had, on the contrary, become obsequious in the extreme.

It was eight forty-seven by the clock in the hotel lobby when in strode a lady to check in. She wore a scarlet designer trouser suit over a low-cut peach blouse and white high heels. Attractive in a willowy, hard-faced way, her lips and eyes made-up immaculately, she was in no sense beautiful. A bellboy was bidden to retrieve her luggage from the hire car and to park it in the lot. She signed in with a practiced flourish and made purposefully for the saloon doors. Her eyes caught the attention of the bartender and, having driven for hours, she treated herself to a glass of chilled Chablis.

Sholtz had noticed her come in; his gaze had alighted upon her as quarry most likely if he were to tick all the boxes this night. He had made a fool of himself already with a variety of women but this one had raised his antennae in a way that the younger, better-looking ladies had not. Perhaps he felt that he was in with a chance with this one, more of a parity of pulchritude perhaps, or simply because he had taken an instant shine to her in an uncalculating way. Whatever the reasons, conscious or subconscious, he leant across to her and formally introduced himself.

"Hello there. Robert is the name. Can I buy you a drink, ma'am?"

He spoke slowly, concentrating so much on his enunciation that he had forgotten that he was Bruce Watson as far as booking into the hotel went.

"No thank you. That's most kind of you, though," she replied, smiling with all her features save her eyes.

"Come on honey! Let me buy you a drink," he persisted, almost snarling the words that came with a subtext which she did not fail to pick up on: that drink did not equate to drink alone and that the tacit suffix to the offer were the words 'or else'.

"Please Mr..." she responded.

"Watson," he intoned self-consciously.

"Please Mr. Watson," she went on, keeping her composure. "I do not want a drink – thank you very much."

Sholtz now went up thru his pathological gears and again the myriad of conversations in the large square room ended on his cue.

"You fucking bitch. You're just like all the other tarts in this dump – frigid and up your own ass. Get out before I get angry, you whore... you bitch!!" he declaimed, as if on stage, which in a very real sense, in that setting, with those luminaries of the movie industry hanging on his every word, he, of course, was.

The businesswoman had driven three hundred and fifty miles for a peaceful weekend and some great panoramic views and within minutes of arrival had been insulted like never before. She remained calm however and, picking up her glass, left for the restaurant.

It was a matter of seconds before Sholtz followed her, to general disquiet, thru the double doors. The barman hurriedly called security and relayed the incident.

Within the confines of the hotel lounge a TV in one corner was on with the volume turned low. Suddenly an image of Robert Sholtz flashed up on the screen and a number of people instinctively pointed it out to their respective circles. The sound was turned up and an F.B.I. man being interviewed about a dangerous absconder reduced everyone to a hush.

It was Sholtz's good fortune that September 11th had happened on the day he had taken off. The news of a maniac like him on the loose would otherwise have been much more widely promulgated – to the extent that he would not have been able to travel as freely or to have been able to sit unrecognized in a respectable hotel for so long. He had pushed his luck too far and now the harassed young man was again on the phone, dialing the number the G-Man had given out.

******

"Oh there you are," said Sholtz prosaically, on finding the object of his affections in the restaurant poring over a menu.

He placed his bulk in the chair opposite, his thighs spilling out over the edges of the gold and damask, an image exacerbated by the shambling suit that hung off him in all directions.

"I like you, you've got class," he added.

"That's not what you just told the whole hotel," the lady answered, her outward placidity belying inner tumult.

"I'm sorry about that," Sholtz said. "Let me buy you dinner to make up it up to you, lady."

"You don't have to do that and I'd prefer it if you left me alone," she stated boldly, her knees beginning to knock under the table.

At the entrance to the restaurant appeared two hotel security men, regarding the vignette with not a little unease.

"I'm awful sorry if I frightened you, ma'am. I can see I should go now. I apologize again for my uncouth mouth."

He finished speaking, aware now that he was in a tight spot.

The mirrored wall of the dining room and her furtive glances beyond his right shoulder had alerted him to his predicament.

She did not say anything now, merely a slight incline of her head to indicate that she had heard his repentance speech, as a priest in the confessional, acknowledging simultaneously both the gravity of the sin and the intention of atonement.

Muzak was playing as usual throughout the lobby as four cops turned up. They were ushered over to the security men who looked relieved.

51

Sholtz could see their reflections retracting automatic weapons from their holsters and preparing to effect an arrest. The lady viewed the scene with astonishment, having had not an inkling that the obnoxious man who had been pestering her was worthy of this degree of paramilitary attention.

Sholtz had, in his own lexicography of logic, no option now if he was to avoid going back to jail. At worst he would die in the attempt but would give himself at least a chance of escape. The continuance of life anyway held no meaning for him if it meant not being able to follow his own course – the sick self-impelled trajectory of his own internal Mr. Hyde, destined never to be free of the tourniquet of societal norms, even as he knew he could never hope to control his dark core. He had at least profound insight into his own warped, irreparable, untetherable id.

"Sholtz, the game's up," cried the senior officer. "Raise your hands slowly and stand up."

"My name's not Sholtz," he shouted back, keeping a weather eye still on the silvered glass wall and edging his left hand into his inside pocket very, very slowly. "My name's Watson. Look, I've got ID"

"Put your hands up!" shouted the policeman.

"Sure I'll put my hands up if you want me to," Sholtz replied, as if having the most normal of discourses. "I'll show you my driver's license."

He held his arms aloft. In one hand he had what appeared to be the documentation.

"Go get him," the officer ordered his lieutenant, who stepped forward, gun focused on the man's lumbar region.

"Take my ID," Sholtz invited, the cool of a confirmed megalomaniac driving out the last vestiges of alcohol-induced slack from his criminal mind.

The younger policeman went to cuff him. The steel ring went onto the right wrist first. Tension in the room reached a critical point as the first metallic click was heard.

"Okay. Now the other hand… nice and easy, fella," he said, switching his stance to the left of the prisoner and tugging the free handcuff and the conjoined arm over to the other side of Sholtz's body, preparing to conclude the arrest.

Sholtz looked subtly sidelong into the mirrors and saw a distinct relaxation in the faces and body language of his three other would-be nemeses. They all still had their weapons pointing at him directly, but his native wit, honed to a sharp edge over a career of confrontation with the forces of law and order, spelt out to him that a crucial moment had been reached.

As the officer went to put the other cuff on Sholtz's outside wrist, the lady, who had been watching the whole drama unfold like some surreal nightmare, finally discovered her true voice.

"He's got a gun! Watch out!" she exclaimed in an increasingly accelerating high-pitched voice, loaded with nerves.

At the second consonant of 'got' Sholtz elbowed the officer in the solar plexus.

He fired at the policemen in the doorway as he turned around, taking care to keep the bent-double body of the other lawman between him and them. The cornered con let off one round, the officer's midriff taking the bullet. He groaned and loosed a shot by reflex into the far kitchen door as he collapsed in a defunct heap. Blood seeped from beneath his tunic onto the parquet floor. By now the other diners had curtailed their culinary indulgence and ghosted away.

Sholtz kicked the weapon out of the nearest cop's grip and dodged a bullet each from the two still standing, their inaccuracy due, not only to the aftershock at seeing their colleague killed, but also to their reluctance to aim at the only partially visible target for fear of hitting their comrade-at-arms.

"I'll kill this one as well," the killer screamed, grabbing the man's neck with his forearm. "Drop your pieces, gentlemen, or this guy is a goner like your buddy!" Sholtz asserted, pulling the officer to him and pressing his semi-automatic against his temple.

"I won't warn you again!" Sholtz screamed, ratcheting his arm into the young man's throat, thereby reducing the available angle to his own chest so that even an Olympic-class marksman would have had only the riskiest of shots.

"Okay, you win," the captain admitted, having quickly weighed the odds.

He disengaged the clip on his firearm and threw it down so that it landed approximately six feet away from both himself and Sholtz.

He nodded to his colleague to do likewise. Both items of ironmongery now lay uselessly within fifteen inches of where the lady was sitting, she by now crying hysterically.

"All right. You've made the correct play."

Sholtz spoke the words very deliberately as he stretched out his left foot to retrieve the two guns. He caught each steel-gray short on his heel, dragging each in turn across the floor and putting them at his disposal.

"Now you two move over there into that corner," he directed and they promptly did, stepping over their slain colleague with respectful gait.

There were still two items that he had to secure. One was covered by the newly deceased and the other was in the near corner.

"Lady, go get those loose pistols for me," he ordered.

He sounded as if he had more verve in his tone, as if he felt a burgeoning confidence in his ability to, against all odds, actually marshal this situation to his advantage.

She raised herself from her seat and made first for the doorway, stooping low to pull the sidearm from underneath the policeman's partially eviscerated trunk.

"Now place it with the others," he drawled, alternately flicking his eyes from her to the male captives and back again.

He watched as she did his bidding, her mind in temporary paralysis at this situation that she found herself in, her physique full of newly acquired tics and tremors.

Now Sholtz possessed a wealth of semi-automatic weaponry. Gradually he lowered himself, putting the snub-nose of his gun into the hostage's nether regions as he did so. One by one he picked the pieces up, cramming two into his belt and the other two into suit pockets.

He could see one of the hotel security men speaking on the front desk phone. Elsewhere it seemed it was void of people – only the strains of Vivaldi fractured the eerie silence.

The psychotic realized the necessity for decisiveness if he were to convert a chance into an opportunity.

He pushed the young officer, sending him flying. In a follow-up motion, which was as seamless as it was unexpected, he pulled the woman to him with his right arm and stuck his Beretta up against her Dolce and Gabanna belt.

"Okay, lady. Let's move out," he said briskly. "Thru to the lobby, no funny business or I'll drop ya."

Almost as an afterthought, Sholtz turned to the law enforcement lookers-on and, with a flourish of his 92F, warned them what would happen should they try anything.

"You too. It wouldn't be good for yer health!" he laughed, demonically.

Hotel security had evacuated the whole of the ground floor during the standoff and so it was that the couple made for the main entrance unhindered and uncommented upon. Only the unarmed hotel detective and the policemen gazed upon the curious pair.

"Where're your car keys?" Sholtz yelled as they skirted the reception desk.

"I, um, I er… they must be …the bellboy parked my car" she flummoxed, her normally fine, confident Boston accent, now reedy and hesitant.

"Well they must be on your hook," Sholtz riposted sharply. "Go on, get them. You know your room number, don't you?

"Come on!" he exploded, forcing her bodily thru the little gateway to the desk, her lithe frame vibrating like an activated pager.

"Fifty-two, I mean three. No. Fifty-one. Yes. Yes, fifty-one," she floundered, then urgently reached for the keys.

"Come on. Let's go now!" Sholtz ejaculated edgily, thrusting her across the lobby and thru the revolving door.

It was a cool and star-filled night, the moon looking like a brightly lit station clock in its heavenly berth, languorous and yet somehow spiritual, as if recorded, deep in its white pristinity, were all the accumulated inhuman crimes throughout history that man has done unto man on the surface of her mother planet.

Within thirty seconds they had located the black hire car, a stylish Lexus, and she had started the ignition – Sholtz's body wedged in the well behind her seat, his favored weapon aimed above the automatic shift at her kidneys.

"Come on, drive!! DRIVE!!" he let rip. "Remember one false move and you're dead meat, lady!"

"Which way shall we go?" she replied, as the car negotiated the parking lot exit and approached an intersection.

"LEFT! LEFT!!!" screamed out Sholtz. "Step on the gas will you!" he commanded.

"Where are we going?" the woman asked, the necessary act of hand to eye co-ordination seeming somehow to have had a calming effect on her nerves.

"Hit the interstate and keep driving fast!" was all he would say.

He managed to turn his head uncomfortably, grazing the upholstery of the front seats with his temples as he did so, just in time to see three figures running down the steps of the hotel entrance. He shot three times in quick succession thru the rear windshield, dropping two of them. The killer screamed with unrestrained joy as he saw his victims buckle noiselessly. Retaliatory rounds from the remaining officer peppered the chassis and the side-window, before the car turned out of the line of fire.

It was all the driver could do to keep her shaking hands resolutely on the wheel, her eyes determinedly averted from the rear-view mirror so as not to make accidental eye contact with the madman's crazed expression. Even fleeting connection with those staring eyes, bright with insanity against the black backcloth of the car interior and the night beyond, made her sick to the pit of her stomach.

Within a short time Sholtz realized that there was no following siren. He could quite believe that the sole remaining guy had called for reinforcements – discretion being the better part of valor.

The road was not busy at this time of night and after five miles of hard driving the fugitive was gaining in confidence by the second. He was acutely aware however that the mobilization of the police helicopter always took a little time. They were going at a hundred miles per hour and so would be in North Dakota within an hour and a half if they continued their tarmac-burning progress along Interstate 90. One boon was that they were under cover of night; it would take some time amidst the chaos of the hotel for the license plate number of the vehicle to be gleaned from the rental company.

"What the hell is your name, lady," said Sholtz after a hiatus, his sight line level with her bosom, imbibing her profile with renewed gusto.

"Janet...Fielding," she replied, glancing around for a split second, as if to gauge what mood he was now in.

"Keep your eyes on the road," he berated her mildly, "And take the next turning off the highway, Miss Fielding."

"Okay," she answered, wondering to herself what reasoning he had for this change of course.

"That's the one, Janet," he said, as she took the car into the inside lane, preparing to turn off.

"Are you sure?" she enquired, noting the sign that stated that the next road was unmetalled and led to an old abandoned gold town.

"Yep. That will do for now," Sholtz replied. "Turn right and let's take it easy all the way to the old saloon bar," he chuckled.

He had seen the sign a mile back alongside one to Diamond City and had decided that he fancied a little detour with historical interest thrown in. Diamonds would always be a girl's best friend but for Sholtz, who, whatever else he was, was no gal and who sported two gold teeth, the glistening metal had always exerted a powerful draw. However, the primary motivation was that by getting off the main turnpike then he would certainly be safer. In an old place like this there would be plenty of shelter for them and cover for the Lexus too. The shantytown had for so long been devoid of people that the trees which encircled it would provide by now, he deduced, a useful canopy to park beneath, out of the way of helicopters and binoculars.

"Pull over on the left," instructed Sholtz, pointing to a grove of ancient redwoods at least thirty meters high.

There was a slot thru the trees and into this Janet Fielding drove the car and parked, ominously hearing the wild hubbub of the forest fauna reverberate as she switched off the ignition.

In the not too far distance a, sepulchral ghost town hoved into view thru the mist. Dung gases rose in wispy columns from the forest floor, dealing an unaromatic shock to her city slicker's olfactory sense.

Janet shivered as she looked around this place that the world and time had forgotten – she sensed a foreboding that seemed to emanate from every stick and stone, each fallen leaf and omnipresent owl.

In the midst of these thoughts she felt a cold hand on her cheek. In silence the kidnapper stroked it with momentary tenderness and inherent anticipation. No reciprocation of his touch was either required or forthcoming.

She sat ensconced in the velvety cloak of night, bolt upright, and yearned to be anywhere else in this vast and imperfect world.

For her however it was too late.

For her aroused kidnapper she was the vassal and the vessel into whom and into which he poured all of his long, long caged-up proclivities. Having used her, she was all used-up and would, could only slow him down.

He put her down like a veterinarian does with a sick dog.

It was almost humane after what he had done to her.

Chapter V

Creet took a slug from his bottle and slurped the amber liquid around his ulcerated mouth, allowing the alcohol to cauterize. He replaced the distinctive bottle on the shelf and strolled outside onto the veranda.

Taking his usual seat, he lit a cigarette. He glanced up at the range of mountains which hailed their full alpine majesty in the clear air. He sat, his face muffled by a scarf against the harsh northwest wind, his already chapped lips smeared with petroleum gel. How he wished he could somehow have inveigled that lovely woman, Desdemona, to have stayed with him, to have been his first sexual benefactress in over a decade.

There was a je ne sais quoi about her that he could not get out of his mind. It was not her obvious line in womanly charms that had taken hold of him so powerfully, rather some other something in her that he had liked. Rational thought did not any longer come easily to Creet and he sat on that rotting bench for hours, the cold biting, yet he oblivious to it, so immersed was he in his own internal monologue.

Finally, concentration flagging, he retreated inside and made himself another cup of coffee, lacing it with a prodigious amount of J.B.

His mental faculties, he believed, had deteriorated whilst doing his time, not just because of the lack of external stimuli, but because he consciously tried to switch off all of his intellectual processes in order to survive. The fact that he had been innocent of the crime and had hitherto led a blameless life compounded his psychological warp factor. He could not, in essence, deal with life anymore. In the penitentiary, if he had yielded to the potent impulse to reflect on his life, even on other things as he had used to, he knew that he would not have survived cerebrally intact. He would long since have gone cuckoo; the mental acrobatics, the internal discourses that he had 'enjoyed' with himself on all manner of things, scientific and philosophical, he had curtailed from the outset. To not do so would be to invite a long-term sojourn in the sanatorium. The tortuous mental furrows that he had ploughed in the past, leading him into depressive spirals lasting weeks, would have been completely untenable in the captive state.

Now that Creet was free he did not know anymore who he was or what he was to do with his future. Only the whisky gave his existence a veneer of pleasure and thereby a validity unto his own mind. It was the sine qua non of his existence now without which he could not envisage himself persevering.

The tranquil beauty of the landscape, which had indeed afforded him such peace these last weeks, was as nothing in the scales in comparison to the alcoholic prop which was now an ever-present in his bloodstream.

Gradually his brain, for so long inactive by design, had begun to fill again with all the flotsam and jetsam of tangential enquiries which he had once continuously entertained. Unlike air rushing to fill a vacuum, the obsessive-compulsive behavior swamped his mind by degrees, forcing his faculties only incrementally into their former template of self-inquisition – into discovering an infinity of solutions which for merely a few seconds may flatter to deceive and furnish an answer as elegant as it was unexpected. At that damascene point, of course, he felt completely vindicated by his quest, a heightened sense of animation in everything that he did and heard and saw and felt until the next query rising spoilt his party and the whole aberrant, futile cycle began again. He could however do no other. In truth he knew that he should have kept the iron discipline of the jailhouse going once he had served out his term, yet he knew that in fact he had not a snowflake in hell's chance of so doing, of fending off these inner dark forces forever – that in a very real sense his sentence was only now starting – and that he, having been freed, was now a lifer.

He sat, idly looking up at the apex of the mountain. A coot sounded in the distance, cutting thru his self-absorption. Creet wondered if this bird was truly free, exploring his own most contrary predicament by the avian parallel – that of a newly released man who was actually far more at liberty when behind bars, freed at least from himself. If only he could conquer his personal demons how happy he could be, he mused, yet he had harbored this delusional aside since adolescence and he knew by now, in his very guts, that it was an impossible flight of fancy to even consider this as a genuine possibility.

A mechanized noise in the distance impinged upon his otherwise engaged consciousness. He looked at interruptions as a double-edged sword, resenting anything which might divert him from his task and yet secretly fantasizing that this may be the precursor to an unblighted future, that this may be analogously the flapping wings of the proverbial Amazonian butterfly which leads on inexorably to a cessation of his own mentally exhausting internal storms.

Presently a black automobile pulled up outside Creet's property and a late thirties man with a gunmetal gray helmet of lightly oiled hair got out.

"Good Evening, sir," he offered Creet as an opening, igniting a slim cigar with his gold lighter.

"Evening," responded Creet, slightly disconcerted by the man's evident confidence in these environs when he had never seen him before.

"Have you seen anyone acting suspiciously around here recently?" asked the suited younger man, languidly puffing smoke out from the side of his mouth..

"Can't say I have, no," answered the homesteader.

"Here, take a look at this picture will you?" asked the man, putting a foot on the second step and leaning forward with a photo.

"Who are you anyway?" enquired Creet.

The man took out something and held it up.

"Officer Marvin Pentavsky of the Montana Probation Service, at your service, sir," he said courteously. "Please look at the photo, sir."

"No, I don't know him. I haven't seen him before," Creet said firmly, taking in the heavy, dark features.

"Well, sir, he's a dangerous convict who's taken off and we have reason to think that he could be around here somewhere".

"Okay," responded Creet. "I believe I heard something about him on the radio. He's taken a hostage ain't he?"

"Yes, that's right, sir. The guy's dangerous, very dangerous. If you see or hear anything at all call 911 urgently, won't you? He may be driving a black Lexus."

The probation officer put his card and mug shot away and slipped back into the driver's seat of his 1998 government issue Chrysler. He closed the door and drove off towards Moonstone.

Creet withdrew into the cabin and shut his door tight, applying the two bolts and chain. He pondered his action for a second or two, wondering at the fact of his own spirit for self-preservation, even now extant, and concluding that his life surely must mean more to him than perhaps even he himself had truly realized hitherto.

Bunkered in for the night, he started making his evening meal.

He ate slowly and thoughtfully and had finished his dinner of chili by seven, relaxing at the window with his hipflask fully charged, admiring the setting sun over the glowering forest. It was a strange sensation – the silence and the knowledge that out there in the semi-darkness a megalomaniac might be planning his next move, might be watching the self-same scene.

At length Creet heard a knocking on the door. After the visit of Pentavsky this startled him incredibly and he went directly to get a serrated knife from the kitchen. He peered thru the window but could not see who was there because of the angle, although he could just make out, in the gloaming, the outline of a woman.

'Could this be a trick to get him to open up?' he thought.

It must be the woman hostage, sent by Sholtz to deceive him. As soon as he unlocked the door the madman would overpower him. This man was highly dangerous. He must know that his life expectancy was not great with the law all over him like a rash. Sholtz would kill him as soon as look at him, he conjectured, and then make use of the cabin for a while knowing that the authorities had already checked it out and would not be back. The murderer and his unfortunate hostage had been probably watching from the woods when the probation officer had come by before, he speculated.

Creet felt his heart racing and globules of sweat rising to the surface of his forehead. He quietly perched on a stool in the deepening gloom wondering what the hell he could do. All the lights were off – that was one saving grace he told himself. Perhaps Sholtz would realize nobody was in and call the woman back. Maybe he would not wish to take the risk of breaking in to an unknown cabin, not knowing who was inside and what arms the occupant possessed. This was not suburbia after all. Furthermore by the appearance of the ramshackle edifice, Creet told himself, any fleeing convict would think twice about holing up inside, not knowing even whether the place would yield any food or even a telephone. No, there must be far better prospects to overnight for a man like Sholtz in his present predicament.

Creet ran these scenarios thru his neurological processors coming to the conclusion that he must not, under any circumstances open the door, nor turn on any light, nor make any sound at all until the danger was passed. It was still possible that they did not know anyone was in and would shortly give up and leave. This was the most optimistic scenario that he painted for himself and yet he also knew that in the context of his life it was also the least likely. His whole continuum of existence had often seemed to be one long QED of Murphy's Law.

The rat-a-tat-tat on the door restarted with more vigor and he thought back to what Pentavsky had told him – that he must call 911 immediately if he saw Sholtz. He had not mentioned that he did not even own a phone both out of a combination of sheer embarrassment and the feeling that it would serve no material purpose if he did.

The perspiration was running off him now, as the stakes seemed to have been raised. Creet sat stock still, poised with the kitchen blade.

"Bryan."

The female voice floated thru the window, a totality of stunned shock and yet absolute relief all effected in him within the nano-second of his hearing it.

It was the sultry voice of Desdemona, the uncertain provenance of her accent as memorable to Creet as any he had ever come into contact with.

"Desi, what are you doing here?" he shouted thru the glass.

"I left something behind yesterday. Awful sorry to trouble you," she answered.

"Hold on, I'll get the door," Creet said.

He unfastened the locks and there on the threshold was this woman that he thought he would never see again, this woman whom he had spent the previous night dreaming of. Add to that the feeling that he had been reprieved from a terrible fate and he smiled the widest smile that he could ever remember smiling.

"Come in! Come in!" he invited.

However, she hesitated at what she should do, seeing the figure of Creet enveloped in the blackness.

"Er... you gotten no electricity or something?" she asked cautiously, recoiling a little.

After the extreme emotional turmoil of the last forty-eight hours it seemed that this was just what she needed. Not!

"I'm sorry," replied Creet. "I'll get the lights."

He fumbled for the switch at the side of the door, and he could, even in the midst of his first full admiring glance at her as she became visible in every gorgeous detail, see the fear evaporate from her blinking cornflower eyes and be replaced instantly by two orbs of melancholia.

"Thank you," she intoned, stepping inside. "I'm sorry to disturb you, Bryan."

Her eyes shone like luminous queries onto the knife that he was still nursing.

"No. Don't mention it," Creet replied, her concern an undiscovered planet to him.

"I left my bracelet in your bathroom," she explained. "You didn't find it did you?"

"Nope. Didn't notice it – help yourself," he said, smiling affectionately, looking at her tumbling dark hair and remembering that morning finding a few strands of it in the bath, filaments that he had raised to his lips and softly kissed.

"I won't be a second," she said, heading for the far door, the tight cut of her jeans making her host draw breath.

"I'll make us some coffee," he faux-shouted after her, walking over to the kettle, only then realizing that he still had the knife in his left hand.

He placed it on top of the breakfast bar, speculating on what the object of his lust would have thought of this; amazed now, yet also gratified that she had trusted him enough to venture into the lair of his knife-wielding alter ego without requiring even a word of reasonable exposition. Little did he know that she may have been almost indifferent to oblivion at this time, certainly subconsciously, may have embraced her own fatalistic end as a way out of the searing pain that she was laboring under.

Desi returned from the bathroom and he saw that she was now sporting a silver bracelet on her right wrist.

"Thank you very much. It was where I left it. I better get out of your hair now."

She spoke fast, looking at him fitfully, not wishing to engage in too much serious eye contact. If she could leave now, having achieved her objective, then she would much prefer to do so.

She walked over to the door.

"Desi, please. Leave if you want to but I'd really like you to stay for a coffee."

His invitation seemed to disarm her with its guileless charm.

She removed her hand from the catch on the door and turned ninety degrees to face him.

"It's not that I don't want to…" she murmured, meaning just the opposite.

"Please," he intervened, before the excuse could be vocalized and therefore made more concrete. "I don't have many opportunities to entertain," he went on. "I really enjoyed talking to you yesterday. I know I scared you with the knife but I thought, when you knocked at the door, that you may be that crazy that's on the run."

"Oh! No! No! You don't frighten me. You're a nice man. I know that," she gushed lightly, dissembling thru her teeth, yet somehow also, as she listened to her own words flow forth, believing them at some deep-down part of her mental motherboard.

"Great. Well siddown and I'll get the coffee," he said, smiling, doing an assumed close on her like a past master at the art of seduction.

Desi, all alone at night in the back of beyond, told herself that she was playing the percentage call – if she did not stay for one coffee he might well turn nasty. It was better to go along with it now than regret her decision in a minute's time. He could, in truth, be a complete loonytune.

"Okay," she said and sat down on the stool.

This really was the last thing she needed.

"So what's the story?" Creet asked, placing a steaming cup in front of her.

"Well my car can't be fixed. It's a write-off," she replied, warming her hands on the china, taking refuge in mundanities rather than wishing to unburden herself to this total stranger.

"Too bad. So where've you been staying?" Creet rejoindered.

"Do you mind if I smoke?" Desi asked, looking at him properly for the first time, taking in his shaven chin, his hair neater than she recalled, the quite fetching scar above his left eye.

"Here have one of mine," he offered.

She took a Marlboro and he struck a match and lit it. She sucked in the smoke and exhaled in one long stream of tobacco effluent, feeling the calming effect instantaneously. He waited, watching for her to return to the conversation in her own time.

"Do you know Kim from the coffee-house? I'm staying with her."

"Why didn't you hire a car to get back home?" Creet asked. "The insurance would pay, wouldn't it?"

"No. I couldn't face that long drive after hearing…"

She trailed off, her eyes misting over, her left hand twisting the bracelet forlornly – the bracelet Trip had bought her on their most recent anniversary.

Suddenly she was sobbing uncontrollably, her mind consumed by the inferno of the Twin Towers.

Creet watched her with a mixture of fascination and tenderness. He pulled out a Kleenex and gave it her. She clasped it in her hands, dabbing her fluid mascara with it, all the while flashbacks to the happiest of times with Trip reeling thru her mind. He waited for the tempo of tears to slow.

His own eyes smiled down on the salt-moist, bloated face of the woman he had almost come to think that he loved. He now judged the moment ripe for a solicitous enquiry.

"Are you okay?" he asked softly.

"I'm s...sorry," Desi stammered, looking up at him, feeling for the first time on her shoulder the somehow comforting weight of his hand.

She remembered those minutes of silent companionship on his veranda and felt that maybe she had let the knife and her vivid imagination cloud her judgment of him.

"Don't be, you had to get whatever it was out," Creet responded banally, yet so often in the depths of despair we do not yearn for high-concept originality but rather comforting cliché.

"Thanks for being so good about it," she whispered.

"Here, drink this while it's still warm."

He spoke gently, handing her the cup.

She sipped it tentatively at first, then voraciously until finished.

"It's your husband, isn't it?" asked Creet, retrieving the bottle of bourbon from the shelf and pouring a double unbidden into Desi's empty cup before she could protest.

"Thank you," she responded, looking at him searchingly. "Yes it is my husband… or should I say was…"

Creet swallowed hard. It was as he had thought.

"I'm really sorry, Desi," he said weakly, downing his own measure in one.

"Thank you," she mumbled, droplets welling again in her eyes – tears now due to the sudden dawning that people do care, that she was not completely alone in her despair, that others' compassion could touch her and bring a touch of solace.

Creet instinctively moved towards her and in an instant had encircled her in his bearlike arms, her face fragile as an orchid and sobbing tremulously.

For two minutes stillness descended upon them. They were as one, as the day before when they had shared an intimacy of tacit empathy. Sympathizer and sympathizee merged by degrees into one; the isolated ambience of the cabin and the undraped windows looking out onto nothing but sepia landscape, advancing the effects of synergy between them.

It was impossible to say which one of the couple orchestrated the first move in the inevitable progression towards the bedroom. Suffice to say that one of them did or perhaps even both in unison. Comforting touches became kisses, reciprocated sympathy turned into acquiescence, holding into stroking, sensual transmogrified into sexual.

Creet carried her across the boundary and laid her reposed frame diagonally across his bed. Every opportunity he gave her for rejecting his advances was always spurned. It was as if he, by his every action, his loving tactility, was giving her the essential balm that she required in this hour of her utmost need.

May the Lord remember the evil of his ancestors
And never forgive his mother's sins.
May the Lord always remember their sins,
But may they themselves be completely forgotten!

(Psalm 109)

Chapter VI

Pentavsky came out of the general store and placed his cell to his ear.

"Dirk, where are you?" he asked.

"I'm in Butte, Marv, chasing up a lead on the other fella. Where are you now?"

"I'm in Moonstone, a little place with nothing to recommend it, I tell you. No sign of the bastard so far," he remarked, dourly.

"Look, Marv. I know you've got a personal stake in catching the son of a bitch, but why don't you let the Feds and the police do their job," recommended Niemeyer.

"Okay, Dirk. I know what you think. But I've got to do this." Marv spoke flatly, his eyes focused ahead of him into the mid-distance.

Between Moonstone and Petricki was the old gold-town where they now knew Sholtz had laid up for the night. He had raped and killed a Miss Janet Fielding before dumping the body and, according to the Lexus's tire tracks, driving due east. This much they knew, but nothing had been heard from him, nor any sighting all day now, even though on the regional channels Sholtz's barbarism was second only to the World Trade Center at the top of the news. It was Friday evening now and the madman's macabre tally had reached four in as many days, and they were only the known ones.

Pentavsky replaced the phone in the top pocket of his dogtooth jacket. He had been liaising with the F.B.I., the police and with Niemeyer all-day and still there was zilch on Sholtz's whereabouts. No- one in Moonstone had seen anything out of the ordinary nor noticed the distinctive car driving thru. He had called on every shop, every property along that stretch of road, all to no avail. He was thinking of calling it a day and heading for home before nightfall.

Marvin Pentavsky sat at the wheel, mind reverberating with images of his wife and child, perfect pictures of family life that Sholtz had ripped to smithereens. Even the most joyous memories were now forever occluded by the taint of the killer's destructive force and by Holly's infidelity.

Pentavsky drove off in the direction of Helena. He saw a formation of Canada geese above the redwoods, heading for the bank of the lake, and he wondered whether perhaps one day he could again somehow experience these creatures' simple joie de vivre in the basic necessities of life. He ruminated whether it was not too late; whether he were in fact destined never to see a glorious sunset again without the gauze of his own tragic history interfacing between his eye and his mind. The answer however seemed so self-evidently negative that he would not even indulge himself in idle speculations but rather pressed the button on the radio, hoping to blot out the pain with some loud rock.

Presently the stereo sprang into life with the news:

<<…reports in the last half hour indicate that escaped killer Robert Sholtz has been shot and possibly critically

wounded by police whilst driving in the vicinity of Moonstone, approximately fifty miles south west of Bozeman. The stolen Lexus, we understand, was involved in an incident with a police vehicle and a chase and then a firefight ensued. The automobile has now been abandoned. Police have issued a warning for local people to stay in their homes and not to approach the fugitive under any circumstances. He is six foot three, dark matted hair, unshaven; he is wearing a navy blue suit and blood-spattered white shirt. No police casualties have been reported so far, but we shall keep you up to date as we obtain more information.>>

<<...And now the news from D.C. is that President Bush has indicated that he believes Islamic terrorist organization Al Qaeda to be responsible...>>

Pentavsky speed-dialed Special Agent O'Hara of the Seattle Feds. It was busy. He threw the phone down on the passenger seat. It was darkening now.

He picked up the phone again but before he could select the contacts option there was a ring. It was Niemeyer.

"Marv. Did you hear the news?" he asked urgently.

"Yeah. Sure as hell did. Why wasn't I told?" Marv questioned him angrily.

"I've only just found out myself. It only happened twenty minutes ago and O'Hara never realized you were down there, Marv. He wants you to get the hell out. This guy's very bad news... I'm sorry Marv. Fucking stupid thing to say. I'm sorry, but O'Hara wants you to go home NOW. Listen – you can't do anything there by yourself anyway. Leave it to the Feds."

Niemeyer completed his plea and there was a pause, a hiatus during which time Pentavsky felt for his shoulder holster and weapon, patting it as if to ensure his old ally was still good for its occasional run-out.

"Are you still there, Marv?" asked a jumpy Niemeyer, concerned.

"Yes," said his boss. "I'm still here."

"Did you hear what I told you?" he went on.

"Yes. I did," answered Pentavsky.

"Okay, signing off then. See you tomorrow," said his deputy.

Pentavsky dug out a packet of cheroots. He lit one, winding down the window as he did so. He was in the middle of nowhere in the rapidly deepening dusk with one solitary and only workmanlike revolver. It would be enough, in most cases, for his own protection, but he had his doubts whether it would be of sufficient caliber to stop Sholtz with the first shot. He was after all not like other men. He was built like one of those granite outcrops that Pentavsky could even now see protruding from the escarpment above the road.

Moonstone was about three miles back now. All he knew was that he was not going to go home, whatever O'Hara or Niemeyer or the police had requested. He was on the spot now and he was not about to take the easy option. The nemesis of his family, of his very life indeed, was close by and he would see it out to the bitter end. Sholtz would not escape again, whatever it took from him – even his own emotionally impoverished and blighted life. He would not, could not allow this man to perpetuate his evil reign. He owed his darling baby Sabrina that much at the very least.

He finished smoking and tossed the end out. No other vehicle had come down this road since he had been stationary. Coldness closed in on him and Marv pulled his collar up. All was quiet but for an occasional cackling of his amphibious entourage enjoying their fish supper.

The exchange of fire must have been a few miles away otherwise he would have heard it whilst he was reconnoitering the town, Marv decided. He knew that every police officer in the state had had their leave cancelled for the duration. The hunt for this psychotic was the most wide-ranging the state had ever seen.

Pentavsky had determined to check out the small towns of Petricki, Goldbush, Mount Firefly and finally, Moonstone itself in the hope of getting a lead. Nothing would give him greater pleasure than to be the bearer of the weapon that killed Robert Sholtz. Revenge, they say, is a dish best eaten cold, and yet for Pentavsky, after nearly two decades of gruel, he was at last feeling that the entrée could be his.

The net was closing in even before the latest gun-battle. Now there would be a massive police operation coordinated by the G-Men to flush out the maniac. It was going on all around him and if it was not to be himself who administered the fatal shot then at least he knew that Sholtz would not be able to slip the net again. Whilst the attention of the country was on the heroics of the New York Fire Department, here in Montana public abhorrence at Sholtz's rampage meant careers were on the line.

Pentavsky realized that he had to make a decision; if he stayed where he was then he was merely a sitting duck. Sholtz, it seemed was on foot and injured. He did not know where the incident had taken place exactly; only that it was somewhere close. If Sholtz was ten miles away then what was the point of him sitting in his car and smoking cigars. He could hardly call O'Hara for more information on Sholtz's movements. If, on the other hand, he was in the immediate area then he had something the madman needed desperately – his departmental Chrysler – and in that context it would be suicidal as well as superfluous to remain where he was parked. Either way he had to move out.

Marv revved the engine and began to do a three-point turn. The town was the only option. It was, he convinced himself uncertainly, the only logical course. He had made his decision and now, as he drove along, he kept his headlights dipped.

Something suddenly caught his attention on the concrete ahead. No way could he be sure in the dark but a sixth sense cried out that there was something different. He focused hard, utilizing every sinew of his ciliary muscles.

He could see a trail of spots across the road; the nearer he came, gradually decelerating, the more certain was he that this was no mere trick of the light.

He did not want to risk exiting the car and taking a closer look but that this was blood – of that he held no doubt, its shimmering hue providing a definite contrast with the gray surface. He saw that the bloodspots were still wet. He realized that Sholtz must have just crossed, may in fact be watching him from the cover of the woods.

Quickly, he slammed his foot hard onto the gas.

Sholtz caught him with a slug to the shoulder thru the passenger seat window. A whoosh of pain flooded down Pentavsky's right side and as his body twisted involuntarily to the left so did the steering wheel viciously. The car crashed into a culvert, Marv's head banging on the windshield, he only saved by the fact that the vehicle had been traveling at pedestrian speed. Somehow he forced himself, with newfound adrenaline, to restart the car. Out of the corner of his eye he could just see the limping figure of the psycho looming. He tried to reverse out of the ditch but one wheel was in mid-air, the others trapped in wet clay, unable to achieve purchase.

Sholtz let off a round, aiming at the head. Fortunately his quarry had sensed the imminent threat and dived beneath the dash. Marv realized reluctantly that he could no more utilize the car as transport and so threw himself out – he would use its steel body for cover. He could hear the shuffling of his would-be executioner coming ever closer, and so edging towards the bonnet, he assumed the stance.

Pentavsky's next action was to retract the weapon from his holster. He gauged that he was about six feet lower than his target, that he would have to aim at an angle of approximately fifteen degrees to the horizontal; he would have no choice but to expose himself to danger if he was to give himself the best shot. A distraction was called for in order to maximize his chances.

Marv cast around for a likely piece of branch or a rock. He found a heavy stone. His ventricles were pumping full blast, adrenaline in laboratory-type quantities coursed through his veins.

Sholtz, his wheezing breath now audible, was only twelve or so yards away. Pentavsky recoiled his arm, ready to throw a skimmer like he had done many times at the ocean when a boy. There was a clump of bracken twelve feet to his left. It should make a fit-for-purpose rustling noise when agitated.

It was now or never.

Die or do. Do or die.

The one great advantage that he possessed, he appreciated, was the element of surprise. Sholtz would not know that he was armed, being as it was that he was in an unmarked car. Albeit that this was the best thing in his favor, it was also the most transitory. The law of diminishing returns did not so much apply as define this calculation.

He let rip with the stone, simultaneously transferring the gun back to his good hand. Never before in his life had he so wished that he were ambidextrous. Rising above the parapet of the car bonnet he squeezed the trigger, catching sight fleetingly of Sholtz's head switching back from the bushes in the direction of the blast, an expression of astonishment on his face as he realized that he, the hunter, had suddenly become the prey.

"What the fuck!!" he screamed automatically in an alto-bass voice, as the 9mm. smashed into his tertiary rib, doubling him up for one and a half seconds before he fired back, gritted teeth shining devilishly in the moonlight. He had however no target.

Pentavsky had begun to drop beneath the level of the wheel arch, as soon as he had fired. Now, imbued by the confidence of a successful plan well-executed, he went over the top again and let off two shells in super quick succession: the first missed but found him his line, the second slammed into where it hurts most in a man – Sholtz's career as a rapist surely over forever.

Meanwhile, at first sight of his adversary, the killer had shot back round after round but the paroxysms of agony which he was laboring under had drastically affected his aim. He landed none out of five. Marv was able to withdraw once more unscathed, and the wounded wreck of the maniac also retreated whence he had come.

It was pitch black now bar the perihelion moon shining an ethereal tablecloth of white across the Montana landscape and the headlights of the Concorde traversing the road at an acute angle.

Marv called out into the darkness:

"Sholtz, you son of a bitch! Give it up! I'm an officer of the Montana Probation Service. Throw your weapon down!"

Sholtz did indeed lob his firearm into the road; he had four more guns metaphorically, if not literally, up his sleeve. This guy may or may not fall for the sucker punch, he had conjectured; it did not matter. It was worth a shot.

"Okay. Now come out with your hands above your head," called Pentavsky, cautiously.

There was no movement from the other side of the road.

"Come on, you need hospitalization urgently," he shouted, still hiding behind the car, not willing to place a bet on Sholtz's honesty.

Still there was no sign of the shambling gunslinger, nor any sound. Marv's shoulder was hurting bad, but he knew that it would be a small price to pay if he could bring the convict in, although he viewed this as by far the least desirable outcome – a clean kill would be the optimum scenario.

Maybe he had fainted from his injuries and was lying off the highway in an ever-deepening pool of his own blood. It was so dark in those woods however that as Marv ventured a quick glance around the back of the trunk, he could see nothing.

In the distance Pentavsky could hear police with tracker dogs. He wondered idly where the policemen were who had found the madman. Were they victims of Sholtz too?

No way did Marv want to be just another gruesome statistic. He would stay where he was, in relative safety behind his metallic friend from Detroit. He would await reinforcements.

"Man! Man! I need help real bad! Call an ambulance for me! Please, man!" Sholtz suddenly screamed, in a broken, agonized tone, as if just returning from the very edge of consciousness.

Marv heard him with a start and somehow, newly reinforced within his psyche, was an impulse to finish the slime-ball off once and for all, before the police arrived and the psychiatrists and the attorneys and the liberal press and he was put back into the system: that same institutionalized sop to traditional thinking on punishment and reform that had just released him after sixteen years to kill again and again and again.

He could not, on the memory of his wife and child permit this monster to end up in a nice, cozy, private room in a hospital, watching cable and salivating over the nurses – other men's daughters and wives. Time was short as he heard the baying canines getting on the scent. Something in him had snapped. He would finish the job that he had started. He suddenly could do no other; his career trajectory was about to nosedive if discovered, but he did not care anymore. His blood was up. For the first time in almost seventeen years he felt totally engaged in LIFE – yet even at that moment, when the red mist had descended, he was self-possessed enough to realize the profound irony that it was an overweening preoccupation with the taking of life that was the catalyst.

He raised himself to his full height, feeling a little cramp in his legs from prolonged crouching and began to walk fearlessly up the slope to the road, his mind a raging foment of long-overdue vengeance and terrible memories of that night – that night that had defined his life.

"Where are you," shouted Marv, looking now at the wood and not seeing anything but trees. "I'll help you if I can, Sholtz."

"Man, I'm dying. Help me, help me," cried Sholtz, just loud enough for it to be audible and yet also to sound weak and helpless.

"Where are you? I can't see you," said Marv, approaching now, his gun held gingerly in front of him, as if he were bent on the mercy mission alone, yet also proceeding with caution in case of a trap.

"I'm here to your left," shouted Sholtz. "Please hurry, man."

Pentavsky turned and went forward.

Sholtz, lying prone on the ground, had already taken aim. He pulled the trigger with his bloodied forefinger, releasing the jet of gas which propelled the firing pin onto the percussion cap of the shell at two hundred and eighty-six miles per hour. The bullet left the Beretta 92F at a velocity such that Marvin Pentavsky heard the blast only a millisecond after he had been shot – the active tip of the casing, traveling supersonically, the sound merging with the sluicing noise of brain fluid cascading down his forehead.

He was clinically dead 0.62 of a second after the lead impacted, his body gracefully collapsing as an antelope on the Savannah, legs buckling first, the capacities of his exploded mind no sooner reacting to the soundtrack of his own final rite of passage than being capable of processing only the silence of his final eclipse.

The police dogs reacted to the far-off report of the gun with frenzied barking.

Sholtz reckoned that they were about a mile away; however the unpolluted air of the antediluvian forest and the echo chamber of the topographical amphitheatre carried the sonic waves further even than that.

Sholtz picked up the MP5 and his previously surrendered weapon and added them both to his expanding arsenal. He knew that he would have to get out of there double-quick and find a place to be his sanctuary if only for the last hours of his life, until he leaked that critical mass of corrupted corpuscles to take him into the kingdom of Hades and Manson.

The only thing that he did not want now was the German Shepherds all over him. Ever since he had been a child he had had a debilitating phobia towards dogs – it was his own Orwellian nightmare, his personal Room 101. His ears pricked up suddenly. He could hear a chopper over the woods.

He felt inside the dead man's jacket. There was a driver's license and an ID card. Ignoring the wallet, he purloined the two items. Neither knowing where he was going, nor caring, he set off away from the baying hounds. The pure savagery of the last three days had made him happier than he had been in sixteen years. His was an evil animus, his soul long ago pawned to Satan and never redeemed.

The night air, mid-September, contained a chill which he was unable in his tawdry, polymer suit to shut out. Keeping off the road, yet following it, he began jogging along as best he was able.

He knew that he was as good as the corpse that he had left behind – only the timing and location of his final demise still hung in the balance.

In agony, and losing plasma at an alarming rate, the killer drifted into a routine. He would run for a minute or so, then rest for thirty seconds against a tree. If there were an award for stoicism for wounded megalomaniacs then it would be he on the rostrum.

A car was coming along the road so long empty. It was essential that he had an automobile, he thought; even if it was impossible that he could escape the ring of steel, then merely to meet his own end at a place of his own choosing.

He halted and took cover behind a tree. The car was doing forty-five. It was a police automobile, manned by two officers. Sholtz prepared himself, a piece in each hand. He remembered the fairgrounds of his youth in Jersey where he had habitually purchased two tickets and fired at the little tin cowboys with both pistols simultaneously. He had gotten good, winning lots of furry stuffed animals for his delighted ma.

The car was a good hundred and twenty yards away now, lights strobing blue and orange, the two officers oblivious to the figure standing off-road, waiting with both barrels leveled at their respective crania.

At twenty yards Sholtz fired. There was a screech of rubber as the car did a pirouette and slid to a stop. The driver slumped forward, blood splurging from his head, the entry wound clean between the eyes testifying to the immediacy of death. The second cop was more messed up – his right cheek blown away by two bullets, his face leaning grotesquely against his partner's shoulder.

Sholtz wasted no time in admiring the gory tableau but he set to in removing the bodies, like so much garbage. Now the dogs were gaining. As the shots had rung out all hell had broken loose. The forest sounded like a menagerie on acid.

He did not purloin their weapons. He did not need to. Well within a minute he was sitting in the vehicle, knocking out the shattered glass with the Beretta. He could not quite believe his own marksmanship skills were so excellent, given his condition, and he roared out an ecstatic 'Yeaaaaaaa' as he sped off.

For a couple of minutes he drove on fully expecting to see a police car blocking the road, yet he did not. Plus the agony was lessening, perhaps merely psychosomatically. His latest double murder had given him an endorphin burst that somehow negated the pain.

He knew, nevertheless, that he required serious medical attention, but he also knew that this was not exactly a realistic option. Anyway the art of survival had always come as second nature.

He saw a sign in the headlights: 'MOONSTONE – POPULATION: 220'. Taking his foot off the gas, he could hear the dogs only indistinctly now. He saw lights in a cabin and pulled off the road. He took out the ID card. Sholtz memorized the name, placing his finger casually over the photograph of the man still lying warm two and a half miles down the lane.

A frisson of acute recognition flooded his senses abruptly, transporting him back in time to Holly, the only woman he had ever really loved, the only woman who had ever given herself to him naturally. Even in the heat of battle Sholtz had had a feeling of déjà vu about that guy. Now he knew why.

He brushed himself down, rather futilely, and knocked. He had, after all, a chance to give Pentavsky life again; he half-smiled at his own mental bon mot.

******

Bryan Creet was lying in bed enjoying with his new lady friend a post-coital Marlboro. They had heard the vehicle come up to the house in trepidation. Both of them had met Pentavsky during his door-to-door enquiries in town and knew of the massive police operation. Their lovemaking had been punctuated by the distant crack of gunfire and the heavy whirring of police helicopters. All of this had only added a certain evocativeness to their debut together between the sheets.

"It's all right, Desi. It's a police automobile," shouted Creet into the bedroom. "You stay where you are. I'll see what he wants."

"Okay," she called back, this unexpected intervention of the outside world making her apprehend for the first time coolly what she had done, somehow breaking the spell which she had seemingly been under.

She had never before been unfaithful to Trip. She was not sure now whether she had indulged in infidelity, or whether the emotionally crippling weight of grief under which she had been laboring, and which had led her vulnerability to seek solace in another man, made the act more a testament to her love for him than a nullification of all that they had shared.

Creet opened the door in his robe, his hair less unkempt than usual due to the happy, sweat-plastered visage that he had acquired, the dark strands stuck down now as if by brilliantine.

"Hiya," he said.

"Good Evening, sir," the visitor responded, holding forth the card, index finger strategically hiding the photo. "Officer Marvin Pentavsky of the Montana Probation Service."

"Yes. What can I do for you, officer?" asked Creet, taking in the three days' growth of beard, the disheveled attire, the caked blood.

Creet knew that this was not Pentavsky. Who after all could forget a name like that? He also knew that he had to pretend it was and hope against hope.

Again, for the second time in as many hours he felt a life-affirming desire to survive, now increased a thousand fold by the incredible sexual experience on which he had just gorged.

"May I come in? I've been in a shoot-out with the escaped convict. I need to call an ambulance urgently,"

"I'm sorry, officer. I'd help if I could but I haven't got a phone here," said Creet, truthfully.

"Well, I need some bandages…"

"Sorry, but I don't think I've a first aid kit in the house, officer," said Creet nervously, knowing the end of the charade was drawing nigh.

Both men now knew that the other knew that the other knew.

It was the most nerve-racking conversation to which Creet had ever had the misfortune to be a party. Suddenly there were footsteps behind him.

"Hi! What's the problem?" asked Desi, sidling up behind Creet.

She appeared at the door, bed-tousled in her blouse and panties, shapely legs luminous in the soft light.

"Hello, I'm Officer Pentavsky…"

"Oh my God!" Desi screamed. "Bryan, close the door! It's the psycho!"

The impostor heaved at the shutting door with his bulky frame, taking out his Beretta as he did so.

"Let me in or I'll kill you both!" he promised in a rasp.

Creet and Desi resisted with all their might but, both in bare feet, it was a task they were unequal to against the heavy shod brawn of Sholtz, who for every inch gained could consolidate his progress with his instep.

Finally and not without a titanic struggle lasting thirty seconds or so the fugitive was inside his new lair, his semi-automatic primed and poised at the unlikely, trembling couple.

Sholtz was not stupid. He knew with utter certainty from the bottom of his hemorrhaging innards that this would be the scene of his glorious last stand.

He was in for the duration – and so quite possibly were the unfortunate Desdemona and Bryan Creet.

He is the Lord, our Lord,
Who rescues us from death…
God will surely break the heads of his enemies…
So that you may wade in their blood,
And your dogs may lap up as much as they want.

(Psalm 68)

Chapter VII

Niemeyer had come off the phone with his superior, feeling peculiarly anxious, somehow unsatisfied that the boss had absorbed the imperative nature of O'Hara's missive.

He had never seen eye to eye with Pentavsky but since finding out his full traumatic life story he had warmed to him in a genuine way.

"I'll have another scotch on the rocks, bartender," he said, taking out his cell and placing it on a cardboard coaster.

"New in town?" stated the middle-aged hospitality worker conversationally, his starched shirt and bowtie an unassuming parody of the breed.

"Yes, I was just here on business for the day," Niemeyer answered, peeling off a note from his money clip, admiring the cool, modern lines of the bar. "Keep the change," he instructed, good-naturedly.

"Thanks, mister," he responded. "So what line of work are you in, if you don't mind my asking?"

"I'm in recoveries," Dirk replied without thinking, feeling the scotch soothe him, like a million micro-masseuses in every golden molecule.

"What, is that something to do with insurance?" enquired the steward, smiling his smile, the one he used on customers when he was intrigued and wanted to draw them out.

"Yeah, kind of insurance I suppose; insurance for society and recovery for all the misfits who need help on getting another stab at life."

He spoke smoothly, enjoying relaxing over a drink and being the center of attention for a change.

"I know, bud, I know. You're a G-Man or something, aren't you?" he mooted.

"Almost," responded Dirk. "I'm in the Probation Service."

"Okey-dokey," said the bartender, picking up a glass and filling it with lemonade from the pump. "I betcha you've got a few stories to tell," he continued.

"Yeah, a few," said Niemeyer, downing his drink. "See ya, fella."

He walked towards the illuminated 'Exit' sign. He had only intended to have one.

He emerged into the fresh air knowing that he must call his boss straight away.

Niemeyer speed-dialed the number but it went eventually to voicemail. He tried Marv's home number but there was no answer. Now he was seriously worried about his colleague – concerned enough to drive down there. Pentavsky had unfinished personal business with the maverick psycho. Surely however even he would not be such a goddamn sucker as to… Niemeyer could not bring himself to complete his virtual semi-formed fear.

He had no choice but to try to save him from himself.

He turned the key and began to negotiate his way out. The day had been a write-off thus far – he learning nothing to his advantage about the other absconder. That was why he had so needed a bolstering tincture before returning home to Helena. The guy was nowhere in the same league as Robert Sholtz, but it was still nonetheless disheartening to have made no headway in the case.

Niemeyer took the turning that led to the main interstate. In an hour he would be there if there were no hold-ups. He prayed that this would be in time to prevent Pentavsky doing something rash. Once again he picked up his cell phone from the passenger seat, pressed the cursor down to his superior's name and activated the call – no response. This time he did leave a message – reconfirming that O'Hara had specifically ordered Pentavsky to vacate the area.

He then apologized for calling again but said also that he had some news to discuss with him about the other case – this no more than a smokescreen to oil the wheels of their often-fraught professional relationship.

By now Niemeyer was doing eighty. He glanced at the L.E.D. time display on the dash. It was six thirty-three. Thoughts of a relaxing hot shower and a pizza would have to be put on hold, but that his mission was of more importance to him than his own R and R he was in no doubt. In any event, he mused, he would not be able to relax anyway until he knew that Marv was safe.

He dialed O'Hara. Perhaps he would have some good news by now. The dialing tone beeped away, he hoping with all the positive thinking that he could muster, that Sholtz was no more at large.

"O'Hara, here," the F.B.I. man answered, impatiently.

"Hello, sir, it's Niemeyer."

"Yep," he returned.

"It's just that I can't get hold of my boss," he explained, cringing at the thought of the invective Pentavsky would lavish on him if he somehow got wind of this conversation.

"Look Niemeyer, I'm in the middle of the biggest fucking manhunt the North West has ever seen. I haven't gotten time for this right now!"

O'Hara shouted the last sentence, and behind the New York accent, Dirk could hear barking.

"I'm sorry," said Dirk. "I just want you to look out for him. I've got a feeling he might go after Sholtz alone. You know what the bastard did to his family."

"Yeah. Yeah. I know. Right now though I've got two choppers, ten police vehicles and sixteen federal agents all tracking the motherfucking meshugganah," he countered. "I can't be expected to wet-nurse your boss as well, okay! Now clear the line…But before you do – tell me Niemeyer why the fuck did you guys let this son of a bitch out of the State Pen. in the first fucking place ?!!"

Dirk went to speak, but realized that O'Hara had rung off. He felt foolish for even making the call. All he had succeeded in doing was to bring the department, already the barely tolerated bridesmaid agency that the other agencies loved to scorn, into even more disrepute. Niemeyer was severely hacked off by continually having to explain to people that it was not his own profession which released people but the parole boards. If there was one thing worse than having to repeat his familiar exposition then it was not being afforded the opportunity to do so. All that his department did was to try to keep tabs on them and help them to build a new life for themselves on release. His reward for his estimable career was to get it in the neck from all and sundry when one of them made a run for it and the shit hit the proverbial.

He remembered how idealistic he had been when he had joined the service fresh from Berkeley. All he had seen then was the opportunity of giving broken people a clean slate in life – men who had served their time, paid their dues, and yet were harried and harassed by an unfeeling, unforgiving society, unwilling to bestow a second chance.

Now that he had witnessed the true level of recidivism among his clients and had seen how the liberal elite used the parole boards as a political football, with neither scarcely a thought to the safety of the community nor a single backward glance to the victim, he had come full circle. How naïve he now realized he had been in those far-off Elysian days, when the universe seemed so, so susceptible to his youthful idealism.

He carried on driving, relentlessly trying both of Pentavsky's numbers but to no avail. The landscape on both sides of the freeway seemed to match his mood: vast swathes of undulating forest, extant for thousands of years, enveloped the ribbon of concrete. It was as if these lungs of the country were blighted by carcinogenic shadows as he and the traffic sped along, pumping out carbon monoxide and lead into the air. Millions of drivers over a century had blasted out their noxious carcinogens, choking the eons-old purity of Montana by their selfish delusion that consumerism and convenience equate to happiness.

It was one big con.

He cogitated that possibly there were only two ways to go in life – good and bad. Maybe to think anything else was a cop-out; perhaps people like Robert Sholtz were as much a force of nature as the lion killing the wildebeest or the forest itself.

It was time to take the slip road off and this he did with some reservations. He knew now that the killer was still at large and that Pentavsky may be in trouble. He was also putting himself in the firing line of a volatile Irish New Yorker, who would blow his top if he knew the mission that Dirk was intent upon – whatever that might turn out to be?

Ahead he saw a roadblock. Dirk slowed and pulled up by the police car.

"Hello, sir," said the officer. "Sorry, but we've got a maniac on the loose somewhere in this area. Can I see your driver's license, please, sir?"

"Yes, I know. I need to find a colleague of mine," he said, handing him a plastic wallet.

"Thank you, sir, but I must inform you that this man is extremely dangerous," he reiterated, barely looking at the ID.

"I know, officer, but I have to see if I can find my associate. It's a matter of life and death you could say," he stressed, smiling up at the twenty-something whom all the while was chewing gum disinterestedly.

"Okay. I can only advise you, sir, that you are entering a very dangerous zone and that you do so at your own risk. You've been warned, all right."

The officer motioned him to go on, having finished the form of words which O'Hara had deputed all of the roadblock personnel to say if they could not dissuade any driver from passing.

The United States was still a free country and the area enclosed by the ring of steel was so huge that it would be a breach of civil liberty to enforce a wholesale exclusion zone – and if so, then logically why not a total evacuation which would have been both practically and politically impossible?

"Thanks officer," shouted Niemeyer as he drove off along the unlit and narrow lane.

The adventure was commencing.

He was as relieved that the lieutenant had not asked him any more questions as he was as fearful of what he was to encounter as he entered the unknown. With any luck, however, he told himself, O'Hara would be by now congratulating the arresting officer; as for Marv – he was probably in a bar in Helena, his cell phone secure in the glove compartment of the Riviera, oblivious to the stressed-out colleague who was so concerned about him. Niemeyer laughed inwardly; it was the one scenario that he had not entertained hitherto.

His car flowed on. At the side of the lane he suddenly came across the chaotic scene of the earlier reported incident. A black Lexus and a police car were all mangled up with a couple of fir trees. Blue and white incident tape now surrounded the vehicles. Niemeyer wondered casually if the policemen were all right, or whether Sholtz had dispatched them too? It shocked him that he had not even thought about them as real people before, with families and plans and ordinary lives outside of their working hours. Against the long pantheon of Sholtz's victims what practical good did an overload of sentimentality do in terms of hastening the capture of the megalomaniac? The thought was of no comfort however. His professional life had made him hard and the surfeit of death that he saw did indeed demean his humanity, made him inured to all but the most routine expenditure of life. A child dying of leukemia, an old lady having a stroke – these were the type of things which made him cry nowadays, not the violent deaths, not man's inhumanity to man; these, as far as he was concerned, were already discounted by his calcified emotional processes after such long exposure to them in the course of his work.

In the distance across the dense woods to the east he could hear a chopper. He strained to listen and ascertained that there were two helicopters, both converging on the same place. Things must be hotting up, he thought, and then suddenly there it was, so abrupt was the realization that this was it that he was almost physically sick as he braked. On one side of the road was the unmistakable body of his erstwhile manager, on the other the deceased's Buick. Incident tape surrounded both, making them appear in the moonlight like exhibits in some grim museum for the macabre.

He sat and wept for Marvin for some minutes and then drove on, scared now, yet for each and every atom in his brain that telegraphed fear there seemed another two which howled for vengeance. All of his innate liberality had dissipated at the sight of Pentavsky's tragic corpse. He did not deserve to die like this at the hands of the man who had already effectively destroyed his life anyway. He would not turn back.

At the end of this most terrible of weeks for America he could not, even if he wanted to, put his own safety first. He had an obligation, neither to the base wants of his predilection, nor even to the memory of Marv, but to the aspirations of his soul, to be the man he needed to become if he was not to be recorded as yet another time-server.

9/11 had changed people this week in dramatic new ways. One now had to realize that life could be shut down at any time and that the worst thing surely was to swim always in the shallow end. His trendy sociological ideas had been fading fast anyway – now he had to become a man who, if he had to one day seek absolution, would not do it over his failure of courage in pursuit of Marv's murderer.

Further along the country lane, after only a couple of minutes of driving, his headlights picked up a police car. An officer was in attendance around two dead cops, spread-eagled on the grass verge. The cop reacted to the noise of the engine and stood up, raising his right hand as he did so in a 'stop' signal.

Niemeyer slowed the car and peered out, noticing the congealed blood on the face of one policeman like some huge Gorbachovian birthmark obliterating half of his right cheek and jaw line. The other had been shot between the eyes. He could see that things were happening faster than the authorities could cope with. He wound down the window as the officer approached.

"What are you doing here, sir?" he asked.

"I am, er… I have to get to Moonstone," Dirk stumbled, not altogether confidently.

He wished that he had not had those drinks; he felt slightly the worse for wear now.

"Well. I don't think you should continue. The gunman is down the road," he said. "In fact in my opinion you should not have been allowed into this area at all. Anyway the roads are totally blocked now."

"I need to get to Moonstone," Niemeyer flummoxed. "I'll not be any trouble, officer."

"I've told you. The road ahead is closed. You'll have to turn back," he restated more forcefully.

Niemeyer's head was swimming now, yet he had not come all this way in vain.

"Please, officer…" he pleaded before the lieutenant interrupted him.

"Sir, I have to ask you to step out the car, please?" he requested. "I have reason to believe that you have been drinking."

"That's ridiculous," said Niemeyer to the man towering over him.

He had no choice but to get out and allow himself to be frisked, his hands thrust onto the roof of the car. The officer then backed over to his vehicle and brought out a Breathalyzer.

"Now," he went on. "Blow into this, nice and easy, sir."

Dirk did as he was told.

"Okay, very slow now. I have to ask to see your driver's license?" he continued, taking back the gadget. "Where is it?"

"It's in the glove compartment, officer."

"Okay, now you stay there. I'll just reach in and get it," he told Dirk, placing the device on the passenger seat as he did so.

"Officer, please let me explain," Niemeyer gushed, listening to the choppers that seemed so very close now. "I'm the Assistant Chief in the Montana Probation Service," he confided. "My ID's in my breast pocket."

He had come so near and yet so far. He could not countenance losing his colleague and his job in the one-day as would happen if he were convicted for driving whilst under the influence. Nevertheless he had been prepared to risk everything – his job, his freedom, his life even – to avenge Pentavsky's death. Maybe he was all messed up inside, maybe he had drunk one too many shorts. Perhaps the whole decision to come on this nightmare trip was due to the alcohol.

"You're in the Probation Service?" asked the cop.

"Yes," Niemeyer replied, looking the officer straight in the eyes.

"Okay let's have a look at the breath test," the lieutenant said.

He picked up the contraption and tutted.

"It's positive, sir. Not even borderline," he stated with some relish, returning the Breathalyzer to his front seat. .

"Oh shit!" exhaled Dirk, seeing his whole career flash between his eyes. "Let me explain?"

"It's open and shut. No explanation that you could give me could alter the result on the meter," he stonewalled. "Now I'm gonna have to cuff you and read you your rights."

"Please, please don't cuff me, don't cuff me," whimpered Niemeyer, all at once panic-stricken. "I'm only here to catch Sholtz. I'm on the case like you. That's my superior officer back there, Officer Marvin Pentavsky, lying dead at the side of the road. Okay I shouldn't have had all of that whisky, but I was really concerned about Marv…."

All of a sudden a radio blared out from the police officer's lapel:

<<O'Hara to all units! O'Hara to all units! We've got him cornered in a wooden cabin at the extreme southwest end of Moonstone. Repeat — suspect in first house into Moonstone when coming from southwest. All units there now. Over and out.>>

"Come on, let's go!" said Dirk.

"You're under arrest, fella. You're in no position to give me orders. Now let's see that ID of yours?"

"I just mean I'd go with you, but let's go now," Dirk explained vociferously, handing him the card and looking beseechingly at the horizon. "I may be able to help."

"Listen! I've just lost two of my best buddies in the force," he said, pointing his finger at the two corpses. "I'm in no mood for this crap."

He shone his torch onto the ID.

"I'm sorry," said Niemeyer, bowing his head in sympathy. "But we're on the same side here."

The officer's expression seemed to soften a little.

"Niemeyer," he came back. "Get the fucking hell into that police car! Get into it before I change my mind!" he ordered pseudo-gruffly. "And if anyone asks, your automobile broke down, okay."

"Thanks. I sure appreciate it," responded Dirk, striding quickly over to the police car and strapping himself into the passenger seat.

He sighed with relief at the let-off; at least he still had his career. Now the focus was resolutely once again on taking the maniac into custody. However he truly hoped for a more cost-effective solution for the hard-pressed federal taxpayer – a more final denouement.

He looked around. A couple of handguns lay neatly on the back seat covered by two police caps. The glossy black metal glistened under the car's interior light. It was like a provisional shrine to his late buddies, Dirk realized. The way in which the hats were both aligned symmetrically, the nozzles angled likewise, was testament to this and he could not help but feel deeply moved.

They drove the couple of miles to the cabin. The final leg of the journey would be by far the easiest, yet in one crucial respect also the most demanding for Dirk's mind as he examined his heart and soul in confusion, attempting to work out what to do. Could he be a vigilante? Did he have the guts? He tortured himself like this for three long minutes. Charles Bronson he was not.

The cabin's lights were all off. Helicopters whirligigged, shining bright lights onto the rear aspect. The final curtain had certainly gone up. Niemeyer was at a loss as to what he could realistically do.

<<Come out! There's no escape! It's over,>> shouted O'Hara into a megaphone.

Another police car drew up, and then another. At the elongated piece of land at the side of the shack, there lurked two dog handlers and their German shepherd dogs, straining at the leash. Four sets of headlights were aimed at the cabin. It would be a brave man indeed who would bet on another improbable escape by Sholtz. The scene was like something out of a bad formulaic TV film and yet this was in actuality the degree of respect Sholtz had earned from the police and the F.B.I. Now that they had their man they were not going to give him even the tiniest window of opportunity.

In the cabin all was quiet.

<<If you're not out in one minute, we're coming in,>> he shouted.

<<One minute is all you've got otherwise you're dead meat,>> he continued in his singularly street-speak style.

"Officer Harmon, over here," O'Hara ordered, looking behind him at the marksman poised with a telescopic rifle.

"Yes sir!"

"How the fuck do you know he's definitely in there, Harmon?" he enquired.

"Sir, he's in there, believe me…'

"But how can you be so damn sure?" he asked, consulting his watch, the seconds ticking away on the ultimatum.

"Sir, I heard the shots when he killed Esteves and McDermott, then heard the engine of that car and waited just off the road. He passed me in the police auto and pulled up." He pointed to the car with no windscreen.

"I got on the radio right then sir. I watched him force his way in past the guy who lives there, but I was too far away to have a safe shot."

"Fine, Harmon," O'Hara said, looking again at his watch. "It's time-up."

He placed the mike at his mouth once again.

<<Sholtz. Your minute's gone. Finito – you goddamn motherfucking jerk. We're coming in.>>

O'Hara now spoke into his radio softly.

"All units move in to the house – now!" he commanded.

On this cue, four highly trained men, all members of the seconded Seattle Special Weapons and Tactics team, sprinted up the steps to the building and somersaulted against the log walls.

The assault was underway.

A thousand may fall dead beside you,
Ten thousand all round you,
But you will not be harmed.
You will look and see how the wicked are punished.

(Psalm 91)

Chapter VIII

It was a glorious New York morning, the air crisp and temperate under a placid sky and the sun as radiant as a buttercup.

Trip Montifort lay in the hospital bed, like he had done for the previous three days, a man surviving by intravenous drip and saline solution alone, a spaghetti of tubes connected at various angles to his bandaged head. By his side were a plethora of machines on castors, measuring his every bodily function, beeping and flashing on a continual basis 24/7.

A man in his late thirties, he lay inert, eyes shut, face immobile. Probably not even his own mother would recognize him because of the turban that sealed and entombed his terrible cranial injuries. The private room, white and sterile, was not paid for by the patient's personal medical insurance, but by the hospital's charitable fund, for still this man was an enigma.

For all the diligent attention that he was receiving from the top neurosurgeon in New York, the prognosis was unfortunately not good. Even if he pulled thru physically it seemed he may be little more than an unthinking shell of his former self, whoever that was. His brain function may however return at any moment, perhaps even in some limited way – it was often the case that people were in comas for months and then they suddenly came round. It was one of those medical puzzles that, even in the twenty-first century, neurologists could still not fully explain. For that reason the TV in the corner was resolutely switched off. If his brain function did improve unexpectedly, then the constant news transmissions about the events of Tuesday that he may somehow subconsciously absorb could only, according to the doctors, risk setting him back into the deepest nether world of his comatose state.

Nurses and doctors frequented his room at all times of day and night, not only checking on his progress, but because the whole hospital had taken him into their hearts. The word 'progress' was a misnomer however for since his admission there had been only unchanging graph lines on his vital signs' charts. The mystery of the man was that not a single person had so far come forward – no relative or friend or work colleague had deigned to visit. He was, it seemed, both the luckiest man in the world and yet the most unfortunate; not only hermetically cordoned off in his own no man's land on the very precipice of life, but facing this awful trial alone. He did of course know nothing about the position that he now found himself in and that was his one blessing.

No credit card or wallet had been found on him and so he was the most famous non-person ever to be admitted to Cedar Plains. His photograph had appeared on the news quite regularly, but his face was, of medical necessity, half-obscured by white cotton dressings.

Every morning though one visitor did arrive at eight fifteen sharp, before he went to do his shift at Ground

Zero – the heartbreaking, painstaking job of fingertip removal of remains. Fire Officer Rosario de Souza had sat for half an hour each day with the man he had carried out from the second tower. De Souza talked to him about baseball, about movies, about his own children – anything except the cataclysmic event itself.

De Souza therefore was providing a most valuable link to the outside world. He had to be very careful not to stray into talking about the events of seventy-two hours earlier however: a sudden shock might jolt him out of his horrible status quo and into the irrevocable abyss.

De Souza strode into the ward and took the chair by the window.

"Hiya Davey Boy! How you doing today," he greeted him, stroking the almost lifeless lilywhite hand of the man he had saved.

He had called him 'Davey Boy' from the first moment he had picked him up, and now for want of a better one the name had stuck, not only for him but for the staff and the media too.

"Hey Davey Boy, you gotta wake up some time you know. Yeah you have. You see I want to get your photo. Just you and me. I'm gonna put that picture in pride of place in my kitchen. Of course I want you to sign it first. You know like an autograph. Because you're a TV star now. My wife says that you'll have to come on over for dinner when you get out. She's a great cook. We'll have chili if you want, but you might be a vegetarian or something. We'll fit in with what you want anyway. I want you to meet my daughters, Maria and Estelle. They're both so chirpy and pretty. Maybe you could do a dedication on the photo as well like those big celebrities do.

"Maybe: 'To Rosario, the best damn fireman I've ever been carried down twelve flights of stairs by!' – something like that. Well you can make something up. I can tell you're an educated man. Shame about the suit, Davey Boy, but that jacket was all bur…I mean when I found you… Did I ever mention my wife's name to you? Well, it's Angelina – she's Cuban. She sends her love, Davey Boy. If you saw her you'd think what's a beautiful babe like that's doing with me, but anyway she loves me for my mind not my looks I suppose.

"Do you like the movies? As long as there's a romance on that's all she cares about, and as for me, between ourselves of course, I like to see the gorgeous actresses. You know! And we'll have a big bucket of popcorn and two big Pepsis and we'll have the best time. Sure you can come with us if you want, one day soon.

"Do you prefer baseball or football? I'm a big Mets fan myself. Anyway time is running on and I've got to start making tracks. I'll see you tomorrow after I finish my shift – probably about five O'clock. Now be good to those doctors and all those sweet nurses won't you. And the boys down at the precinct want me to say they're thinking about you and hope you get better soon. Okay, see ya Davey boy!"

Fire Officer Rosario, as he was, by now, known throughout the hospital, patted Trip's hand and stood up from his chair. There were tears in his eyes as he looked at this man who had endured the nightmare and had somehow come out from it, only to find himself in a made to measure mausoleum of his own skin and bone. It was thought that it was the falling masonry that had dealt him a most severe glancing blow to the head.

De Souza had found him there, unconscious and bloody, his suit in tatters from the flames.

No one would ever know exactly what had happened to him. All that mattered now was his recovery, a recovery that de Souza, in his naïveté and with his simple faith in God, thought was just a matter of time.

If prayers were enough then Davey Boy would come thru, for as the fireman worked the rubble each day, amid the preternatural stench and the kaleidoscopic particles of dust raining down and up and out and around, de Souza silently prayed and prayed and prayed.

"Officer Rosario, could I have a word with you?" asked Dr. Milsom as the fireman was leaving.

"Sure, doc. What is it?" Rosario replied.

"It's the wallet," the doctor answered.

"What wallet, doctor? He had nothing on him when he was brought in," Rosario replied, looking quizzically at the consultant.

"No. There must be one though, mustn't there," said the doctor, raising his left eyebrow in pseudo-conspiratorial mode.

"Yes. I see, um, what you're er, um, saying, doc – I think," said de Souza falteringly.

"Officer Rosario, I saw on the morning news that there's a lot of stuff, personal effects and so on, that's being found. Charred, burnt, unidentifiable, most of it perhaps, but that some of it is still okay."

Dr. Milsom spoke sotto voce, looking into Rosario's eyes as if the solution was somehow in there.

"Yeah, there is some stuff that's more or less intact..."

"If you can go though every day the... the effects, you know, you may find some ID. I'm also in communication with the executive vice president of Berkeley Brothers Stock Brokers, the company that occupied the floor you found Davey Boy on. He's trying to come up with a list of names and photos of all the male employees between thirty and forty-five."

"That's fine, doc, but even if I find something of his he can't see anything, can he?" Rosario asked, desperate now to have his prayers even partially, even minutely, answered by the good doctor. "What good would it do for him even if we do find something?"

Milsom motioned him down the corridor and into an empty room.

"I've concluded my initial tests now. I believe that the blow to the head was not the crucial thing. It wasn't enough of a hit to affect the whole brain permanently. I think that he's in a state of suspended animation," the doctor informed de Souza.

"You mean there is a chance he'll be normal again?" Rosario enquired, spellbound by the implication of Milsom's words.

"It's more psychological than physical. The brain shuts down for a rest to avoid trauma and then like a daffodil bulb in the early spring it comes back when the trauma's no longer there. If we can just jog along this process with a touch of recognition therapy then great. Remember Rosario, the human mind is an incredible thing. Even whilst in a comatose state people can sometimes perceive voices, touch, even perfumes on some deep level. If we can find someone he was close to…"

The doctor shook Rosario's hand and went off to his next appointment. For Rosario, he had held out hope at last – not against all the odds hope, not miracle hope, but real hope grounded in real medical science.

He went to work with a tiny, well-concealed spring in his step, yet by the end of the day he was in tears – tears for what he had found at Ground Zero and for that which he had not.

Babylon, you will be destroyed.
Happy are those who pay you back
For what you have done to us —
Who take your babies
And smash them against a rock.

(Psalm 137)

Chapter IX

Everyone was in emotional meltdown in the little town of Moonstone, Montana. It was 9/11 +3, but it was the +3 suffix that had contrived the effect behind closed doors. By six thirty p.m. every man, woman and child had heard the news by Chinese whispers or on their radio or television; otherwise they had actually heard the distant shots themselves.

One of the greatest ironies of life is that the very people who value the life of others the greatest, value their own the least. One corollary to the theoretical respect for humanity is the propensity to see one's own life as of only commensurate value with the value one puts on one's fellow human beings. The upshot is that the nicest of people are always the bravest. Self-sacrifice and heroism are rewarded with gongs and ceremonies to inculcate in others less instinctively courageous, a self-interest dimension into the thought processes, perhaps only sub-conscious, when the moment for heroism eventually arrives.

For Kim that time had arrived. She had comforted Desi and found there a terrible truth that somehow this woman's unique pathway of life had conspired to keep from her for more than forty-eight hours. She had given her succor and a bed and when Desi had discovered in the midst of her pain that her bracelet was missing, Kim had advised her not to go looking until morning.

It was advice based less on the fact that there could be a maniac nearby, for at this time he could have been anywhere within a ten mile radius, more it was to do with Creet himself who in some inexplicable way disturbed Kim by his daily appearances in the café. Hers was the fear of the unknown, of the quiet stranger newly pitched up in their isolated town.

Kim sat in her living room and saw that Desi had been gone for half an hour. Creet's place was no more than a five-minute walk and Desi had reassured her new friend that she would be coming straight back. Kim was concerned. As she threw on her coat and went into the cool evening air she crossed herself and prayed that she had got it all wrong.

"Hiya Kim. You okay?" called Mr. Dempsey from across the street. He was shutting up the doors to the garage.

"Yeah fine, Tom," she responded distractedly.

"How's your new friend? Terrible business that. Terrible," Dempsey said, crossing the road to speak privately.

"She's, you know... she still can't believe it," Kim answered, her open face darkening at the very thought of it all.

"Well, you tell that nice lady that when she's ready Todd will drive her to the airport, and there'll be no question of any money changing hands," he said, his face flushing at the thought of his own generosity by proxy.

Kim wondered whether to confide in Tom about her current expedition but decided against it. If there was nothing the matter then the last thing she needed was Tom Dempsey spreading it all over town and everyone asking her the same question for the next week.

"Well, good night, Tom," she said. "I'm just taking a little walk to clear my head."

"Is that a good idea, Kim, with that crazy killer on the loose?" he replied, chivalrously.

"No, I'll be fine. Anyway they don't know really if he's around here or twenty miles away," she answered, nodding at Dempsey and taking her leave.

"Be careful, Kim, anyways," warned the mechanic.

She walked along in the breeze. She felt on her face the last effervescent ripostes of the autumnal sun filtered thru the trees, amidst increasing feelings of disquiet. What if those smiles that she received every day in her pinafore were proof positive that Creet harbored perverted undercurrents? Where had he come from? No one seemed to know. Would it not be better to inform the police of her fears?

She pressed on however, past the Channing property and the old ruined clapboard church that marked the edge of Moonstone proper, and on into the bend. The distant Galletin Range and the sunset never seemed to get any nearer, neither optically nor metaphorically in her own life, but their aggregate beauty was sufficient reason for a walk anyway. She did love this corner of America – the freshness of the air, the clean smell of pine needles and, at this time of year, the fantastic colors on the deciduous trees. She had no regrets in coming here. It was a quiet life compared to Des Moines but it was for her a good one – if not a ringing endorsement of her relocational choice, personal relationships-wise.

Nearly at the cabin now, she hesitated. If nothing was wrong then she did not want to look foolish. She decided to go around the back to ascertain if she could see anything. Crouching, she had to trample thru a patch of nettles and this she did as quietly as possible.

The windows were so low that in order to look in without taking the risk of being seen, she had to lie down below the sill and then get herself in a position to take a peek.

Kim stared thru the glass incomprehensibly, her jaw dropping like a bad actress in a thriller.

There in Creet's bed were the two of them and they were making love with a tenderness which instantly denoted that this was not a forced coupling at all but rather a coming together of two people, damaged and alone respectively, yielding to their basic requirements for comfort and reassurance.

She watched, rooted to the spot, captivated unpruriently by the beauty of the entanglement itself, Desi's slim, milky back arching and straightening in metronomic frequency over his supine body. Her hair flew fast-forward over his pleasured features and then tumbled back exposing her own nascently orgasmic expression. His strong hands held her hips like hinges whilst her breasts grazed his hirsute chest as she rocked to, and lay proud and erect as she came fro. It was, Kim thought, akin to some highly choreographed routine by Nureyev and Fontaine, yet completely natural and far more beguiling for that. Kim's last view as she lowered herself out of voyeuristic accusations was of Creet kissing the glowing forehead of his Desdemona and of her caressing his cheek, whilst the lowering sun bathed their figures in its golden surround wrap.

She was about to start making her way home thru the increasing gloaming when she heard a shot. Her mind focused now on the fugitive madman. She froze as she heard yet another report, and decided that she would be safest staying where she was.

More shots rang out and she cursed herself for her decision to come chasing after this woman whom she did not know. Twilight turned into dusk and dusk metamorphosed into moonlit night. She lay there, cold and wretched by the cabin for what seemed like hours listening to the helicopters coming ever closer. Then two more shots rang out, this time much louder.

She pulled her woolen coat around her and put the collar up. Suddenly she could hear a car coming. It slowed outside the cabin. Kim took a sharp intake of breath. She dimly heard a male voice, then Creet's. Presently Kim heard Desi and then instantaneously a commotion blew up.

She heard the sound of rotor blades coming ever nearer, then more police vans arriving. She did not know what she could do. Then the strong beams of the helicopters hoved into view, traversing the back garden, narrowly avoiding lighting up her skulking form. She knew that she was in tremendous danger. Any slight movement into the torches' light funnels could be fatal. Her eyes searched around for ideas, for inspiration.

The helicopters were doing passes over the house. In one of these the white rays passed right over her, illuminating the old casement window above. Kim noticed that it was unfastened. Still lying down she eased the window open an inch. She hoisted herself up, opened the window fully and hopped inside.

Kim looked around. The bed was in disarray, the door ajar. Thru the six inch gap she could see the grizzled face of the megalomaniac and beneath him on the floor two kneeling, trembling figures cowering under the lethal lese-majeste of a shiny black Beretta 92F.

She closed her eyes and wept silently in the semi-darkness.

She wished that she had stayed in to watch Letterman, wished that the latter man had not turned up or that she had turned back when she had had the chance.

That it was the most exciting event to befall her since her arrival in this outpost of rural sleepiness was, at this moment, of no consolation.

Kim was not a religious woman but she crossed herself there and then and silently prayed that the forces of law and order had a game plan; that if she had to miss Letterman, then at least she and Desi would be delivered.

You gave my father strength to beget me;
You made me grow in my mother's womb.
You formed my body with bones and sinews
And covered the bones with muscles and skin.

(Psalm 10)

Chapter X

The SWAT team acted in synchronicity, each now at the base of the wall readying themselves for the next most crucial stage in any siege. Behind them were positioned the two snipers who would shoot to kill on sight if they saw a clear line to target. That they had not thus far was because the fugitive was adept at keeping the two hostages and himself away from the windows and in the one narrow tract which was safe from marksman fire. Sholtz could, from this vantage behind the front door, cover any movements on the veranda; the position also safeguarded his vision from the blinding glare of the police cars' headlights.

"This is Blue 1 – two hostages," said the officer on the extreme left into his radio mike. "One male Caucasian, one female Caucasian. Target has Beretta in each hand trained on each one. Hostages three feet inside door. Target three feet back. Over and out."

O'Hara knew that to make an omelet one had to break eggs first but he did not want to end up with any further casualties. There had been more than enough bloodshed.

"Blue 4 – this is Control," O'Hara announced grim-faced. "See if you can get off a shot without exposing yourself to undue risk."

Blue 4 whispered, "Roger and out."

The officer stealthily raised himself, then quickly turned his head, bringing his left hand around in an arc and fired.

However a split second before he did so, another bullet peeled out across the assembled professionals. Glass smashed to the floor in the cabin and onto the veranda in equal measure and onto Blue 3 similarly. Sholtz had fired before Blue 4 had quite consolidated his aim. The officer fell to the wooden slatting, his mission replete yet failed, his neck dribbling gore, gushing blood from Sholtz's effective tracheotomy.

"Shit!" cried O'Hara. "This son of a bitch is good!"

All of a sudden, like some bad dream, Blue 3, having taken the insult of the glass, seemed to have a rush of blood to the head. Having seen so many of his colleagues die it was his intention to put an end to it and if his spontaneous combustion meant his imminent elevation to the great precinct in the sky then his body language seemed to be speaking of a philosophical acceptance of this. It was as if by throwing caution to the winds he may just succeed, he may fail, he may well die in the attempt but what would the furtherance of his life be worth anyway if he had a chance to end the glut of killing and yet shrank away in cowardice?

He stood up above the wooden panel and effected a rolling dive and somersault into the floodlit room.

O'Hara, having seen him prepare for action, cried into the mike after him, "No, stay there! No!"

119

It was too late however to prevent another needless fatality.

The psycho picked him off facilely with two bullets, one to the spine, one to the forehead. The guy never even got a round off, so ill-judged had his mission been.

"Fella, chuck the body out of the window," Sholtz ordered Creet casually.

Creet glanced at Desi as if it might be the final time he ever saw her and walked over to the body. Dragging the corpse of the one hundred and ninety pound man was not easy. A trigger-happy shot rang out as Creet's form appeared in the newly unglazed aperture.

"Hold your fire you cretins!! It's the hostage!!!" called out O'Hara angrily.

His blood was boiling now.

On every stakeout he had ever been on there had always been one sniper with an itchy finger; it was one of those things. It could not be trained out of all men, however many psychometric and virtual reality tests they were subjected to.

Blue 3's corpse was hoisted over the ledge and allowed to fall onto the decking. Creet could not afford to show any finesse in the distasteful job into which he had been co-opted. He returned to his position kneeling next to the woman whom he had come to care for. She inclined her head towards him slightly and gave him a little pout of relief, as if to say 'Thank God you've survived that'.

O'Hara got on his microphone anew.

"Blue 2, move over to the other window!" he commanded.

"Roger," averred Blue 2, setting off on hands and knees beyond the door.

120

O'Hara turned to one of the snipers behind him.

"You head to the rear and get back to me," he said.

The helicopters' task had been to prevent any breakout from behind the house and now they had the added responsibility of aiding the snipers' vision by beaming their 280W sodium lights right thru the windows. To this end, at O'Hara's prompting, they began to reduce height until they were hovering a meter and a half from the ground.

O'Hara picked up the megaphone from the roof of the auto.

<<Sholtz, let the hostages go and we'll give you a ride to hospital. We know you're badly injured. Come on, man! You'll die without emergency treatment. This is your last chance! So help me, Mary, Mother of God.>>

O'Hara waited for a response. There was a pregnant pause of about twenty-five seconds until O'Hara accepted reluctantly that it was futile. He concluded his speech.

<<Have it your own way. Nothing will give me greater pleasure than personally zipping you up in your fucking body bag!>>

The chief threw down his megaphone into some bushes, a release not only of tension but of plangent grief too. He had himself lost count of the grisly tally – like a man in a bar, after six or seven beers, who cannot recall precisely the number imbibed. The body count probably always was going to have to rise by one more prior to there being an end to it. If he was honest with himself it was ever thus. O'Hara knew in his heart of hearts that even had he possessed the negotiating skills of a Henry Kissinger, they would still have been surplus to requirements against this level of supercharged, super-efficient evil. He could not concern himself overly with Sholtz's desire to meet his inevitable destiny; it was the thought of how many more he would take with him that exercised his mind. Never in his twenty-five years as a G-Man had he been at such a loss as to know what to do professionally. In purely operational terms it would have been better if Sholtz had killed the hostages, then they would not pose any more that critical deterrent to any action that the SWAT team could take. With the couple out of the equation they could have stormed the cabin in force and by now it would have been all over. Even if Sholtz had shot and killed two more of his men in the heat of battle the situation would still have been better than it was now.

There must come a point where the lives of his men and the further quantity required to be risked piecemeal must outweigh the moral imperative to preserve the lives of the hostages. Already in purely utilitarian terms, he reasoned, the lives of two police officers were surely of no lesser value than the lives of two civilians. In one sense the forces under his command had already paid a commensurate price to try and save their lives. Surely they could not in any sensible moral universe carry on indefinitely sacrificing their own futures purely to uphold the law's fundamental totem that life is sacred. This would in some sense, O'Hara ruminated, bring that selfsame law into disrepute, manifesting itself as having so scant regard for the sanctity of human life, in so rejecting the pragmatic in favor of the philosophical, that it would bear almost a moral equivalence to Sholtz's own nihilistic nonchalance in slaughter.

O'Hara shook his head, trying to focus on the job at hand. He was not an ethicist or a moral philosopher, nor did he get paid for making up policy on the hoof. In a siege situation everything had to be done to safeguard the lives of the hostages – that had always been the dictum drummed into every training session. It was the bottom line and things could be no different now he told himself resignedly.

"O'Hara to Red 1," he said into his radio. "Come in Red 1."

"Roger, chief," it crackled back.

"Are you in position, Red 1?" he asked.

"Roger. In position, but the door to the room is in the way for a clear shot," the sniper replied.

"Okay. Standby. Over and out," he instructed, wondering whether the whole shebang was not some kind of elaborate reality TV show and that he would soon be surprised by the polished orthodontics of a smarmy, blow-dried host assuring him that it was all a big set-up, that nobody was dead at all and to which charity of his choice did he want the $100,000 check made out.

"Blue 1 to chief," came the voice, calm and smooth out of his earpiece.

"Roger Blue 1. What's up? Over." he replied.

"I think I can take him out, chief. Over." he said confidently.

"How the fuck do you think you're gonna do that?" O'Hara replied, his voice bright with skepticism.

"There's a little makeshift repair I've noticed to the shack. If I can pry the wood off with my penknife then I reckon I've got a direct line," he elucidated, his animation exaggerated in volume by the need to compete with the noise of the helicopters.

"Roger. Okay. But only if you're absolutely sure you think you can hit him clean with no collateral damage," the director of operations said, resigned to tactics taking precedence over strategy.

At last there may be an endgame in sight.

"Good luck Blue 1! Remember you'll only have time for one shot. You've seen how good this psycho is. Make it count and spill the son of a bitch's guts! Over and out."

Blue 1 carefully went about his business, of necessity slowly and deliberately, until he had worked the patch loose and had created a hole approximately three inches square. He knew that he would get only one chance to fire at will before either there was a return of fire, in which case he would have only the flimsy wooden slats as protection…or it would hopefully all be over.

He lay down silently so that his feet dangled over the edge of the decking and adjusted the angle of the gun barrel until he was satisfied that he had it perfect. He would be shooting blind to a degree, there being not much more space in the gap to see in clearly with the gun in situ. Nevertheless Sholtz had not moved in the last ten minutes so it was with more than a modicum of confidence that the officer took a deep breath and squeezed.

The sound of the shot rang out in splendid isolation, no follow-on fire ensued. Blue 1 heard the heavy thud of a man's weight collapse to the floor and the horrified scream of a woman.

"Red 1 to Control. Come in Control," came over the radio.

"Roger, Red 1. What do you see?" asked O'Hara. "Does he look dead? Over."

"Negative. Male hostage shot thru the back."

"Oh my God!" exploded the F.B.I. man. "Blue 1, you've fucking cut down the male hostage, you moron!"

"No! No! It can't be, chief. I had it lined up just right," the SWAT man responded balefully.

"Well it's kind of hard for me to understand too," roared the New Yorker. "Now, no more brilliant ideas, okay. In fact you're relieved of duty. Come back here now!" O'Hara ordered.

The officer came back down from the cabin, his head hung in ignominy, his eyes watering with the cold reality of what he had done. O'Hara took his MP5 and gesticulated at him to turn in his badge. He then took his place in the back of one of the police automobiles, hands covering his ashen face.

"Blue 2, come in. Return to base. Over," said O'Hara. "Red 1. Can you see him now?"

"No, Chief. I've got no shot. Over," he replied.

"Okay you come back here too," directed control, realizing that he would have to reconsider the whole situation.

It would be pointless to do anything now until reinforcements could be summoned. He was indeed running low on manpower. He checked his watch. It was nine seventeen. Perhaps they would be waiting until morning. Things were going from bad to worse.

He spoke into his radio again.

"Choppers 1 and 2 – do you receive?" he bellowed. "I want you to land at the back of the property as far back as you can go before the trees. Turn the lights off and stay there until I issue fresh orders. Over and out."

The pilots both acknowledged the command and within a few minutes the landscape was, for all of the protagonists in this high drama, incongruously quiet as the rotor blades gradually slowed and stopped.

O'Hara went to the nearest car and cut the engine. He signaled to the others to do likewise. Then he turned off the headlights of the vehicles one by one. It was going to be a long, long night. In the final automobile he found a geeky-looking guy in civilian clothes, a man who had watched the scene unfolding from the safety of the back seat in growing incredulity and mounting immobilization.

"Who the hell are you?" accused O'Hara, taking in the suit and tie, the white-collar attitude of his eyes.

"Niemeyer, sir," he answered courteously, looking him full in the face.

"Fuck me!" blurted out the native New Yorker who had, up until this point, only ever communicated with him down a phone line.

What the hell was he doing here?

As if he did not have enough problems without a useless probation officer on site, probably more concerned with the human rights of the maniac than the remaining hostage or indeed his own brave men.

He had high blood pressure at the best of times but now he felt abnormally short of breath. Only a Montechristo Number 3 would do to relieve his anxiety.

He cut the end off of a huge Havana with his stainless steel cigar cutter and played his Dunhill lighter over the end. As he puffed the expensive smoke into the night air, he repeated the choice phrase:

"Fuck me!"

He looked around whimsically, hopefully, for a grinning Master of Ceremonies to appear.

Alas, to no avail.

See how wicked people think up evil;
They plan trouble and practice deception.
But in the traps they set for others,
They themselves get caught.

(Psalm 7)

Chapter XI

Nurse Sheryl Baker arranged the latest floral bouquet in a vase. It was about the fiftieth she had done in the last three days, all for the same patient – this man who would in all probability never know their loveliness nor sniff their fragrant perfume. Even the fact that so many people had made the decision in their pocket book to show that they cared, would, she reflected, in all likelihood never be appreciated by the comatose man in the bed. They were running so low on vases that she had already brought in all of her own and still the flowers came, each addressed simply to Davey Boy.

It was incredible that no one had come forward to say who he was after all this time and yet Nurse Baker thought to herself, as she trimmed two inches off of the stalks of the pink carnations, who would miss her amid the metropolitan anonymity of the Big Apple should something similar ever happen to her?

She did not know her own neighbors with the possible exception of the old lady on the ground floor who never watched anything other than reruns of Star Trek on cable and never bought a newspaper and most probably thought that a worldwide web was something woven by a giant spider in some cheesy 1950's sci-fi flick.

As for family and friends, they would not be alarmed if for a few days she did not answer the phone, knowing as they did that she worked shifts at irregular hours. In fact even if her face was plastered all over the media, who would recognize her with all those dressings and tubes?

If a friend should call intermittently over a few days and receive the voicemail service each time, why should they panic? They would just think that she is too busy to return their calls.

As a single, hardworking big-city girl Nurse Baker could understand all too well that she might fall thru the normal social net and appear unloved should an unforeseen tragedy happen. If in addition all of her workmates had been caught up in the selfsame tragedy then it was even simpler to understand.

She looked at the man lying there in front of her and felt for him with every ounce of her fellow feeling. He was alone in the world with no special loved one to help bring him back from the brink.

Maybe thirty years ago, she mused, it may have been less likely that this could have happened, but in New York in 2001 people's lives had become increasingly denuded of community ties, familial links, for all of the zeal with which Mayor Giuliani had gone about his reforms. Even friendship seemed a rarer commodity. It was an unfortunate by-product of modernity it seemed.

She touched the patient's hand tenderly, her clear-varnished fingertips lingering in pity on his knuckles. As she went out into the ward another stray thought occurred. What if out there, there were people who did recognize him but were too shell-shocked by events to bring themselves to call the hospital?

It was nearly two O'clock – almost time for Dr. Milsom's rounds. In tow he would have his usual nurse and three or four junior doctors.

The master clinician bounded into the room. He ran his expert eye over the instruments that monitored the patient's status.

"Very interesting!" announced the doctor, picking up the ream of paper that constantly fed the EEG machine and then formed a neat concertinaed pile. "What does this mean, Dr. Webber?" Milsom asked the handsome twenty-something, who was the self-appointed Clooney of his year's intake.

"You mean this non-uniformity in an otherwise straight line?" replied the young man, describing what he could see for the benefit of the nurse whom he was out to impress. "Very peculiar. Have there been other occasions like this Dr. Milsom?" he enquired, raising an eyebrow at the consultant.

"You've been here every day with me since the patient was admitted, have you not Dr. Webber?" he intoned in his best teaching voice.

"Yes sir," replied Webber. "But I've only ever looked at the current page and that's always been stable background brain activity, nothing more."

"Nurse Ponsonby," he stated. "Do you think that we keep these machines churning out paper every minute of every day just in order to waste the hospital's money, not to mention the Amazonian Rainforest?"

"No, doctor," she said fluttering her long lashes at him.

"So why, nurse?" he asked reasonably, smiling back at her.

"It's a diagnostic tool, sir," she responded.

"And you Dr. Webber?" he said, looking almost affectionately up at the taller young man whom he was certain would one day make a fine surgeon.

"Of course, sir. I know all that. But sir, this is good news isn't it?" he asked.

"Yes it is," said Milsom, smiling quite broadly now.

"What exactly have you seen in the paperchase before now, doctor?" Webber asked him, shooting a look at Davey Boy and then taking in the pretty features of the young nurse.

"This sequence indicates frontal cortex faculty coming back on stream, Webber. As you know the Johansson Signature is always the first sign of a return to brain-wave normality as the cortex re-establishes connections with the cerebellum and the nerve tissues to the spinal column."

"You mean he's on the way back?" said Nurse Ponsonby, her heart-shaped face glowing with transparent joy.

"Of course it's too. early to say for certain, nurse, but..."

"So how often are these Johanssons coming, sir, at present?" Webber interrupted.

"Have a look for yourself," the consultant said, opening his hand in the direction of the paper.

He liked the junior doctors to experience the practicalities of the neurological discipline as much as possible by dint of their own devices. It was how he had learned; it was the best way, the only way. It was the beginning of Webber's career and although it was time-consuming for a busy consultant neurologist like himself to teach like this it would pay dividends for Webber's patients in the future.

In fact none of the young doctors present would ever forget this tutorial and so many lives that might otherwise have been given up as hopeless cases may instead be regenerated.

Webber took the paper and, with Nurse Ponsonby attending to the task of holding each sheet up, the intern studied each one with his notebook and pen poised. Every so often he would make a mark, then he would murmur something to the object of his current affections and she would let go of the sheet and pick up the next.

At length he raised his head out of his notes.

"Well?" said Dr. Milsom.

"Every ten minutes at the end of yesterday, increasing in frequency to every seven minutes thru the night and now for the last few hours they seem to be heading towards five minute intervals," he announced, closing his pad in triumph.

"Good. Very good," whispered the eminent neurologist.

"It means the synapses are working at least in some parts of his brain," said Webber. "Even if the Johansson signatures are not Johanssons at all it's still very good news."

"But they are quite distinctive lines, are they not?" asked Milsom, ignoring the nurse now, concentrating on searching his prodigy's face for clues as to the comprehensiveness of his understanding.

"Yes they are," answered Webber.

"Johansson Signatures do not have to be of any particular format," he explained. "They only have to be regular and of the same basic profile," he went on, deliberately.

"It is akin to the call-sign before a radio transmission," he continued. "In World War 2 the British sent coded radio messages to the French Resistance all the time preceded by the first two bars of Beethoven's Fifth. This brain pattern is like that. It is the brain equivalent to Da Da Da Daaaaaa.

"As the connections are increasingly re-made between different sites in the brain, the brain automatically exercises its new prowess. That is why the Johansson Signature is not amplitude or wavelength specific – because it is purely the try-out for the latest network resoldered. The shortening gaps and differing profiles indicate that there is more and more resoldering going on. In truth the rest periods between the signatures are the most crucial time, when the connections are being repaired."

He finished his lecture. He indicated to the junior doctors to move onto the next room.

The professor placed his palm on the forehead of Davey Boy. By some sense innate to himself, and perhaps people of the medical fraternity everywhere, he could divine nature doing its bio-chemical best inside his patient. He was re-forming centimeters beneath his hand at the rate of thousands of electrical junctions per second. It was for moments like this that he had become a neurologist all those years before.

It made him feel humble in the face of such fantastical natural remedy. All they could do now was stand back and keep him stable and comfortable in his outer shell, for in a short time, perhaps, he would again be requiring it. Hopefully he would be able to walk out of his Cedar Plains hiatus that he would recall nothing of – and this period in his life will be forever but a miniscule, yet crucial, percentage of his existence.

As for Dr. Milsom he may once again be feted throughout the neurological fraternity and possibly the wider world too. If so, then he would be suitably gratified but his wife, Melissa, would be exceedingly gladdened to once more bask in reflected glory.

Milsom had, for many years, rued his decision to marry a trophy wife. She would not give a fig for the miracle of Davey Boy's resurrection, only for her own in the social context.

Davey Boy however would remain his main concern. After what this poor man had been thru he deserved a break.

Milsom made sure nobody was watching and then placed his hand on the patient's.

"Come on, Davey Boy," he said gently. "You can do it!"

He then turned on his heels and went to catch up his contingent, happy that he had never subscribed to the standard advice about never becoming emotionally involved with one's patients.

How much longer will you forget me, Lord?
For ever?
How much longer will you hide yourself from me?
How much longer must I endure trouble?
How long will sorrow fill my heart day and night?
(Psalm 13)

Chapter XII

Kim had endured the most terrifying hour of her life. She huddled against the wall in the bedroom, hoping that the helicopters' lights would not flash on again, that the officer with the rifle would not return, but mostly that the badass psycho would not discover her. When the SWAT man had come up to the window to see if he could get a line to Sholtz thru the sights of his SA80, that had actually been the most nerve-racking moment of all. One false move and she would have betrayed herself to this man not twelve inches away diagonally thru the thin pane. She had witnessed thru the crack in the door the shot which had almost killed Creet, if not the one that actually did, and both had been due to so-called marksmen. She did not want to take unnecessary risks by identifying herself to any one of them, out of the blue. She adjudged that they would be as liable to shoot first and ask questions later as the hostage-taker himself.

She comforted herself that she was as yet undetected and now that the lights were off she at least felt safer. Kim knew that the choppers would switch them on in an instant if she tried to sneak out thru the casement. Most likely she would be shot on sight. It did indeed look like there was no way out; she was the living quintessence of a person caught between a rock and a hard place. How she regretted that decision to chase after Desi because of some stupid feeling that she had.

She tried to see thru the door to the kneeling Desi, sobbing now uncontrollably. Her heart went out to her. This woman had been thru a most incredible rollercoaster these last two days, so unbelievable in fact, she mused, that if it were a Hollywood film people would say that it was too far-fetched.

Kim could smell the stench of spilling bile emanating from the other room. It was distinctly colder now that the left hand window was smashed in. She felt a sneeze almost upon her and pinched like she had never pinched before, thumb and middle finger above her septum. Soon she became cognisant of her pupils adjusting to the dark.

Into the front room she peered, transfixed by a sight which, even in the half-light, scoured the lowest trough of human baseness, which made her blanch and taste the sweetness of her own vomit in her parched mouth. Merely the silhouette she saw, yet that was enough. In all the annals of recorded Stockholm Syndrome cases no parallels could surely have occurred to match this vignette of complete bestiality. Kim saw the open-mouthed woman and the now seated sub-human, his Beretta pressed to the rear of Desi's scalp, as she pleasured the congealing, ultimate source of his depravation.

She wanted to act, wanted to do something, anything to reassert her humanity in the face of this onslaught to every moral fiber in her being. Pure hatred at Sholtz's vileness propelled her forward in soft padding movements to the door. There in sharp relief she lived the nightmare both visually in close-up but also aurally as the moaning and panting of this devil incarnate filled the shack.

As this observer watched for the second time in two hours the sexual congress of Desdemona and another, the circumstances of which however could hardly have been more different, she tore her eyes off of the scene before her, now reaching its nadir, and looked around the room. In front of her she could see the depleted ranks of policemen and vehicles in a state of abeyance. On the floor jagged shards of glass diffracted the light from outside and shimmered. The front door was locked with two bolts and a mortise, to which she assumed Sholtz had the key. On the other side of the room she could see the kitchenette, a serrated knife lying carelessly on the breakfast bar.

Sholtz held one gun to Desi's head and the other he had trained on the front door, ready to switch either way should a frontal assault materialize.

It looked like the assault would only be launched when more personnel had arrived. Probably they were all in for the night now, thought Kim, listening to the hideous sound of the maniac's urge finally being sated. She might yet get her chance during the night should Sholtz drift off to sleep. She made a mental note of how to tiptoe over to the knife without tripping up on any furniture. As plans went it was not ideal but for the moment it was all that she had and she clung to it in desperation.

When one has nothing but hope then that emotion is always of a level inversely proportional to the logical foundation of that hope. It is indeed an evolutionary tool designed to make one never succumb to the non-procreational depressive gene.

"Now I need some bandages," Sholtz ordered after his recreational interlude. "Go get some sheets from the bedroom."

Kim retreated into the dark corner as Desi, as if in a catatonic trance, pushed the door to and went to the bed.

"And put a strapping over my ribs as well," he called after her.

He held his hand over the entry wound, no longer leaking blood. He felt better since he had received some attention from the woman. She now attended to him again but in an altogether different capacity.

He seemed now to have forged thru the pain barrier and it looked as if the platelets in his blood had done their job well. It seemed as if the damage wreaked on him by Pentavsky was not as life threatening as he had first assumed.

"Now do the leg," he said and this makeshift, brutalized nurse swathed the bloodied tibia.

"Thanks," he uttered gruffly, adding, "For everything," a lecherous smile on his face.

He did not know for sure if he had sustained internal injuries of a fatal disposition, but he felt patched up now by Desi's handiwork and ready for anything.

The door to the bedroom, since Desi's foray there, had now swung to and remained at three quarters open, giving Kim an almost unrestricted view.

She looked on as Desi asked for permission to get dressed and it was granted.

Desi came into the bedroom, the nozzle of his 92F following her constantly. Kim was able to see the left hand clasped around the butt of the firearm. She thanked God that the door had not opened any wider lest Sholtz, head turned to admire Desi's unclothed legs for one last time, should see her own shrunken figure in the shadows.

Desi pulled on her tight-fit jeans and boots and then her blouse and jacket. She looked out into the distance at the helicopters and, it seemed to Kim, directly at her just for a second – not only at her, but into her eyes. She seemed to smile as well. Kim held her breath.

"Do you like my perfume?" called out this most self-possessed of women, improvising a flighty southern belle accent, a la Vivien Leigh in *Gone with the Wind*.

Sholtz was himself taken aback and cleared his throat prior to speaking in a voice less crude than his wont and which toyed with reciprocal flirtation.

"Very nice. What scent is that?" he asked. "Chanel No.5, is it?"

Kim went cold all over. 'What was all this about?'

She watched as Desi went to Sholtz and sat on his knee, stroked his cheek.

She was subsumed by the craziness of what was occurring now; she attempted to make herself into an even tighter ball. Kim fleetingly wished that she had brought her cell phone with her but even if she had done it might itself have condemned her to a premature grave – if it had accidentally rang or if she had been heard calling 911.

"Baby, what perfume is it then?" she heard the killer ask, watching in amazement as this whore of whores kissed him and looked coquettishly into his hangdog eyes.

"Didn't I tell you then, sweetheart?" she asked rhetorically, running her fingers thru his mangy hair.

"No, you didn't tell me, baby," said the madman, now feeling that he was more enjoying this 'romantic' twist than the enforced fellatio of a moment before.

"It's called Carmen Vitis," stated Desi. "Now do you want me to pull the drapes so that we can have some privacy?" she went on.

"Yeah, hon, you do that," averred Sholtz, unconsciously licking his lips in anticipation.

In a flash Kim saw what was going on. Carmen Vitis was her own favorite brand and on the previous night Desi had seen the elaborately wrought bottle on the bathroom shelf and commented on how striking it was. She knew that Desi was not wearing it, as she had seen her dab on her own scent on leaving the apartment. Desi had been trying to tell Kim that she had seen her, that she knew she was there. It had not been in Kim's imagination at all.

Kim watched as Desi edged over to the windows with some trepidation and slowly pulled the drapes. On the left side the cheap, red fabric billowed in the night air.

"Now I'll draw the drapes in the bedroom," said Desi, walking up to the window and pulling them completely closed.

'Thank God,' thought Kim, 'that no one outside had mistaken her for Sholtz and fired a shot in error,'... but then this remarkable lady looked anything but a rampaging two hundred and fifty pound psychotic.

It was now almost fully dark in the cabin save for some stray moonlight diffusing in thru the unlined drapes at the front.

Desi lingered by Kim and placed her hand on her face for a second, looking back over her shoulder all the while at Sholtz.

"Where are you, honey?" he called out.

"I'm just coming, darling," Desi responded, and then in the briefest, lowest aside turned to Kim. "Did you see the knife in the kitchen?"

"Yes," said Kim softly, more mouthing the word than consciously using her larynx.

Desi went and sat again on the monster's knee, no sooner sitting than also stroking and petting.

Kim could feel her heart thumping so hard that she scarcely could think straight.

"I need a glass of water. Is that okay, sweetheart?" Kim heard her say; saw her rise.

"Anything for you, my lovely," he replied languidly.

It were as if he were back in Philadelphia with Holly.

She had been the only woman until now who had spoken to him with such feeling, such tenderness – apart from the odd hooker, but even he knew that that did not count.

Desi went to the sink and took a glass. She let the tap run for ten seconds, then filled it up and rinsed the wretched, salt taste of the megalomaniac from her tongue.

"Why don't you take your clothes off for a massage," she trilled demurely.

"Um. Yeah. Sure honey. I sure could use a massage," he said, taking his boots off.

Desi picked her moment and secreted the knife within the inside pocket of her blouson.

She returned and took his hand in hers, leading him into the bedroom, caressing him until he was lying down prone on the bedclothes.

"I'm going to give you the best work-out on your shoulders you've ever had," she told him. "Now relax."

140

"You take your clothes off as well, honey," he directed, his arms dangling over each side of the counterpane, a gun still held in each hand.

"Sure thing, baby," she said, softly.

She threw her jacket to the side of the bed, watching it land by the window, within a foot of her hidden ally. Then she undressed.

"What's your name anyway?" Sholtz asked at length, after she had massaged his gargantuan neck for a couple of minutes.

"Desi," she replied. "And I know yours is Bob, isn't it?"

"Yep! I'm fucking famous now ain't I, Desi," he said, feeling the sensual pleasure of her tapered fingers on his body.

"You sure are, Bobby darling," she remarked, looking around surreptitiously at Kim cowering in the darkness, wondering if her new friend had it within her to kill – knowing that one of them absolutely needed to – or they were both surely now only auditioning to be his next wretched victims.

> *To God my defender, I say,*
> *"Why have you forgotten me?*
> *Why must I go on suffering*
> *From the cruelty of my enemies?"*

(Psalm 42)

Chapter XIII

Niemeyer had watched the siege in all of its developments with growing disquiet. It was not that unusual for him to see the recapture of one of his 'clients' (in the modern PC-speak, now so much a part of the service's culture), but no operation he had ever been on had been as remotely as intense. He had been too late to save his colleague, but to see two more police officers butchered and then the householder himself was so disturbing that he had taken two valiums whilst the scene was being played out like some super-violent X-box game.

If this was what his career was all about, then he was not sure that he would want the promotion that would now be his, so affected had he been. He had had enough of having to deal with ex-cons who paid merely lip service to the idea of going straight and of the parole boards and the whole of the psychiatry profession that seemed to make a virtue of repeating the same mistakes over and over. Continually they had the wool pulled over their eyes, without ever once admitting so or apologizing to the long-suffering public who paid their inflated fees thru their state taxes.

It had given him time to think, this last hour of the standoff. He did not want to die at thirty-seven. There was still much that he wanted out of life. He heard an engine and looked up to see an ambulance arrive to take away the dead.

O'Hara came over to Dirk and commiserated him on the loss of a fine man. Niemeyer reciprocated regarding the deceased officers, asking also what had happened to the two who had apprehended the fugitive earlier, whose car he had seen with the abandoned Lexus.

"Dead," he was told. "Shot thru the head. This guy don't take no prisoners!" O' Hara snorted.

Dirk muttered the conventional thing about being very sorry for the losses sustained by the police and went on to say that if there were anything he could do then he would be only too willing to oblige. O'Hara thanked him peremptorily but said that there was nothing he could do and that he should go home.

"In fact that's an order," he went on, calling to Blue 1 and asking him to give Dirk a lift to his car and then return home himself.

Pending an internal investigation into the incident in which the hostage had been blown away, Blue 1 was on indefinite leave, he had stated.

The car journey passed in silence until they reached the spot where Niemeyer's vehicle was parked. He alighted and thanked the SWAT man. He noticed with relief that Marv's body had been removed. He got into his vehicle and drove off.

It was a long journey. Still the same policeman was at the roadblock, but he was no longer advising people not to go thru, only to not stop anywhere near the siege-house. Niemeyer wished him a good night and went on his way, thinking of his late colleague, dreaming of another life away from all of this.

Everyone needs a decent reason to wake up every day and go into work; currently he was blind to his own raison d'être. He neither felt valued by the department nor felt that what he did was of any real intrinsic moral value.

He drove along the freeway on automatic pilot, his mind replaying time and again recent events. Finally he rolled into the sedate city of Helena and onto his own apartment block. Having lived there for three years one may be excused for thinking that it felt like home by now, but somehow it did not. It lacked any real warmth, any individual touch in the décor. He poured himself a scotch and sat down at the computer. He began to type.

After an hour he awoke and studied the screen in front of him. Almost half a page he had written until the combination of tiredness and liquor had made him fall asleep.

He recommenced tapping out his letter of resignation.

Dirk signed it and addressed the envelope to the department's head of human resources. He went into the kitchen, found some potato chips and Ritz crackers that he then ate voraciously, flicking channels on the remote all the while, stopping only when he got to the local news broadcast.

He watched the latest report from Moonstone, the item informing him that one hostage was dead and six further policemen.

Dirk watched forlornly, as the segment progressed:

<<The name of the owner of the property, we can reveal was a Mr. Bryan Creet,>> the reporter went on in the typical, breezy style.

<<We understand that he had only been released from the Montana State Penitentiary two months ago. Investigations are ongoing, as we speak, to determine if there is a link between the gunman and Mr. Creet.

<<This has been Marcus Paradiso for MSB News in Moonstone, Montana.>>

Niemeyer clapped his hand to his head in shock, both startled and numbed at the reference to Creet. How stupid he had been not to realize that this was Creet's house, for he had loved the guy almost like the elder brother he had never had – 'almost' being the operative word here – and he had once stayed there as a callow youth of nineteen with Creet himself. Now he knew why he had been inexorably drawn to the place – not for Marv alone but for Bryan also.

Dirk went to the crystal tantalus and poured himself a large measure of scotch before going to his desk. He took out an A4 size manila envelope. He tipped the contents onto the keyboard and out spilled a selection of old photographs. All of them were of Creet and himself: playing pool in a bar in Tucson, swimming in the Pacific, sparring in the YMCA gym in Savannah, Georgia.

Creet had been ten years older and had shown him how good life could be – how life was supposed to be fun.

Dirk downed the whisky like tonic water and studied the photographs, a sentimental gleam in his eye. Those were the best times of his life, he reflected, raising his tumbler to his chin and proposing a toast.

"To Bryan Creet, the best friend a man ever had," he gabbled and he smiled at the memories which were flooding back, recollections he had not taken out of cold storage for years.

Having sat there for an hour reacquainting himself with the snaps, Dirk went to a file and pulled out a letter. He reread it in silence, a frown cantilevering his forehead: -

Montana State Penitentiary
7/22/01

Dear Dirk,

I write to let you know that I will be released in a few days now. I will be buying the little wooden cabin off of Alec McKenzie. Remember us staying there with Alec all those years ago. He's going back east and he's letting me buy it virtually for nothing – well 10 years' prison wages anyway.

Speaking of 'for old times' sake', I know that I should have wrote you before now, but I couldn't bring myself to drag you into my own dire life. I know that you do believe me when I say I'm innocent because I got all your letters in the early days. I'm sorry that I refused to see you that time, but I did not want you to risk the career you've worked so hard for by any association with me.

I was in a terrible state then anyway and I couldn't face anyone. Why am I writing now, you ask? After not seeing you for ten years I just want to say that I would love to see you again if you wish to. I really do hope that you could perhaps pay me a visit or vice versa, if you prefer.

I'll leave things like that for now but when I've settled in I'll write you again and give you the proper address. I'll understand if you would prefer not to see me, after all these long years. You've probably moved on – onwards & upwards! – why not, eh? Good Luck to you! All I know is that in those far-off days when we went on trips and worked farms together and loved life and lived it to the full each day…..they were the best days. I'll always be grateful that I met you that afternoon at Berkeley back in '83.

Yours sincerely,
Bryan Creet

Dirk closed the file. After all those years of being locked up for something that he had not done, of not spending any money inside, of having bought the cabin and then after only a few weeks of freedom to be gunned down in his new home by a cop... it made no sense.

Neither rhyme nor reason was there in this whole tragic, sick series of events. He had never been lucky – that now was the only sense Dirk could make of it all.

Niemeyer only knew that he was pleased that by some weird, circuitous route, he had made some kind of contact with Bryan before he had died. Unknowingly for both parties maybe, but the connection was indubitably there at the end of his miserable life and Niemeyer felt kind of right at that knowledge. He would make sure that he had a proper funeral. It felt like the very least he ought to do.

Nevertheless there was nobody to call, no family, no friends. His had been a life that generally fell into the cracks between other people's lives, perhaps by dint of personality or maybe circumstance, but never quite impinging. Even when Dirk and he had been close there was always a distance that could never be breached, forever a far-off glaze in his eye, even when enjoying intimacy of sorts.

Niemeyer glanced at the clock on the VCR. It was nearly midnight. 'What a week this has been,' he thought and turned off the television. It was Saturday tomorrow. He prayed that there would be no more slaying.

In the bathroom cabinet a man with sallow complexion, rheumy-eyed and prematurely jowly stared at him. He was old before his time; he was lonely, he was miserable. Those photos may as well have been of a different person for all the correlation that they had with this middle-aged face reflecting back at him.

In the bedroom he climbed beneath the duvet and took respite on the fresh, blue pillowcases that he had changed that very morning. If there was one thing he liked it was cleanliness – yet he had chosen a dirty profession. He saw that now.

All the good that the probation service could possibly do to address the problem of re-offending by the more malleable ex-convicts was far outweighed by the one or two who got away – like Sholtz. The malleable certainly were already converts to a life of righteousness... because they were malleable and had been converted to the path of good anyway by simple incarceration. What therefore was the point? Surely it was far and away better to have a safety first policy so that the detritus of society were not allowed to prey on the innocent? Surely to allow one such murder from one released killer was one too many? Better wasn't it surely, to punish the guilty properly rather than the innocent improperly?

Niemeyer awoke, aware that he had been dreaming, a sweat moistening his neck and forehead. He could barely remember the dream...or was it a nightmare? He sighed and got out of bed for a glass of water.

He speculated what course his life would have taken if he had not met Bryan Creet on that fateful day, driving a tractor over the Berkeley lawns. It was all hypothetical. It did happen – nothing could alter that now or ever. We are all, Dirk thought, turning off the bedside lamp, merely biological automatons. We can do no other than what we do.

Sholtz, Creet, O'Hara, Pentavsky himself, all shared that one primary human failing which everybody thinks is the absolute zenith of human power and the source of all of the arts, the sciences – that thing which we call free will, which is a complete misnomer and in the form that it is meant cannot exist. None of us have it and if we did we would not know what to with it anyway. It is a universal design fault, not in the usual sense of the term however, but in a hypothetical, conceptual sense, because there is nothing but a complete lack of free will in every atom of the universe.

Dirk comforted himself with this thought. It was a very reassuring thought, now that he had thought about it clearly.

He went back to bed, altogether made placid in his head by the reverie which had transpired from nothing more than umpteen thousand unthinking collisions and releases of molecules.

However, in the antecedent, there were millions upon millions of chemical and electrical, magnetic and mechanical events in his body over which he had no more conscious control than O'Hara had over Sholtz – and in the outside world countless trillions, each of which impinged on him in some imperceptible way.

All of which had led him to here.

If this was the case he could do nothing other than hand in his letter of resignation in the morning. There was no reason to doubt anything anymore. He was on the inexorable conveyor belt of life. His life – a life that could be no different to that which it now was.

He fell into a deep, restful sleep.

I am abandoned among the dead:
I am like the slain lying in their graves,
Those you have forgotten completely,
Who are beyond your help.
You have thrown me into the depths of the tomb,
Into the darkest and deepest pit.

(Psalm 88)

Chapter XIV

"Officer Rosario, you asked to see me?" Dr. Milsom said, looking de Souza up and down, wondering idly if he had to wear a special non-contamination suit at work.

"Hiya, doc," Rosario greeted him, shaking his hand. "Any progress?" he enquired.

Milsom half-smiled and sidestepped the question. He looked warily at his palm and wondered what the hygiene arrangements were at Ground Zero.

"Well, you know Rome wasn't built in a day," he responded that 0.25 second too late to sound completely natural.

The doctor had no intention of raising Rosario's hopes any more than he had already done so. It was one of those skills that he had acquired over more than thirty years. Everyone always reads more into an optimistic prognosis than is really there. It was best to sometimes dampen down the burden of hope one had conjured up in loved ones by merely telling the truth. It was, he thought, like playing good cop, bad cop – but by oneself. He was after all tending to the psychological welfare of the patient's family as much as to the patient himself. It was part of the job description.

"But doc, you know…um, er…what you said yesterday," Rosario stuttered. "I thought things were, you know, hopeful, doc."

"They are, but it's very early days. Now I'm sorry but I've got two more patients to see on Vanderbilt Ward," he replied.

If he was undetained, if his bleeper did not go off, he was looking at being at the cocktail party in Staten by eight thirty. His wife was meeting him there. He had booked a reservation at Cavasta for ten fifteen.

"Yeah, doc. I'm sorry to keep you. I know you're a busy man," de Souza said, animatedly, fishing in his sports bag and pulling out a clear plastic pocket. "But, doc, I've found something. I've actually found something, doc…at, you know…on …site."

He realized that he was speaking so ebulliently that he immediately went down an octave and whispered the last word – people were coming along the corridor.

Milsom smiled nervously for an iota. A dozen thoughts flashed thru his medical brain, his layman's brain and touched on his essential humanity all at once. In one part of his 'husband's brain' he felt a twinge of foreboding – something from deep down in his neuron processors told him that he may have to let Melissa down by baling on dinner. She would not be pleased.

"You better come to my office with that," said Dr. Milsom brusquely, as if addressing a courier, yet it was not rudeness which informed his manner but a professional urge not to betray his own heightened excitement.

"Sure, doc. You lead, but doc, I thought you've got things to do?" Rosario tried to clarify, taking in an attractive nurse as they walked thru reception.

"Yes, yes, yes, I have. But this – this I have to see," he answered, walking into the plush elevator and pressing 'Fifth'.

"Hello, prof. Hello Officer Rosario," said an orderly, jumping in as the doors closed and pressing the console. "How is Davey Boy today?"

"Seems about the same," responded de Souza.

"We're all rooting for him!" said the young man, exiting at the fourth.

Thereafter they were silent until they arrived at the surgeon's consulting rooms.

Black and white framed prints of old jazz musicians littered the walls, only outdone in number by certificates of medical qualifications and association memberships. Jelly Roll Morton vied with an honors degree in Neurophysiology from the University of Chicago and Bix Beiderbecke with certification from the American Association for the Advancement of Science.

"Sit down, please," said Milsom.

Officer Rosario sat down at the polished walnut veneered desk, clear but for three tiers of stacked red plastic in-trays and then waited while the doctor busied himself with cutting open a sachet of coffee and pouring a jug of distilled water into the percolator.

"You'll have a coffee, won't you, officer?" asked Milsom, once the machine was up and running, dripping its hot brown elixir of late nights and hangover morns.

"Yes, please Dr. Milsom. I'll have mine with no sugar," he replied, looking around as the doctor garnered milk from a mini-refrigerator.

Finally Milsom returned to the desk with two cups, indicating to his visitor by guttural coughs and a scimitar eye-flash, to pull two coasters out of a pretty, little EPS holder.

"Thank you for your understanding and for your forbearance," he started. "I've been thinking up a lot of questions but if that thing is what I think it is, it's better that we do this here rather than in full public view. "

He completed his sentence and took a sip.

He felt dumb for having to ask his first question, being a man of science, but he thought he had a responsibility to his hospital and to his Hippocratic oath to ask anyway.

"Could that thing be hazardous in any way?" he interposed.

It was very remiss of him, he knew, but he had been so busy that he had not had time to read any of the articles on what exactly was going on in the recovery enterprise at that Hades of a place.

"No, doc, it's quite safe. We take all sorts of precautions like X-ray machines, Geiger counters, de-contamination chambers…"

"Yes, but has this… um… item been thru all of these?" the medic interjected.

"Oh, I see, you think I've just found this, put it in my pocket and come straight…?"

"No, I didn't think anything," Milsom said, shamefaced, then paused, took his hand off of the cup and

153

placed it open-palmed in mid-air, as if to calm down what was rapidly becoming an awkward dialogue.

"The thing is, I'm just asking what goes on there? I need to know the exact provenance, here, before we can conceivably use it? I have to consider hygiene, safety, all of that. Remember this is a hospital and if we start waving it around in front of Davey Boy and it's...well you know... we may as well switch off all of his life-support machines right now."

The doctor felt bad at having to be so pedantic with someone who so obviously was one of the good guys and who so self-evidently cared at least as much for this stranger whom he had rescued from the mire. He finished talking and stretched his lips in an approximation of an apology.

"Look doc let me talk now," the fireman rebounded, putting the clear plastic case on the desk. "It's hell down there, but it's efficient. I won't go into detail about the things we find... but a lot of it is heart-rending – totally! Now, when you mentioned yesterday about finding a wallet or whatever to speed his recovery, I was, of course, happy to oblige.

"Of course, I didn't really believe it ... I mean, that I could find anything worthwhile. Needle in a haystack, huh, doc! Well you've seen the pictures on the TV news. There's hundreds of thousands of tons of rubble and it's still burning."

Rosario stopped talking and took a mouthful of coffee. Milsom glanced at his watch.

"Excuse me Rosario, but I'll just make a call if you don't mind. It won't take a second.

"Hello, Randolph Hearst ward? Is Dr. Chambers there, please? Yes I'll hold… Hello, doctor. It's Dr. Milsom. I've been delayed in seeing those two cases of yours, doctor. I should be there in half an hour. Yes. Sorry. Yes. See you then."

He replaced the receiver and looked at Rosario once again, inviting him to proceed.

"Dr. Milsom, like I said … I didn't hold out much hope, to be frank, not when I got thinking about it, but any hope is better than none, ain't it. So I thought I'd give it my best shot. That's the least Davey boy deserves. Anyway, 'the problem created the solution' as Officer Ibrahim said this morning."

"Who's this Ibrahim?" asked Milsom.

"He's the officer I went to with our problem. He's got everything found on site neatly recorded on computer, once it's been thru all the processing, of course. Every item is catalogued alphabetically. What he then did for us was run a program cross-referencing each found item with the names of all the victims, so far known."

Professor Milsom hesitated, not sure if all this was strictly kosher or should one say halal?

"So he gave me this, only two hours ago. There were only thirty-one items so far unaccounted for in terms of named personal effects. Out of these eighteen were women. That leaves thirteen possibles to rule out.

"Ten of these were ID with a photo. None of them was our boy. That left three items – a Diners Club card, a wholesale store card and… one was a wallet with a credit card – this one."

He waited for the doctor to pose the question which he had been on the verge of for the last ten seconds.

"But Rosario, it doesn't mean anything," he said wearily. "If there's no photo identification then you can't say with any conviction at all that this is our man."

Officer de Souza carried on regardless.

"So anyway, Ibrahim eliminated the charge card by calling the guy up. He had lost his card a year ago. He used to work there.

"The store card, that was trickier because the guy's name was Jones. Anyway after thirty-six calls he found the guy who said he had lent it to a friend, three weeks ago – and he knew he was okay."

"So that leaves this as the only possible?" said Milsom, shaking his head now in profound skepticism.

"No, certainty!" exclaimed the fireman, his broad Bronx vowels dominating the office space.

"Well?" asked the older professional quizzically.

This had all the hallmarks of a wild goose chase conducted by two well meaning but naïve firemen playing at being detectives. The thought occurred to him that he may be able to make the drinks party after all, so long as he rushed thru his meeting with Chambers.

"Open it up. Go on," urged Rosario.

"I really must be somewhere in an hour and a half and haven't got time for all this right now," Milsom protested, thinking to himself that to avoid any embarrassment on Officer Rosario's part, it may be better that he brushed him off now and arranged to meet him on Monday. By then no doubt he would have realized that he had let his optimistic outlook and desire to help outweigh his attention to forensic detail.

"Please, Dr. Milsom. Open it up and then I'll go."

The fire officer spoke the words coolly, this time less like a time-wasting ingénue, but rather more like an intelligent man on a mission.

The room succumbed to an uneasy silence, the silence of anticipation. And yet still Milsom believed it must be a long shot; it could be an article from the Lost and Found, discovered and retained months, even years ago, with no relevance to Davey Boy whatsoever.

Gingerly the surgeon took the envelope and emptied it onto the desk. For some reason now he felt humbled in the presence of this object. Perhaps it was that it was tinged with the stamp of history he thought, but no, that was not it. This mere dog-eared artifact was of no more significance than any one of a trillion grains of dust from that terrible vestibule of destruction and death. It was a black calf leather wallet – that was all – singed around the edges. He wondered whether it had been completely sterilized or whether it may contain germs and viruses. There were indeed fears that the terrorists may have smuggled biological or chemical weapons on board.

Rosario seemed to read his mind.

"It's 100 per cent clean, doc. It's been thru the processes. Go on, open it," he said, his eyes blazing now in keen anticipation of the professor's first reaction.

Milsom flicked it open. In front of him, laid between the leaves of the wallet, was a folded up sheet of paper. At first glance he saw that it was an application form for a credit card, folded into quarters. Dr. Milsom opened it up ponderously and then started as a wave of comprehension and profound amazement flooded, in equal measure, his whole being. It was the most genuinely incredible moment he would ever experience as a clinician and one that went directly to his core, making him feel chilled as if someone had sprayed him with liquid nitrogen.

Staring back at him from the top right hand corner of the sheet was a color facsimile of a blue eye. It was instantly recognizable, and beneath it was printed the legend: – 'CORNEAL RECOGNITION SYSTEM' and then a barcode. Quickly Milsom saw that this was an application for a platinum credit card from the United Bank of New England and Maine. He saw the time of the fax: 17.03 - 9/15/01.

Milsom could hardly imagine Rosario's joy when that fax came out of the printer and he saw that eye, jumping right out of the machine at him. It had been indeed a long shot but sometimes in life long shots come off, otherwise there would be no long shots, only impossibilities. He removed the paper and next looked at the card itself. It appeared like any other credit card, but with a biometric barcode on its reverse.

"Well what do you think?" asked the fireman, smiling his easy smile at the evident redundancy of his own question.

"Incredible, just incredible!" Dr. Milsom answered quietly, the news still sinking in, then louder, "Fantastic Rosario! Great work! Great work!"

He stretched out his hand to the elated fireman and shook his hand with brio for a job well done.

There was every possibility that this whole episode would remain forever of academic interest only. On the other hand if this information as to his identity led to someone close to the patient coming forward, then there was every reason to hope that this may prove a major step on the road to recovery. It was sometimes incredible to see what a loved one's familiar voice or touch could do to penetrate the layers of unconsciousness. He had seen maybe a handful of ultimately successful cases of this ilk across his long and distinguished career.

The human mind is a veritable myriad of neural connections and often the simplest thing can activate the whole process of regeneration. The Johansson Signatures were by themselves a definite cause for optimism. Now there was this as well.

He picked up the form again.

"Mr. Trip Montifort!" he announced, articulating each syllable with exuberant intensity. "Mr. Trip Montifort. I'm pleased at last to make your proper acquaintance."

God remembers those who suffer;
He does not forget their cry,
And he punishes those who wrong them…
Be merciful to me, O Lord!
See the sufferings my enemies cause me.

(Psalm 9)

Chapter XV

Kim cowered in the corner of the room as if spectating at a nascent gladiatorial event at which the bookings manager of the Coliseum might himself have baulked – on grounds of offence to public taste and decency.

She was perhaps the lynchpin of the whole scene, and yet as she shivered off stage, cold by the rickety window frame in the night breezes, and watched her friend massage the perverted beast, she felt physically and mentally incapable of making her long overdue appearance from the wings. For all that she knew what she must do, she could not bring herself to stir from her spider hole of dubious safety. Paradoxically though, she knew that the longer that she left it the more difficult it would be for her, psychologically speaking. There would be an ever-increasing chance that her subconscious would become overwhelmed with doubts – and moreover there was the intimidating sight of Sholtz's impressive prison gym physique.

Never in her wildest dreams had she ever envisaged having to kill a man. The depths of her respect for Desi, so cool and in command, knew no bounds as she went about

160

her plan of calming the pathological sex fiend, lulling him into a false complacency, gaining his feral trust – in order to afford just one clear opportunity to ensnare him, to finish it. There would be only one clear-cut chance to strike to end his reign of terror. Both women knew that. Kim felt herself somehow belittled in comparison by the strength of this other woman, her moral courage in deciding on a strategy and sticking with it. Now all Kim had to do was to keep up her side of the tacit bargain.

She reached slowly for the blouson and drew it to her, feeling within the impedance of the knife. Silently as possible her fingers roamed inside the fabric and withdrew it, feeling the weight of it in her hand; it was not heavy. The blade was not designed for combat however but for fruit and vegetables, bread and cheese, salami...

She ran her finger lightly along the serrated edge and felt its cool, stainless steel power properly for the first time. She absorbed a sense of its compact potential energy thru her fingertips and thrilled to it in a fashion which both simultaneously alarmed and yet intrigued her.

Kim heard a groan of pleasure from within the inky, blue-velvet enclave of the bed. For thirty seconds or more she had been quarantined in her own mental isolation from the unspeakable acts Sholtz was now performing on her new friend.

She had to act and fast.

Out of the shadows she raced, wielding the knife at head height, gripping it with all the adrenaline-fuelled strength that she could muster. She brought it down on his heaving back, its tip penetrating thru the epidermis, quelling instantly Sholtz's onslaught and eliciting a shriek of baritone agony. Down thru the dermis it traveled as Kim applied her other hand to the task, blood pouring forth everywhere as it crudely ripped into the stratae of subcutaneous fat.

His face took on the stricken expression of a pained gargoyle in the moonlight as he screamed with the elemental force of one who knows that the game is finally up. Desi leant forward and punched his mouth and then squirmed out from under him.

Kim pulled the blade out of his flesh and in one flowing movement stabbed it with venom into his left eye, splitting open the iris, as if a juicy nectarine.

The totality of the attack had taken no more than three seconds but time, for all protagonists in this backwoods coup d'etat, had become elongated into a series of discrete actions and reactions, each when post-mortemized, a lucidly recollected episode. The senses of each woman were working overtime with vivid, clearly delineated sights, sounds and smells but above all, their minds were processing a newly minted cornucopia of ascending and descending feelings.

Sholtz had dropped one of his Berettas immediately on impact.

Now the madman, even madder, his head pyroplasmic, let off a shot at his initial assailant; so damaged now was his eye however, and so incoherently responsive now were his muscles and ligaments, that he missed. Kim but managed to dive into the shadows against the internal wall as he lined up his next.

She was terrified now that this was it. As she watched him raise his gun hand and prepare to shoot, she crossed herself and recited silently a fragment of a prayer she had learnt as a girl and had not thought of in at least twenty years. Religion is like riding a bike – one can shirk it off yet one can never forget.

Sholtz concentrated all of his fast-diminishing faculties on trying to hold himself steady and fire at the fuzzy form now desperately backing into the shadowy hinterland of the wardrobe. Her sightline was still focused unstintingly on the knife still protruding from his eye like some Viking god of vengeance and she thought that that would probably be the last thing she would ever see. Only then did she receive a reprieve.

"Take this, you animal, you fucking monster!!!"

A single blast.

Desi felt the unfamiliar recoil of the fire-arm, as the steel alloy entered on an upward path into his left temple and the brute slumped.

Instantly both women tasted the sweetness of life renewed as his preternaturally suppurating cadaver dropped to the floor. Three rivulets of blood oozed from the entrance wound, a veritable torrent of fluid and plasma rushed from the exit.

He was finished, and as a hysterical Desi bestrode his abdomen, gun poised, two-handed and cocked at his head for a repeat shot, she suddenly demurred.

He was dead. Even an amateur could see that.

Both women remained stationary in the half-light for what seemed to each an eternity, until finally Desi dropped the weapon onto a pillow and fell in an uncontrollable deluge of tears into the embrace of her friend.

Sholtz lay like a slaughtered walrus, his pathetic demeanor in death irreconcilable with the mammoth nightmare that had been his life; in point of fact, the nearby town of Mammoth was one place Sholtz had not visited his unique brand of 'charm' upon.

"It's over, it's finally over," soothed Kim.

"I can't believe it. I just can't believe it," sobbed Desi.

"Come on, let me help you dress," said Kim, picking up her blouse.

"Yes, thank you," said Desi, looking down at the warm bulk of the man whom together they had vanquished.

All of a sudden the cabin was full of the hustle and bustle of a serious crime scene post-siege, and the two women were being shepherded out to one of the squad cars. O'Hara comforted them as best he could, until they were calm enough to go thru some preliminary formalities.

"Thanks, ladies. Just the main points will suffice. It's just for the paperwork," he would say and then they reeled off the salient moments in five minutes flat; a still, leeside composure strangely propelled both women in their unemotional recollections.

"If it was down to me I wouldn't ask you any questions at all," the G-Man said more than once, his voice brimful with sympathy.

Thus their ordeal came to an end and O'Hara himself drove them back to Moonstone.

"I'll make you an appointment with a counselor. She'll call you," he said. "They'll be no need to give any more statements or answer any more questions. On that you have my word."

There would be no day in court either because Sholtz, the sub-human homicide machine was not about to have his day in court – not anyway an earthly one. There would be no cross-examination, no testimony to give to a high-priced defense lawyer out to make his or her name out of defending the indefensible.

It ended as prosaically as it had been extraordinary.

It was finally in the past, at least chronologically speaking, if not cerebrally; but then that would never be an option for either of the two women. They would have to relearn how to live their lives, but it would always be there, like an advertising jingle one cannot help but replay subliminally all the time. This was no catchy tune however that would be supplanted in a few weeks by the next one. This would be there forever – an emotional trauma that could never be healed, only ever managed.

******

Once inside the apartment, Kim poured them both a brandy and in perfect unison they sat on the buffalo-hide sofa and quietly drank the restorative alcohol down in needy gulps. No words were exchanged and Kim continually filled the glasses with the reviving distillation.

They sipped from these for an hour or more, and as they ingested the burnished liquor and haplessly tried to wash the rampaging images of their experiences out of their minds, by degrees, they became calmer. The cabin took on an air of other-worldliness as if it did not exist at all but was in some kind of fourth-dimensional loop.

Nevertheless the more cognac they imbibed, the more the memories of this dreadful night did evaporate in a silent collusion between them and the detensioning springs of their overwrought brains.

It is a peculiarity of human existence that time is sometimes one's enemy and sometimes one's friend. This was how it was here in this cozy functional apartment above a shop in the middle of Nowheresville, USA.

At first the casual glances at the clock by Desi were rewarded with intervals of twenty-five minutes and she was pleasantly surprised that time was rushing by, the more to put some clear space between her and Sholtz. Then gradually the intervals became merely quarter hours when really she wanted the oblivion of slumber. She knew her own body too well. If she went to lie down now she should not be able to sleep. After everything, she was too wired still. She felt that after the last thirty-six hours of loss, abuse and debasement, all that she wanted for the moment was to sit.

Most women would perhaps have needed a bath to rid themselves of the effluent and odor of the ravisher's body; she, however, did not have the proactive energy required for that, nor indeed the motivation. It was as if having suffered such a double whammy of life-diminishing crises, so quickly one upon the other, they had in the large part cancelled each other out. The usual benchmarks for feeling emotional pain had been so transcended that it seemed that her brain was insensible to the true depth of each trauma that she had endured.

They had another drink and then Kim, at length, decided that since neither of them had eaten, that they should do so. It was by now nearly one a.m. and she went into the kitchen and began to prepare a meal.

Both women ate with relish, realizing how famished they had been. The occasional word was exchanged between them. They relied on the most transiently trivial as a source of conversation and for both women at this time, that was sufficient; they felt no need to rake over it all.

What they each needed and obtained from the other was, however, even more important than discussing things – that was the simple proximity and empathy which they shared.

They were just finishing their bowls of tagliatelli and pesto when the phone rang.

"Leave it, it's far too late," said Desi.

"No I better get it in case it's O'Hara," replied Kim, putting her fork down and reaching across.

"Hello,"

"Hello," said the male voice at the end of the line. "Is that Kim? How are you doing, Miss? Sorry to call so late."

"Who is that?" asked Kim, agitatedly, looking into Desi's eyes and giving a tiny shake of the head.

"My name, Miss, is Marcus Paradiso of MSB News. I'm really sorry to disturb you but I wondered since you're still up could I come over and ask you a few questions – and Mrs. Montifort too, if she's all right about it."

"I'm sorry, but how did you get this number?" asked Kim, her brow knitting into a pre-emptively disbelieving frown.

"Now, Kim, we have our means you know. The main thing is I want to give you both the opportunity to put your side of the story before the National Enquirer puts its."

"It's very late now. Couldn't you…?"

He smoothly interposed with a dressed-up question.

"I'm sorry, Miss, but I'm only doing my job. Now can you just tell me whether you thought you were going to die?"

"Of course I thought I was …" she began.

"Fine, thank you Kim. You don't mind if I call you Kim, do you? Now tell me which one of you actually fired the bullet that killed Robert Sholtz? Just tell me that one and I'll let you go."

"Please, it's not for me..." she stammered.

"So it was, let me see now, yes... Mrs. Montifort who pulled the trigger," he said falteringly, obviously referring to his notes.

"I'm sorry, I'm going to put the phone down now," Kim said, emphasizing the last word.

"No, no, no, no. Please put Desdemona on if she's there."

"No way, she's going to bed," responded Kim, boiling-angry now.

"Is it true that she was raped by Sholtz while you watched?" he asked nonchalantly, as if asking about her taste in music or something equally nondescript.

"Goodbye, Mr. Paradiso, and don't bother calling again."

"Who was it? I presume a reporter," enquired Desi.

"Yes, for the TV news. He seems to know a fair bit of what happened. I think he must have been talking to one of the cops," Kim explained.

"I'm going to bed – are you?" asked Desi.

"Yes, I'll just use the bathroom first though," Kim replied. "Will you be okay tonight, Desi?"

"Yes, thank you. I'll see you in the morning, Kim," she said, preparing to rise and follow Kim out of the living room.

The ring tone sounded once again.

Desi would have preferred to ignore it but she was a guest in Kim's home and if Kim were not in the bathroom then she probably would have answered it – on the assumption that it must be Special Agent O'Hara this time. Before the third ring she had the phone at her ear.

"Hello," she said, softly.

"That's not Kim, is it?" enquired the male voice. "That's Desdemona…isn't it?"

"Are you the reporter who just called…"

"Yes that's right. My name is Marcus. I'm just ringing back because the line seemed to go dead just now."

"Well, it's very late isn't it? Kim's gone to bed."

"No, Mrs. Montifort, that's all right. I would like to ask you a couple of questions though if that's not too much trouble."

"Well I don't know…" she began.

"You see, my boss is a real stickler for accuracy," he interrupted. "He won't let me put out anything on TV unless it's 110% correct."

"That's good, I suppose," replied Desi, stifling a yawn.

"Can you tell me what it felt like when he was raping you, Mrs. Montifort?" Paradiso asked.

His brief was always to get results and sometimes it was astonishing how the most unsubtle approach could draw a direct answer. Sometimes people actually wanted the opportunity to tell their story in all its personal and unedifying minutiae. It was perhaps somehow cathartic.

There was a long, long pause. Desi's eyes began to water as the degrading pictures, which she had in the main suppressed since returning to the apartment, flooded back with a vengeance.

"It's obviously a bit too raw for me to want to go into that right now," she stammered nervously. Then she added with conviction, "Or ever!"

"Now I know this is terrible for you, but could you tell me exactly what your relationship was with the other hostage, a certain Mr. Creet?" Paradiso asked.

"I really would rather not answer any more of these impertinent questions," she replied firmly.

"Please, Mrs. Montifort. I won't keep you any longer than necessary."

"No, really. I want to go to bed," she said, her head spinning from the inquisition.

"Is it not fair to say that you were having a sexual relationship with this Bryan Creet, ma'am, otherwise why were you in his house in a state of undress? Can you answer me that at least, Mrs. Montifort?" he finished sharply.

Desi was now crying hysterically.

She handed the phone to Kim who had just emerged from the bathroom, having heard the commotion.

"I'm awful sorry, Mr. Paradiso," she told him, sarcasm injected into every word, " but you've really upset my friend. Now, good night!"

"Kim, please don't hang up. I'm really sorry. I didn't mean to do that," he protested, disingenuously.

"Listen, Mr. Paradiso, she's been thru a hell of a lot these last forty-eight hours...please leave us alone," Kim pleaded, watching Desi's back disappear into the guest bedroom and start undressing.

"What do you mean forty-eight hours?" Paradiso fired back quickly, his reporter's curiosity suddenly piqued.

"Just leave us alone, will you."

"I will, but my editor will kill me if I get my segment wrong in any material aspect. What do you mean forty-eight hours?" he persevered.

"Okay. You promise; no more calls, no more questions?" she reiterated, her head dizzy with drink and emotion.

She watched Desi's perfect and very nude size 8 figure cross the room to switch off the light.

She hesitated for a second, but the computations in her exhausted mind seemed to come down on the side of telling him. He was human after all – surely if he knew the truth he would leave Desi alone out of compassion.

"Okay. She lost her husband in the World Trade Center disaster," she gushed. "And now I'll say goodbye, Mr. Paradiso. Good night!"

"Goodbye, Kim," he said, completely taken aback by this startling intelligence.

He heard the click as she hung up – but only vaguely, distantly. Already his mind was working in overdrive.

He could not quite believe his luck.

This woman was involved in the two biggest news stories of the week, of the year, maybe even the decade. What an unfortunate woman she must be, and what a million to one chance could that be…and he had it, he had the story… exclusively!

Marcus Paradiso put down his cell, licking his thin lips in mercenary anticipation. He had the best damn human-interest story he had ever had. If this did not get him a job at NBC or CNN then nothing could. He poured a vodka from the half size bottle he kept in the car and started talking into his voice-activated Dictaphone.

It was a list of all the research he would embark upon the next day in order to get a grip on the story. It was already the next day however – he completed his aide memoire and turned off the machine. He lit a cigarette and contemplated his world exclusive and what it would mean for his career if only he could play his cards right.

Paradiso fell asleep off-road in his BMW not two hundred yards from the cabin.

That night he dreamt of being a ten million dollar a year anchorman on the NBC Ten O'clock News. He would sell his own grandmother, if that were required as part of the deal. Putting the squeeze on the two women was going to be easy in comparison.

He quite liked his grandmother.

God rises up and scatters his enemies.
Those who hate him run away in defeat.
As smoke is blown away, so he drives them off;
As wax melts in front of the fire,
So do the wicked perish in God's presence.

(Psalm 68)

Chapter XVI

Niemeyer awoke the next morning and knew exactly what he had to do. His head felt groggy from the hard drink and from the carnage that he had seen.

He had a funeral to arrange and so he made a few calls. Soon he had established the whereabouts of Creet's body. It was in the city morgue.

Niemeyer picked up his letter of resignation and went out of the apartment and down the stairs to his automobile.

He would drop off his letter and at the same time clear out his desk of his personal possessions: a platinum nib pen that had been a 21st present from his father, a rotary pencil sharpener, a selection of maps, a couple of paperbacks by Joseph Heller and a scientific calculator. He knew every one of them like old friends. It would not do to leave them behind, he mused as he drove thru the bright morning rays.

It was Saturday so he should not see anyone at the office and would thus avoid any explanations as to why he was leaving so abruptly. In fact, after the certainties of the night before, he did not know himself quite what he was doing and why. All that he knew was that he owed it to himself to put the stresses of the last chapter of his life totally behind him and to try to plough a new furrow. He hoped that it would be as diametrically opposed to the former one as one could possibly conceive.

He parked his car and used his key card as he had done thousands of times before to enter the building. It was only then that it struck him. He still did not know the denouement of the siege or even if it was still ongoing. For all his hitherto professional conscientiousness, it now seemed like a matter of almost complete indifference to him. As his deputy, nominally he had assumed Pentavsky's position at the moment of his death, and therefore responsibility for ensuring Sholtz was captured with the maximum of speed, yet now he realized that since waking not two hours previously it had barely even crossed his mind.

Dirk saw that there was an agency security guard on duty and so he signed the visitors' book. He went up in the elevator and entered into the all too familiar office space. Nobody was in; he would be able to go about his business without interruption.

Having placed his letter on the desk of the Human Resources head honcho, he hesitated for a minute.

No, he told himself, it was now or never. He left the letter in her in-tray and was about to leave when some vanity within him determined to go into the goldfish-bowl room that for so long he had aspired to inhabit.

He entered Marv's office and sat for the first time ever behind the desk, seeing the floor as his late boss would have done. By only a little stretch of the imagination he could picture the scene on a weekday: the desks full of people, the muted noise thru the glass, an officer's occasional catching of his eye as he looked at him in envy or admiration or resentment.

Absentmindedly, he opened the top drawer. Inside was the usual paraphernalia. Opening the middle one he saw a few papers, personal statements for utilities in the main and underneath a racing form book and some notes about horses in a ring binder, in Marv's own scrawl. He was surprised. He had never had Marv down for a 'ponies kind of guy'.

The title on the spine was "Horses to Follow 2001". He flicked thru the leaves out of curiosity at this hitherto hidden side to his erstwhile superior's life, chuckling at some of the codes next to horses' names which seemed to denote how they had last ran. It was a view into another world, another language of hieroglyphics and squiggles, abbreviations and figures.

Having turned casually thru to the last leaf he noticed something flutter out and fall onto his lap. He put the file down on the desk and picked up the sheet. On closer inspection he ascertained it was a letter.

He read it in a low murmur to himself, his growing incredulity heightened considerably as he reached the center page numerals:-

9/11/01 11 p.m.

Marvelous Marv!

Congratulations! You've finally hit the jackpot! I'm very pleased for you (though I wish I'd followed you instead of doing my own thing – my nags were all shit yesterday).

Anyway I've just been round to Johnny Fingers' place and he had this envelope waiting for me. Good as gold.

175

As you will see, I've deducted my 10% and I'm gonna take a vacation starting today. I've just come in to leave you this package as per our phone call. I can vouch for the security in this building! I'm sure you'll find it okay in the morning. I know how discretion is important so I've marked the jiffy bag with your full title as you'll have seen by now. Anyway let's do the math:

> *3 winners – 10/1, 8/1, 20/1*
> *$100 triple = $207,900*
> *- 20,790 (my cut)*
> *- 1,300 (owed to Johnny this month)*
> *= $185,810!!!*

Don't spend it all at once. I'm off on a fishing trip for a week, so you won't see me. I've told the boss my mother-in-law's just passed on! Wishful thinking!

See ya 'n Congrats again

Dunk

(P.S. Checked money twice.) Oh yeh, almost forgot - Johnny says to say Mazel Tov!

Dirk finished reading the note. It was unbelievable. Even he, with his scant knowledge of the sport of kings, knew that the odds on getting three up were next to impossible and yet Marv had miraculously pulled it off, only to get himself blasted to kingdom come by a con a day later – certainly the odds on that would have seemed even greater than picking a winning treble at the time Marv had picked his selections. Maybe the universal imperative that is the law of averages had been at work, Dirk considered, evening up the score.

In a way it made Marv's actions in endangering his life when he had been explicitly ordered not to even more admirable, but then what is money compared to the motive for revenge?

Suddenly he was aware of someone else entering the floor. He looked up and saw it was the security guard doing his rounds. The fresh-faced young man lingered inside the doors and Dirk felt impelled to give him a sociable wave. Although there was nothing wrong with him being there in Pentavsky's office so far as the agency guard was concerned, Dirk felt a tingle of guilt — like when one is caught looking fleetingly at an attractive woman's breasts and in the act of looking sharply away it only compounds the guilt both in her eyes and in one's own.

Some flavor of Marv's extra-mural life was now coming to him. It had been pretty bleak, he thought, in terms of normal men who had a real family and an extra-curricular meadowland of life-affirming pastimes and social engagements. He sensed that Marv had seen his one chance for happiness demonically terminated and that he had never been able, out of some species of loyalty, to commit again to any woman. Possibly, it was that he thought it would be a waste of time as no other woman could ever come remotely close to his Holly. Although she had been unfaithful to him, it was as if the violence of her end had obviated this point in his mind and preserved only a perfect impression of their marriage forevermore.

Dirk shook his head as if to banish these speculations from his mind and watched the guard stroll out of the office and into the elevator lobby. Niemeyer rose from the swivel chair for the first and last time and made for the door himself, picking up his personal effects on the way.

His own existence outside these four walls was not that very different to Marv's, he thought – both single men with no real purpose in life anymore after their one true love had, for completely differing reasons, departed the scene. He had few, if any, real friends to give himself a place in the order of things out in the real world; no great interest in anything much, hedonistic or sporting, artistic or political, stamped his life with meaning.

Of course, he mused, the senior man had his horses but that was such a singularly money-oriented and solitary activity that it should hardly count in the great scheme of what he was reflecting on. Neither man was a part of some Platonic 'good' beyond himself in the wider community, except for within working hours, and even this, in his current state of mind, was debatable.

Niemeyer paused at the exit. Who would really care now that Marv was dead? He himself did not want to end up like that and he had determined now that he would not. It had to be the right thing for him to do – to resign – to find that elusive existence which had some real human interaction and quality at its core, some intrinsic value in his downtime and preferably the outlet for creativity that he yearned for in his career. Other people achieved it so why not him? He would find his real vocation in life if it killed him, he decided. It was not the Holy Grail, but how long he would have to wait before finding it, he could not hazard a guess.

In the interim, whilst the search was engaged he would need as much funds as he could muster.

Dirk doubled back, put his key card thru the swipe apparatus and went back in, hurrying over to the glass office.

On the floor in the far corner was the forty-two inch Lemington XT5. It was used for sensitive reports, firearms for issue in special circumstances, electronic tagging devices. Sometimes cash was kept there overnight for rent deposits for ex-cons and, rarely, newly purchased power tools for 'clients' returning to their trade. Only Pentavsky and Niemeyer had the combination to the safe. It was by no means certain but it was at least possible, with all that had been going on, that Marv had put the money in there temporarily until he could deposit it at the bank.

There was only one way to find out:

6.….2.….7.….9.…..

Having punched the code into the electronic console, he turned the key and pulled the handle.

There in the midst of the regular stuff was a large jiffy bag, marked in black ink with Pentavsky's full bureaucratic title.

Dirk looked around, then emptied out the contents onto the floor. There were nineteen bundles of notes, one smaller than the others, each secured with a brown rubber band. Swiftly, his hands shaking, he closed the safe door and then stuffed the money back into the envelope. He could not believe his luck. He went to the desk, retrieved the letter from Dunk and put this into his pocket. There would be no evidence remaining of Marv's good fortune. No one would be able to link Niemeyer with this 'perfect crime'.

He vacated the office and walked in ungainly style to the main door, the cache held within his jacket under his left arm. The most shocking thing to he, himself, was not what he had done but the fact that he did not feel one twinge of guilt now that he had actually done it. No one would miss it, and Marv, where he was now, could have no use for it. It was, it seemed to him, the apogee of victimless felonies. He strode out of the elevator, walked up to the unmanned reception desk and signed out: 9:57 a.m.

He went out into the harsh Helena sunlight, shriveling up his eyes as the glare hit him. For some reason he thought Saturday's sun was always of a qualitative difference to any other day's, or perhaps it was just because Saturdays were always ripe with the promise of the unexpected, the freedom of the weekend stretching ahead replete with the potential for a thousand good times. That his sixth day was more usually spent in activities more redolent of domesticity and paperwork than partying was neither here nor there. There was always a quantum leap from the sweetness of anticipation to the actual execution. Now, however he had his opportunity for play – a new life beckoned. First though he wanted to pay his final respects to Bryan Creet.

He had had no one either.

******

The mortuary was only ten minutes away. At the front desk he asked for Dr. Ramirez and was waiting three minutes when a short, mustachioed man in his mid-thirties walked up and shook his hand.

"Ah, Mr. Niemeyer. Pleased to meet you," the doctor greeted him with a pronounced Hispanic accent.

"Yes, Dr. Ramirez. Likewise. As I said on the phone the department have to organize the funeral arrangements for Mr. Creet."

"Yes, of course. Horrible business. Terrible, being shot by the police like that."

"Yes. A tragic accident, without a doubt," murmured Dirk. "Can I see Mr. Creet's body, if that is possible?"

"Yes, no problem. Follow me, Mr. Niemeyer," he said briskly, leading on along a whitewashed corridor.

"Now I'm afraid I'm not allowed to leave you by yourself in there because the body is going to be subject to an autopsy later this afternoon," Ramirez stated. "Also you must put on these overalls, hat and mask, and slip-ons. It's very important not to risk any contamination."

"No problem," replied Niemeyer.

He started putting the outfit on whilst the doctor talked about the events of the previous night. Dirk listened with utter detachment to the account, occasionally uttering a 'Yeah' or an 'Ummm'.

"First your friend is shot by a cop. Then the convict is stabbed in the eye by a hostage, whom the police did not realize was even there and finally shot thru the head by another woman hostage…"

"Oh yes," replied Niemeyer deadpan, noting with academic interest only, that Sholtz at least was no more.

"Well, it's a terrible end to a terrible week, isn't it, Mr. Niemeyer," he summarized.

"Ummm."

"And in the middle of it all is this woman hostage who was raped by Sholtz and had an affair with your friend…"

"What?" said Niemeyer. "What was that?"

"This woman who killed Sholtz with his own gun...she was having an affair with your Mr. Creet...didn't you see the TV news?" he enquired, looking for clues as to the visitor's real interest in Dirk's preoccupied eyes.

It was highly unusual for a request to see a body from anyone other than family or one who had a direct professional input into the case. Ramirez could not fathom exactly where Niemeyer's purpose lay. He was curious, but was careful not to betray this to the probation officer. He, after all, had every right to see the cadaver if he wished to – he was the de facto head of the Montana Probation Service now. It was not Ramirez's job to second-guess a fellow professional's actions or motivations.

Something, to him however, stank a little – and it was not the refrigerated bodies in their steel caskets.

"No, I didn't," replied Dirk, at length, suddenly feeling somewhat queasy, as he put on the green sterile hat.

"And of course this friend of yours was purely a professional acquaintance only, was he, Mr. Niemeyer?" Ramirez probed discreetly, unable to resist a chance to satisfy his own inquisitive nature. "He'd only just come out of the pen, right?"

Niemeyer hesitated in answering.

"Yes, of course. Professional acquaintance only," he said offhandedly, his mind racing as fast as Pentavsky's geldings.

"And in the middle of it all, this woman hostage...the one who was your Mr. Creet's lover and was raped by Sholtz...she's just lost her husband in the Twin Towers. Unbelievable! Completely crazy! We live in a mixed-up world, eh, Mr. Niemeyer?" he commented.

182

"Yes, we do. Indeed we do," agreed the ex-probation officer distantly. "Am I ready now?"

"Yep, all set. I'll open the drawer for you," Ramirez said, holding the door to the morgue proper for his guest.

Niemeyer could feel the change of temperature as he crossed the threshold from the anteroom. All of a sudden he felt like he did not know why he was there.

"Sholtz is not here as well?" he asked instinctively, suddenly, as the doctor pulled open the 24-inch deep drawer and exposed Creet's penultimate resting place on Earth.

"Of course. He's in there."

He pointed to a casket three along and one up, as if he saw nothing strange in this.

"Surely that's not right," Niemeyer protested unenergetically, watching the man walk back towards the entrance.

"That's life," answered Ramirez. "If you'll pardon the joke. In death we're all equal, Mr. Niemeyer, are we not?"

Niemeyer braced himself for the view of his old paramour, the man with whom he had spent the happiest times of his life. He could feel the refrigeration system kicking into his metabolism. Abruptly, he felt that he required some air – he pressed on however, aware that he would now see that which he had come for, that he would hopefully attain, at last, some closure.

A tear welled in each eye simultaneously and then the two lachrymal dewdrops were smeared in the normal process of blinking, brightening and moistening Niemeyer's irises until they shone with the fervent regret of one whom has only latterly apprehended that which he had once had and that which he had now lost forever.

"I'll be over here if you need me," announced the doctor, seeing the pallor in Dirk as he made to look into the metal box. "It takes people funny sometimes. Don't worry about it, Mr. Niemeyer."

Niemeyer nodded without turning around. He needed a glass of water desperately; felt that he was about to retch. Nevertheless, he somehow managed to compose himself.

Creet looked much older than when he had seen him last. His blonde hair had been replaced by a gray receding hairline. The complexion which had been so much a testimony to his healthy outdoors lifestyle had accumulated a decade's worth of anemic veneer. It was scarcely Bryan at all yet, of course, he knew that it was. There had been a lion-like quality about him, now there was merely meekness – not just because he was gone, but in his whole facial muscle tone there was no sense of the embracer of life whom he had once been.

Niemeyer was an avowed atheist and so he did not cross himself or say a prayer or linger over the deceased. He did not envisage his friend in the afterlife driving a celestial lawn mower around the pearly gates of St. Peter.

Shutting the receptacle in which he had come to see his old friend lying in state, he realized that this man had in reality left his life a decade before – ten years in which they had both been imprisoned. His was a self-inflicted two-cell subsistence of career and solitudinous life-evasion, for which up until now he had not sought penance nor relief from himself. Now he felt at the end of a long tunnel. He had no excuses left.

"If you want to arrange the funeral then I…" commenced Ramirez, convivially.

"No! No! I've decided against it. The state will take care of him won't it?" interjected Niemeyer with feeling.

"But of course," said Ramirez, taken aback. "But it will be the basic crematorium deal."

"That's how he would have wanted it, I think," said Dirk, pensive now, looking into the casket at his past and thinking how easily it could have been his future. "Did you say cremation?" he asked distractedly.

Ramirez's eyes were lizard like, trying to take in every facet of the visitor's expression, as if to analyze what their true relationship had been.

"Yes," Ramirez said simply.

"And the ashes?"

"I don't know Mr. Niemeyer. I think …on the flower bed outside the furnace building, no?" he responded, watching as Niemeyer closed the drawer and turned on his heels.

"That will be fine, then," he said, beginning to take his green coveralls off in the anteroom. "Thank you, doctor."

Ramirez washed his hands with liquid soap from a clear plastic dispenser above the basin.

Niemeyer finished dressing properly and washed up.

He dried his hands on a paper towel and then both men walked back to reception. They parted cordially.

The pathologist stared after him, nonplussed, yet only in an idle way.

It did not really matter. For him, death and all of its sometimes Byzantine ramifications had long ago lost all real fascination.

God is our shelter and strength,
Always ready to help in times of trouble.
O we will not be afraid, even if the earth is shaken
And mountains fall into the ocean depths.

(Psalm 46)

Chapter XVII

It was Saturday September 15th 2001 in the semi-metropolitan sprawl of Newark, New Jersey. The rain was beating down like it would never stop, as if the gods of Southern California were taking their sanction on those residents too poor or moribund never to have migrated west.

The scene was a decrepit kitchen in a tall twenties redbrick long since converted into apartments. In the basement that they had inhabited these last forty years, a couple was watching a syndicated report on the TV News.

"Turn it off," the man said. "You'll only upset yourself."

"No! Leave it," retorted the gray-haired woman, her face etched with the decades of grief and shame that was all that her son had bequeathed her.

She took the remote control into her heavily veined hand.

"At least it's over at last. We know we don't have to worry about him ever coming back now," spoke the husband softly, his normally avuncular face distorted by the events of over two thousand miles distant.

He was still a strong and virile looking man and he was now late for his part-time job at the abattoir.

"Did you know Bobby was due to get parole, Albie?" asked her tiny, cracked voice, looking sideways at the television.

She was unable to watch directly, yet equally incapable of switching to the cable channel showing continuous *Friends* which she habitually enjoyed over her first coffee of the day.

"No, I didn't, love," he said, sipping his tea and deliberately avoiding his wife's eyes.

"What was that letter you got a fortnight back?" she questioned him, catching sight on screen of a black body bag being carried out of the cabin.

She felt a sudden catch in her throat and swallowed twice.

"Darling, it was nothing. You saw the envelope. Just one of those Florida condo scams again – that's all," he answered.

"Why did it have a Montana postmark then?" she cried loudly, then, at last, breaking down into tears.

"I don't know. Probably because if they send them from Florida people know its timeshare crap and so they don't open the letter at all – just put it straight in the trash," he answered, sliding his stool nearer and putting a comforting arm around her.

"Albie, he's gone. He's finally gone," she wailed.

"I know it's hard. But it's surely for the best," he said. "He won't be able to kill any more innocent people now, will he, love."

"I know that, but I'm still his mother and whatever he's done, he's still my only son… *was* my only son," she sobbed, latterly correcting her tense, and in so doing, making herself convulse all the more.

"Was *our* only son, Alice. Was *our* son," Albie stressed. "Don't leave me out of this, will you. He was my boy as well."

"Sorry, Albie…I didn't mean nothing…" she started.

Her husband interrupted, "I loved him so much. I did. Like you. But there's only so much love a man can give when it's thrown back into his face so often."

His eyes misted over now, recalling happier times when their son was a floppy-haired altar boy with the face of an angel.

Albie made a grab for the roll of kitchen paper and tore off a perforated square, his nose wet with bright memories of his pride in the twelve year old Bobby, when he had learnt the catechism for Father Thomas and been word-perfect in front of the large congregation, swollen by friends and extended family.

"He was evil," uttered the big man, blowing his nose like a harmonica. "We must never forget that."

Albie enunciated clearly each syllable, as if determined not to allow himself to slide into sentimentality of any description. Then he tenderly touched the lined parchment-like face of his wife, still listening to the TV, but unable to look.

"He was the devil's spawn – let's face it, Alice. Let's not shy away from saying it like it is."

"Don't Albie, please don't. He was our son, our son…"

"He was evil, evil… evilllllllll…!!!"

He trailed off into paroxysms of pained sobbing, his shoulders traveling vertically at a great oscillation, as he let out the long, long, pent-up emotion that he always knew he could not betray whilst his progeny lived.

How could he, lest, by the finality of this admission, cause even more harm to the fragile woman whom he adored? Now it was over, he truly felt that the long overdue wake-up call to his wife would be cathartic. He had to be cruel in the short term to be kind in the long.

Over the years they had barely been able to speak of him in any terms other than that of their boy who had gone off the rails – never in anything other than sadness and pity – never outright condemnation, never ex-communication from the bosom of the family, jail terms notwithstanding.

Both had been good parents and they had maintained the charade that Bobby was basically a good boy, long after it became seriously unhealthy for them to do so – by which time of course it was all too late and they had found a niche for themselves to stay in, warm and comfortable, safe and easy. All the while they had cherished, in die-hard fashion, the belief that their boy was still a normal son. Disingenuously perhaps, but whatever the weight of evidence against him they would be sure to think that he was not as solely at fault as the court made out; that however guilty he appeared, he was, if not more sinned against than sinning, then at the very least a man given the short straw in almost every sphere of his life from jobs to women, friends to juries. Only his own mother and father were beyond reproach, in regard to his upbringing, in their rose-tinted worldview.

"He was our son," declaimed Mrs. Sholtz, tears now flowing like sequins under the fluorescent light over the curve of her cheek, and then, in a moment of revelation, for her so long-suffering spouse, she said, "however damaged... however bad he was."

"I know, sweetheart," Albie averred, wiping away a tear from her downy jaw line.

He was the creator of the monster in equal measure with her; he could not, nor did he seek to, deny that biological fact. He was the donor of the corrupt spermatozoa which had created this one in a million freak, this dud who could only prosper at the expense of other people's most basic right to carry on with their lives.

He watched the screen as the reporter spoke to camera in sepulchral tones.

This ordinary couple, this man and this woman of certain years, fell into a hug of mutual condolence, sure in the knowledge that whatever feelings they ascribed to themselves as parents, the other party was no less strained emotionally from every which angle.

Meanwhile, as if to underline this watershed, the reporter was reaching the winding-up part of his broadcast:

<<...and so at the culmination of this most terrible of weeks for our nation we have here another tragic story which in any other week would have been the headline news. As things are this particular terrible episode will be not even a footnote in the history books of our time.

<<A terrible indictment of our civilization at the beginning of this new millennium is that a man who is responsible for the deaths of at least thirteen people and very probably many more that will never be definitely attributed to him, has come to his demise – not by the forces of law and order but at the slender hands of two young demure women, each of slim build, yet each with the guts and the courage to crave life over certain death and to take untold risks to save the other.

<<With women like this in America today who stand up against a madman weighing 250 lbs – whom has already assaulted and raped and killed, and would have thought nothing of doing the same again – we can at least know that we live in a great country.

<<Somewhere out there in America are the grieving widows and widowers of thousands of our compatriots who died more apocalyptically than they or we could have ever imagined this time last week.

<<In a poignant postscript to the whole litany of misery, I can now reveal that one of these brave selfless women is herself a new widow, as a result of Tuesday's events in our greatest metropolis, New York City.

<<Yes, in a terrible compounding of exponential odds, I can now reveal that the lady who so courageously shot the bullet that killed Robert Sholtz had lost her stock broker husband in the carnage of the Twin Towers.

<<To come up against one such tragedy per lifetime is surely so statistically improbable in the extreme as to enable us to go on about our daily existences, barely even admitting the possibility that things like that can happen. And for the vast majority of us, fortunately, in going to work, buying the groceries, visiting friends, these terrible possibilities are beyond the normal range of our thoughts and our fears. However for this woman who has suffered so much not once but twice in three days, the nightmares will be with her forever. Our thoughts are with her, with the other lady and with all of the police and other victims and families at this time. God Bless America.

<<This has been Marcus Paradiso for MSB News in Moonstone, Montana. >>

Albie took the remote out of his wife's hand and pressed the stand-by button.

"It's over," he intoned, looking leaden eyed at his wife.

She was crying heavily now.

"Why? Why?" she screamed, rhetorically. "Why Bobby? Why did this have to happen to us? Why, Albie? Why?"

Her husband shook his head at her, raising one side of his mouth until one cheek bulged under his eye, as if to express that he could think all day or all year and not come up with a fitting answer or one which could even remotely do justice to the question.

"What about the funeral?" Alice asked, as if thinking out loud.

"I don't want to go. That's my last word on the subject. We ain't got money to throw away in any case. Let the authorities do what they do," he said. "There'll probably be no funeral – and let's face it no one would come. It would just be us and a load of press vultures and cameras."

"I want to go whatever it is or wherever it is," announced Alice, her lower lip trembling with conviction. "I want to be there when our boy is buried."

"Fine, darling. If you want to waste 500 bucks we ain't hardly got on going out West…" he spluttered, finishing mid-thought.

He was suddenly conscious that he had made a pledge to himself that he would display supreme sensitivity to his wife when the moment finally came. He realized now that that had been a forlorn hope that he had already blown to kingdom come – that sometimes the pre-eminence of truth supersedes all else.

A silence ensued for at least five minutes; each of these seniors, who for so long had lived under the shadow of the prodigal son, then the black cloud of the criminal son and then these past nineteen years or so the torment of the pathological killer son, now reflecting on the fact that they now had no son.

At length, Albie began sobbing again. It was a lament for all the things that he could have done just one per cent better – that iota of difference, in all his dealings paterfamilial, which may have altered his son's course sufficiently to save the innocent lives he was to extinguish.

The phone, situated in the front room, began to ring its obey-or-die tone. Albie, in no fit state to abandon the breakfast table for its insistent advances, stayed where he was.

Alice, ever the one to spring to the challenge of convention, wandered on auto-pilot into the chintzy living room and answered the phone, as ever, with light panic rising in her voice. It was as if this nineteenth century invention were the bugbear of her life, when in actuality it was the one thing that kept her actively engaged with real people and not merely soap characters on the television.

"Hello."

"Hello, Marcus Paradiso here from MSB News. Is that Mrs. Sholtz? I'm sorry about your loss. Now could I ask you a couple of questions?" he said in the brisk journalese that is always the first refuge of the present-day news hound.

"I'm sorry but how did you get this number?" Alice asked.

"We have our means and methods, Mrs. Sholtz. Now when was the last time you saw your son?" Paradiso enquired smoothly, squeezing feigned sincerity into every word.

"I visited him in the federal penitentiary about three years ago," she replied, flustered into answering by the just-dawned realization that she had, a minute before, been watching this man on screen.

"Have you had any contact since then on the phone or by letter with Robert?" he asked, thinking that if this elicited a response then afterwards it would be plain sailing.

"Who is it? Who's on the phone?" Albie shouted, entering the living room.

Paradiso heard the gruff voice and mentally cursed.

"It's that reporter from the television, Albie," she said, covering the mouthpiece.

"We don't need no damn reporters calling us and camping out on our doorstep at all hours. Tell him you can't talk," Albie barked.

"I've just got a couple more questions that's all, Mrs. Sholtz," the reporter said in practiced fashion.

"Albie, please. If I want to speak with this gentleman then I will," she said firmly, yet calmly. "Now go back into the kitchen, darling, and finish your breakfast. I won't be long."

Sholtz senior tramped off dejectedly, muttering to himself.

The interview continued.

"Mrs. Sholtz, you were saying, did you speak regularly on the phone?"

He picked up where he had left off.

"He would call once in a while, and we would exchange letters regularly," she admitted.

"Did you know he was being released this week?"

"No we didn't, Mr. Paradiso."

"Okay, when was the last time you spoke with your son, Mrs. Sholtz?"

"About a month ago, I guess."

"And how did he seem to you then?"

"Normal, just normal, I suppose."

"Okay now, Mrs. Sholtz, I can't keep you any longer or your husband will be upset and anyway I can imagine how difficult all of this is for you right now. If I can give you my cell phone number would you be prepared to be interviewed for a program about Robert?"

"I don't know about that," she said not wholly frankly, already imagining the make-up girl powdering her face, and the limousine picking her up from the apartment.

"If you want to think about it, that's fine. Have you got a pen?"

"Yes, I have one right here."

He read out the number and Alice noted it down.

"Well, goodbye and thank you for sparing the time. Give me a call in a few days."

"Thank you, Mr. Paradiso,"

Already she felt a kind of catharsis in just the act of talking with a third party outside the stultifying insularity of her home and husband. She stared at the phone number for a good twenty seconds and then tore off the sheet and secreted it up the sleeve of her housecoat.

She had always wanted to be on television, she mused, as she went back into the kitchen to face the wrathful silence she knew would be her lot for at least an hour. No matter, she told herself, taking the remote control console and turning on the channel that showed Oprah repeats.

What had happened to Bobby could have happened to any boy, any family in America. She owed it to the hundreds of millions of people out there to tell it how it was, warts and all, and maybe, just maybe, her tale may somehow prevent another mother, another father having to go thru what they had been thru, as well as possibly saving the lives of a myriad of putative victims – if others could learn from *their* parenting experiences, *their* mistakes. Maybe – but then they did not know, could not know what their mistakes had been, that had so transformed their son from an innocent boy into an infamous rapist and multiple-murderer – it was indeed an unknowable question.

Whatever her self-justification for wanting to be on TV she would do it.

Albie would just have to accept it.

Save me from my enemies, my God;
Protect me from those who attack me!
Save me from those evil people;
Rescue me from those murderers!

(Psalm 59)

Chapter XVIII

Kim and Desi woke late. It was a bright morning. Kim rose first and looked out. It was a scene of small town people doing small town things. She was thankful that she had survived the worst night of her life physically, if not mentally, unscathed. She showered and then ran a hot bath for her friend.

Looking thru the door at Desi she saw that she was laying, staring at the ceiling, as if the traumas which she had been thru were being replayed on the white polystyrene-tiles.

"I'm running a bath for you. I've put a lot of bubbles in it. Now do you want coffee or tea?" she asked.

"I think tea, please, Kim. Do you have chamomile?"

"I think so."

Thus the day began for the women, like millions of female flat-mates across the Western world, in banality and beverage, their shared experience still so close yet so, so yesterday. They both knew that the episode was forever now mired resolutely in the past and it would be best to let it remain so.

Neither of them turned on the TV or the radio in an unspoken pact of two women not requiring the media to be aware of what they had so recently been thru. No one but themselves alone could truly know what it had been like in that cabin. They would each re-enact it, they both knew, involuntarily, in their heads for the rest of their lives. They did not need any more exposure to the nightmare on any wavelength which were not their own.

At eleven O'clock Paradiso called and asked courteously if he might come to the apartment and film an interview with them. Kim, who vaguely recalled herself barring him from hassling them, rejected the overture icily, explaining that it was too soon for both of them.

An hour later they were sitting on the sofa, scrubbed and clean, drinking herbal tea in their bathrobes.

"How are you feeling now?" asked Kim solicitously, the first careful sortie into the uncharted waters of discussing anything even remotely unconnected to the domestic trivia of starting a new day.

"I feel so strange, like I want to feel more but I can't," she replied, staring blankly ahead.

"It will take time to sink in," Kim stated obviously. "Let's just have a quiet day doing nothing, listening to music – not thinking about anything, especially the future," Kim said, placing a hand on Desi's forearm in sisterly fashion.

"Yes," responded Desi, moving her hand deftly over her friend's in a reciprocal gesture.

"You know you can stay here for as long as you want," invited Kim.

"Well, that's real nice of you to say. But I'm thinking that on Monday I'll go back East. I sure do appreciate the offer though. Thanks, Kim."

She spoke quietly and deliberately, as if formulating the plan of action as she spoke, and in giving voice to the future somehow re-staking her claim to it.

"Okay. Well the offer stands," emphasized Kim, sipping her own peppermint infusion.

They sat in repose in silence, until, as was inevitable, the stresses of the last few days' cataclysmic events seemed abruptly to overtake Desi and subjugate her. The aftermath, long postponed, had at last come to demand its emotional quart of tears.

Kim was helpless as the outpouring commenced. She was witnessing an emotionally distraught woman finally given free rein to her feelings.

She felt excluded as the tears drenched her friend's face and Desi's shoulders became a quivering quartz-rock of anguish, a mandatory outpouring of her loss. She looked on uncomfortably with merely a hand cupped on the small of Desi's back to indicate an empathy that could never be. It was like watching a car crash in slow motion knowing that that one could not help in any way until afterwards, when the Third Law of Thermodynamics had done its stuff. It tortured Kim's mind to watch the volcano of feelings unleashed ascend to their zenith of throbbing force, knowing that she was and could only ever be, merely an informed bystander to the uniqueness of her comrade-at-arm's pain.

For the hostess, it was a simple case of do or not do.

Slowly her hand crept up Desi's spine by infinitesimal degrees and then, completely out of the blue, she kissed her full on the lips.

Desi could not disguise her disgust as she shrugged her off.

She could not, for all her 'live and let live' philosophy, disguise the degree by which she felt let down. For Kim, the cringe factor after her clumsy pass was incalculable and, much as she apologized, citing her desperation to offer succor to a friend, Desi's moist eyes looked on unconvinced, newly cynical about this woman whom, for all that they had been thru together, she actually appraised now that she barely even knew.

Kim had crossed the line of her own self-imposed taboo and it had been because she had desired comfort herself – as much as needing to give it. She had wanted to make an everlasting friendship with this remarkable woman whom she so respected, to consolidate in the day what had been between them during the cruel night. Unfortunately Kim had, by her crass action, destroyed all hope of any continuance in their relationship.

"Kim, I thought we were friends," stated Desi delicately, her words permeated however with passive aggression.

"I'm so sorry. I don't know why I did that," explained Kim.

"It's all right. It's everything that's happened. I think I understand," said this woman who had been thru so much and even now was without respite.

"I'm so mixed up. My mind's telling me one thing and my body another," she explained thru a veil of damp atonement.

"It's okay. It's just that I'm not like that," Desi returned flatly, shifting her undressed leg away from Kim's personal space.

"I feel so close to you that I just wanted to make your pain go away," she pleaded, turning thru a right angle to look her erstwhile friend in the face. "Can you forgive me?"

"Don't be silly. There's nothing to forgive, Kim. Let's talk about something else now," she held forth, yet without meeting Kim's needy gaze.

Soon they were busying themselves in the kitchen, preparing a simple lunch and talking about chicken breasts and tomatoes, couscous and the optimum way of cooking rice.

A dialogue about the relative merits of the Atkins Diet and low-fat, restricted calorie regimes followed; both ladies were now pleased to be conversing normally again, the precise topic incidental to their garrulous enjoyment. They ate from dishes on their laps, talking in the familiar fashion that hinted perhaps at their friendship having survived.

"What about that TV guy? When he rings back, do you want to talk to him or not?" asked Kim, finally thinking it was time to bring the matter up.

She could still not quite remember fully what had been her conversation with the reporter in the early hours of the morning.

"Definitely not. No!... No!... No! Of course not! I'm still in a state of shock from finding out about Trip and then...."

She let her voice fall off and picked absentmindedly at her food.

"Okay. Don't you worry about it. I'll tell him not to harass you anymore," Kim assured her. "I understand. He does seem to know a lot about what's happened to us. I don't know how..." she went on, vaguely aware that she may be being economical with the truth – the conversation of twelve hours previously with the journalist was starting to haunt her.

Thru the window came a shaft of watery sunlight. It was a reminder that there was still a whole universe out there, that, in their own time, they would have to gradually re-engage with.

Tea was brewed and sipped by the thimbleful as the cirrus clouds scudded by outside the apartment, a rolling chiaroscuro of blue and white, embedded with the occasional shard of silver.

They could hear the faint sounds of lunchtime in the café, chair legs grating on the old parquet, voices muted as if indulging in gossip.

"Shall we keep in touch?" asked Kim, out of nowhere, going to her stereo to put on some country music.

"I'd like that," said Desi, her mind far away on the East Coast, seeing the husband, whom she had loved in every aspect of his being, bringing her lox bagels and coffee in bed on their last wedding anniversary.

Kim saw the glazed eyes of her guest and retreated to the kitchen with the dishes. She knew with the utmost certainty that they would never be friends, knew that the strange tide that had brought them together was insufficient to sustain a genuine relationship of equals.

She had the good grace to give Desi time alone with her thoughts and by the late afternoon had prepared herself for the inevitable parting.

"Do you want another drink?" she offered, craning her head thru the doorway.

"No thanks, Kim," she answered, lowly. "In fact, you know, I think I will leave soon. I just feel an overwhelming urge to be home."

"I know," Kim said. "I know. I'll call Todd Dempsey."

"If you wouldn't mind?"

Desdemona smiled at her hostess.

Kim went to the phone and called the mechanic. Within thirty seconds it was all arranged.

"He'll be over shortly," she announced, replacing the mouthpiece.

"I'll go to the bathroom and then start taking my luggage down," Desi told her bleakly, not quite able to look Kim in the eye.

It was not what Kim had done so inappropriately that mattered, so much as the realization that their nascent friendship was not really equal on both sides. They frankly had nothing in common, Desi thought, and never would have. Briefly sharing a few moments of connection was not enough raw material from which to crystallize a real friendship in any enduring sense. Moreover she suddenly felt, with a strident fervor that she wanted to be home – to wake up in her own bed on Sunday morning.

"What about flights?" enquired Kim, as Desi humped her heavy case down the stairwell.

"I'll take care of it on the way," she shouted back, finally feeling that she was doing something positive, the awareness that she was again taking control of her life reinvigorating her, if not actually leavening the wretched agony that would, eternally now, be her affliction.

Dempsey Junior maneuvered the car outside the door and loaded the trunk. Three locals regarded her curiously and then looked away shamefaced when she stared back; she was not, in point of fact, even noticing them consciously. Her mind was completely taken up with far greater travails and thought processes.

"Goodbye Kim. Thank you for everything." the departing houseguest declaimed, squeezing sincerity into each syllable.

"Things will get better. I know it," said Kim, lighting up a rare cigarette.

They did not kiss nor hug. It was pointless now. They shook hands instead – rather awkwardly.

The automobile drove off without a backward wave or glance from the passenger and Kim went back into the hallway. She entered the apartment and closed the door on the world, like she had done so many times before. She had wanted a friend and ended up with worse than nothing, after her ineffectual overtures and her sudden Sapphic faux pas.

Kim sat down on the sofa and caught a snatch of Desi's fragrance in her nostrils.

She began to sob – not solely for the tragedy of what had happened to them both, but for the life-long trauma of being her, Kim – cast adrift, rootless, a pathetic shadow of the woman whom above all others she wished that she could be.

The phone rang.

"Hello, good afternoon. It's Marcus Paradiso here. I'm real sorry to trouble you but I just need to check some facts," came the voice, brisk yet charm-offensive down the line.

Kim's face took on a weaseled, lopsided grin.

"Mr. Paradiso, what can I do for you?" she asked, her tone newly bright with dollar-greed. "In fact how much would you reckon on me getting for the full gory story?"

Those who are trying to kill me
Will go down into the world of the dead.
They will be killed in battle,
And their bodies eaten by wolves.

(Psalm 63)

Chapter XIX

Mrs. Milsom brought her husband his coffee. He leant up against the pillows and drank it, feeling the dose of caffeine revive his senses, sodden from the night before. Too much Chablis never agreed with his system.

"So what do you want to do today?" his wife asked casually, sitting down beside him and wearing her ivory satin nightgown like Gloria Swanson in a forties classic.

"What's the time?" Milsom asked, yawning and feeling the prominent vein in his temple throb.

"It's nearly nine," she replied, looking at his befuddled appearance and questioning whether he would ever have been on the cover of Time without her help in the grooming department.

It had been five years now and she was beginning to think that the best opportunities for social advancement were behind them. Even his neurological profile was not as internationally pre-eminent as it had once been, she reflected, viewing his bloodshot gray eyes with cold detachment and thinking of how glamorous that Danish professor had been at the convention in Fort Lauderdale – and fully twelve years younger.

"I've got to have a shower quick and ring the hospital," he said distractedly, putting his cup and saucer down on the bedside cabinet.

"Remember we've got Heinrich and Jules coming tonight," Mrs. Milsom reminded him, as she rose and went over to her dressing table.

She slapped cold cream over her once beautiful features, now less lovely than haughty, and returned to bed, picking up a glossy magazine as she did so.

"Yes, I remember," he called out resignedly, entering the shower cubicle in the black and white tiled en suite, luxuriantly succumbing to the powerful jets.

Once undertaking the steamy ritual he could think, unbridled from the tittle-tattle that Melissa voided from every pore of her being. He had often wondered why he had fallen in love with such a woman – but he had indeed fallen in love with her.

Milsom lathered himself with liberal quantities of gel and then doused himself thoroughly, all the while just one thing on his mind – Davey Boy, or Mr. Trip Montifort as he must learn now to call him.

He knew that he must do a press release straight away. Somebody somewhere must come forward, either family or friend or business associate. This guy was no drifter, no bum. He had worked at the World Trade Center and must be known to many people who were not caught up in those incredible apocalyptic events.

Besides all of that, however, he really believed that this man, who had been thru so much, was on the way back – the return journey to full mental function. With the right stimulus at his bedside the process may be prone to acceleration, but, even without, the Johansson Signatures were insistent evidence of full brain function restoration in a medium term time frame – to use the technical diagnosis. Milsom hoped that he was right and that the man in the hospital bed, connected up to so complex a spectrum of tubes and electrodes, would come thru.

He left the bathroom in his cool, cotton yakata and patted his face dry with the voluminous lapels.

"There's some compote in the refrigerator," Melissa piped up, without taking her eyes from the article. "And there's some potato salad with chives…and there's… er… well you'll see," she went on disinterestedly.

"Thanks," said the doctor, dressing in his Sunday casuals. "I'll be downstairs in the study."

"Okay," she murmured from behind a layer of moisturizer and Cosmo.

In his elegant study, Milsom set up the computer for a press release to each of the news organizations that were pre-existing on his database. He often had to notify the media about his fundraisers for the department and, in the past, when he was a kind of celebrity neurologist, his latest cutting-edge research to 'Nature' and the medical journals. He clicked, entered into cyberspace and within a couple of minutes had imported the Reuters, Press Association and Bloomberg addresses onto his address list.

He started to type under the legend "Press Release', illuminated in Gill Sans Ultra Bold:-

<<Further to the admission of a comatose patient, identity unknown, from the World Trade Center on Tuesday, Cedar Plains Hospital would like to ask for your assistance. We believe that we now have the name of this patient and would like it widely publicized so that his family can know that he is still alive and assist him on his path

towards recovery. Also any close friends who may be able to throw any light on the whereabouts of his loved ones should please contact the hospital urgently.

The name of the patient is Mr. Trip Montifort.

Thank you for your help in this matter. For any more information please do not hesitate to contact Dr. P. Milsom on the above contact details.>>

He read it, re-read it, made two minor corrections of syntax and clicked on 'Send'.

Hunger for the potato salad delayed his prior wish to check in on his most famous patient's progress. Meandering into the kitchen he suddenly felt the potential chill of the downside to the achievement (like a novelist awaiting the critiques in the newspapers, or a scientist the feedback from his newly published research) – he had now to wait to see if any good news would be forthcoming. It was not that much to ask surely, to hope that Trip should expect his own nearest and dearest to be by his bedside whilst he bravely battled his tortuous way back to consciousness.

Milsom poured a full measure of orange juice into a glass and slurped half of it, then retrieved a spoon from the cutlery stand and ladled five lumps of his favorite dish onto a plate. He absolutely adored potato salad. He added a couple of tomatoes, first rinsing them under the cold water, and then a teaspoonful of gooseberry chutney. He began munching his way though the repast, hoping that every gram of carbohydrate that his metabolism extracted would be converted in the coming hours into energetic progress in his quest.

Having enjoyed his breakfast, he placed the plate, glass and stainless steel flatware in the dishwasher. Melissa had him very well trained by now. He saw that it was ten thirty-five by the kitchen clock. It had been half an hour since his missive had been sent out.

He went to the coffee machine and took an espresso. The phone had not yet rung.

'Why did I not send it the previous night?' he demanded of himself, considering that wondrous moment when he had seen Trip's eye staring back at him from the fax, that revelatory moment that would always stay with him. It had been late. He had been in a hurry to see the other patients and to leave for the cocktail party. He was a husband as well as a neurologist.

Notwithstanding all of this, however, he had wanted to think out what he should do, calmly and collectedly.

Over dinner he had been inordinately subdued, to his wife's chagrin, debating with himself over whether to go to the police, to the press or even to hire a private detective.

It was eleven-am now. He drained his cup and returned to the study. He had done what he thought right. He stood by his decisions. Instantly he could see that he had received only one e-mail in the last hour or so and that was a purely social one from an ex-colleague in Vancouver.

Picking up the phone he dialed the hospital.

"Randolph Hearst Ward," the female Brooklyn accent announced.

"Nurse Baker, Dr. Milsom here."

"Hello, doctor."

"Any news at all on Trip?"

"No change, Dr. Milsom," she remarked.

"You gotten my e-mail then?"

"Yes. Good news isn't it."

"Yes, it is. Goodbyes then, nurse. Don't hesitate to call me if there's any change."

He hung up with his usual refrain.

There was no change and yet the Johansson Signatures should by now have increased in frequency once more at the very least. He felt dejected in the extreme.

Milsom admired his Japanese prints which he always found calmed him in a crisis or in one of his regular black dogs, as he always referred to, a la Winston Churchill, his sporadic bouts of clinical depression.

Going over to the bay window he looked out onto the park. By the statuesque elm, children played with a yellow Frisbee in the wind, and people strolled on the pathways in twos and threes.

The leaves were turning russet and ochre and would soon be bestrewn in their tens of thousands across the expanses of concrete and slowing grass. It was a normal Sunday, he realized, the terrible events of a hundred and twenty hours earlier would indubitably hold severe national trauma for generations into the future and yet somehow Sunday would always be Sunday.

The world had been changed forever but Earth had not been blown off its axis nor would it ever be by mere terrorists, cowards every last one of them – lesser people who had never experienced the simple joy of curing life's ills by deliberate, gentle means rather than simply pursuing a trajectory of terror and destruction and hate.

It was however a Sunday. People lay in bed for hours on a Sunday morning, like Melissa upstairs, he told himself, coaxing a smidgen of optimism from deep within. People would be still having breakfast, or by now possibly brunch, the television not yet on, the radio untouched.

Nevertheless it had been an hour and a quarter since he had informed New York about Trip and still the phone had not rung with even a solitary enquiry from a network. Still, he placated himself, his communication to the media had been entirely self-explanatory.

He gravitated back into the kitchen and poured another coffee. Whilst drinking it he would put on the rolling news channel, he decided.

As the small screen sprang into electronic activity he saw images of Ground Zero that required no introduction, nor would for a millennium. He watched and the familiar emotions inside him kicked in, necessitating a finger to wipe away a tear. His was a 9/11 story of one man among thousands: Trip's own teetering humanity was as nothing in comparison with that vast landscape of doomsday horror. He was just one man and yet it was this paramount importance attached to the rights of the individual that so differentiated the creed of Milsom's society from that of Bin Laden's.

At the foot of the TV a video-screenwriter system scrolled the headlines horizontally in less dramatic visuals than the main picture above. Suddenly he saw it flash past in little more than three seconds: -

<Comatose World Trade Center victim identified as Mr. Trip Montifort. In stable condition in Cedar Plains Hospital, New York City.>

It may have been terse but it was there though, out there for all to see in the public domain. Now he thought, as he further indulged his caffeine addiction, he could only wait.

Finally, after what seemed to him to have been an age, the phone at last echoed thru the apartment, its ringing seemingly amplified in direct proportion to his prolonged anticipation.

"Hello, Dr. Milsom here," he almost shouted.

"It's Nurse Baker, doctor," she trilled. "You better come in at once. The monitors are all zigzagging off the scale and the graph-lines…"

"The Johansson Signatures, you mean?" he interrupted animatedly, accidentally knocking his espresso all over the Michelangelo marble surface.

"Yes, the Johansson Signatures are every twenty seconds now," she excitedly explained, her voice vibrato with the responsibility of her pronouncement.

"I'm on my way. See you in half an hour or so," he said. "You've got my cell phone number."

"Yes, and doctor?" she went on, then halted. "…It's all right – it will wait."

"What? What is it Nurse Baker?" he asked impatiently, the vein in his forehead visibly pulsing now with professional ecstasy and ordinary human joy.

"Well, it's just that I've already had five calls from people who know Trip," she elaborated.

"Why the hell didn't they get in touch before now?" he shouted.

"They all said they didn't recognize him with all the bandages and tubes and everything – the photo was not very clear, doctor."

Nurse Baker related what they had said with speed, knowing that she would far prefer to be telling the consultant this in person. She wanted Dr. Milsom on site to deal with any neurological eventuality that may come up as Trip's brainwave patterns weaved their own, entirely unique way, back to original operational integrity.

"I'll see you soon! Keep calm!" Milsom said, addressing the final comment to himself as much as to his conversant.

This was the breakthrough that he had genuflected mentally, day in, day out, to achieve. He bellowed goodbye to Melissa upstairs and took his coat from the ebony hat-stand in the hallway.

His mood had been a minute before tinged a similar color. Now however as he walked to the carport he felt a rainbow of bright emotions each suffused with more optimism than the last.

My strength is gone,
Gone like water spilt on the ground.
All my bones are out of joint;
My heart is like melted wax.

(Psalm 22)

Chapter XX

Meanwhile in an exclusive apartment block named Virginia Point on the northern fringe of Manhattan, Mrs. Desdemona Montifort was entering the lobby. She was extremely tired and of course highly emotional, yet relieved beyond quantification to be finally home

She had been unable to get a flight until the early hours of Monday morning and had been forced to book into a hotel in Seattle on Saturday night. Sunday she had spent at the airport, drinking coffee endlessly and staring bleakly into space when not making her hourly enquiries about cancellations.

Hers was the sort of building where people knew each other's faces sufficiently to make polite acknowledgment in the swanky elevators, but still not know each other's names.

Desi turned the key and went in with her bags, dropping them in the hall. She slumped exhausted into her favorite black nubuck leather armchair. She had imagined, whilst she was on her adventures, this homecoming many times. Not once could she have conceived that she would feel as bereft as she now did.

There on the mahogany sideboard was a wedding photo, gilt-framed, and capturing all of the intensity of their mutual happiness on that perfect summer's day. On the wall was a painting of Mont-Martre, which she had been so delighted and surprised by when Trip had hung it in secrecy on their return from honeymooning in Paris. She felt the silver links of her special bracelet which, in truth, though she could never ever dream of relinquishing it, would forever now hold for her decidedly ambivalent feelings.

The whole place radiated, almost tangibly, the strong bonds between them and evinced in each corner of the spacious room the burgeoning materialistic success of her husband's high-octane career.

She had loved him so very much, and him her – the latter without limit. In hindsight, she formulated vaguely, her epic journey across eight states was no doubt divinely ordained so that she could renew and reinvigorate her love for Trip, and thereby possess forevermore the feelings that she was now experiencing.

Even the whole episode of the siege paled into insignificance in her own mind besides the beautiful memories that would now be with her unto eternity. As she sat, made immobile by bittersweet recall, she reasoned that the crazed psycho had, in his own unknowing way done her a great service. Without him she may never have been fully able to contextualize her deep abiding love for her husband – exponentially more powerful than the, by comparison, paler hatred engendered by Sholtz.

It was almost two when she cast off from her long chrysalis of beautiful memories and rose at last.

She went into the bathroom and turned the faucet. She would bathe, both to ritually try to cleanse away the misadventures of her travels and to wallow in plangent recollections of Trip and their love.

As the mood of sentimental remembrance had gradually displaced shock from her mind she wished to hear again their favorite songs and so Desi turned on the radio.

Celine Dione played out soothingly as she stepped into the bath and sank into the foamy water. Luxuriating in the orchestral sweep of the music, she could, if she closed her eyes, imagine Trip humming along, sitting on the rim, occasionally stroking her wet hair and soaping her back. He had always loved romantic ballads and she had bought him at least three compact discs by the diva. Desi smiled beatifically and soon was sobbing gently in time to the music that at this confluence of time and place, so, so moved her.

As the strings faded the oft-heard theme for the two O'clock news report commenced. She leaned forward to turn the radio off, not inclined to hear of the aftermath at Ground Zero whilst her mindset was still so very fragile.

As she reached for the switch, straining her outstretched arm to breach the divide between the news that she did not want and the bath that she still did, she slipped a little, and in the act of recomposing herself the newscaster's almost upbeat voice began with their new headline story.

Desdemona Montifort stubbed her toe on the faucet as she heard the news; her whole body had convulsed in that nano-second of dawning truth.

She still slapped her own face three times to confirm that she were not dreaming. It was true then – the gods of

Fate were giving her another chance for happiness… and Trip too!

You must no longer be partial to the wicked!
Defend the rights of the poor and the orphans;
Be fair to the needy and the helpless.
Rescue them from the power of the wicked.

(Psalm 82)

Chapter XXI

Father Dupree lit his pipe and sucked in the rich Kentucky and Cavendish notes. The first tugs of the day were always the most delectable – after that it was a downward curve all the way, the law of diminishing returns exemplified par excellence.

It was just after five fifteen in the morning as he made his way to the kitchen. The walking stick click-clacked along the bare unvarnished floorboards and he visualized the cup of Lapsang Souchong tea which Miss Boniface, as usual, would have brewing.

"Bon Matin, Miss Boniface," he said, the salutation as old as her residency in the seminary, a span of service that numbered almost thirty years.

"I've made some scrambled eggs and some of your favorite buttered mushrooms. How did you sleep, Father?"

"Yes, very good – the slumber of the innocent. Probably thinking of your magnificent breakfast, Miss Boniface."

"Oh, Father Dupree. I've always said you must be the sweetest talker in the diocese."

"Well I never," he smiled. "Don't let Cardinal Flaherty ever hear you say that. This is most fine, Miss Boniface," the priest complimented her, tucking in voraciously.

"If you don't want me for anything else, Father?" the housekeeper asked. "I'll go and wake up the girls."

His mouth full, Father Dupree nodded distractedly.

Miss Boniface went up the steps into the corridor carrying a tray with two cups and saucers. She made her way deliberately up the stairs, teaspoons rattling slightly in the crockery as she did so. Along the shabby hallway she went, her stooped frame making for the end door. Out of her apron she retracted a large key, slid it in the lock and turned it.

She looked at the two little figures in the twin beds, long blonde hair falling in waves upon the pillows and made an involuntary inhalation of breath. They looked so perfect, so immaculate in the half-light. All children are God's children, she reflected, but these twin girls looked as if they were cast in His No.1 die, so ethereally lovely were they, so blissfully angelic in repose. Never having had the good fortune to have procreated herself, she loved it when there were children staying. She loved the injection of life they brought with them into this draughty old nineteenth century building – the laughter, the fun and games – and the inexorable rise in Father Dupree's spirits that always seemed to accompany their presence.

"Wakey, wakey, girls!" she called out, placing the tray on a chest of drawers. "Come on, we've got a busy day, today. We've got to get you bathed and dressed before breakfast."

The girls stirred at her shrill voice and gradually came round, stretching and yawning almost in unison, their too-long white night gowns spilling out of the bedclothes, almost to the floor.

It was now the fifth day that they had been here and the accumulation of sleep deprivation for girls of their age was cruel and unusual punishment. If the regime that they had had foisted upon them was designed to melt their will and furnish malleable personalities for whatever was expected of them next, then the priest and his loyal maidservant were not failing in their diabolic mission.

"Can't we sleep a little more?" the braver of the sisters enquired, looking over protectively at her still drowsy twin.

"Now, none of that Sophie, dear. You know the rules by now, don't you? Father Dupree only wants what's best for you and your sister."

The housekeeper spoke the words with a smile playing on her thin, passionless lips whilst shaking Lara into premature wakefulness.

"We want to go home, Miss Boniface. Can't we go home today?" Sophie asked, throwing her legs over the mattress onto the threadbare rug and running her fingers thru her hair.

"Good morning, Lara," Miss Boniface greeted her other, less noisome, less headstrong charge – the one whom, as often is with siblings from a divided ovum, was the second born.

"What's the time, Miss Boni..?" Lara asked, rubbing her eyes.

"That's no concern of yours, young lady", she retorted stiffly. "Father Dupree is having his breakfast already and the first service of the day will be starting soon enough, so let's have none of your backtalk, girls. It's well past the time for you to get washed and dressed. I've been up already for an hour and a half, myself. What would the good Father do if I decided I was going to be a lazy dolly and rest in bed all day? Nothing would ever get done around here, would it?"

Resigned to their early starts, the girls tiptoed over to their lukewarm cups of tea and ingested the liquid with visible distaste. At home they would not be up for two hours yet and there they would enjoy deliciously refreshing cold orange or pineapple juice, not this fetid witch's brew – at least insomuch as their juvenile taste buds were concerned.

The twins picked up their towels and trudged, as they had done every one of these last six days, to the bathroom. They would run the water and share it, one at each end of the grimy tub. It was a salutary lesson, if nothing else, which would forever make them appreciate those simple home comforts that they had previously so naturally taken for granted and that now, it seemed, were permanently erased from their young lives.

Miss Boniface took the tray with the tea things on it back to the kitchen – not before, however, she had locked the bathroom door with the girls in it. She would return in ten minutes to let them out. Hopefully, by then, they would be more amiable with their lot, she conjectured vaguely. If they were not obviously grateful for the great service of charity which Father Dupree had so graciously done for them, then it was because they were still merely selfish young girls, only interested in dolls and hair and pop music and ponies – like young girls everywhere. Miss Boniface knew that one day they would appreciate all that she and the good Father had done for them. For now, she must remember that these girls were newly orphaned and were still coming to terms with their great loss, the greatest loss a child can ever have. To lose one parent is catastrophe enough for a child of ten tender years but to lose both is a crime not only against the minor concerned but against the whole of humanity itself.

"God surely does work in mysterious ways," she asserted under her breath. "Poor little angels."

It was nearly six when Miss Boniface returned to the washroom and let out the girls, all newly scrubbed faces and squeaky-clean apple blossom hair.

While they dressed, locked in the bedroom as usual, she pulled out her needles and carried on crocheting a new sweater for Father Dupree's birthday. By now there would be an assembly of pimply-cheeked seminarians congregating in the little chapel over in the west wing. Father Dupree would have completed his hearty repast and finished his second cup of stewed tea.

There had once been up to thirty students studying in the seminary but as Father Dupree had become older and less contemporary with the latest theological fashions (and as the large rambling building had fallen into a state of tiredness and disrepair) the student intake had fallen to about a handful of rather earnest, young men. The ones who were destined to become bishops or even cardinals in later life were not amongst them; the ones however who would become quiet, unremarkable but well-loved parish priests were the ones who were attracted – or perhaps, if one were being unkind, were there by dint of default more than anything else. The bishop was forever trying to rationalize St. Cuthbert's out of existence, but out of respect for Father Dupree's forty years of service he never quite seemed to get around to it.

"You ready, girls?" the housekeeper shouted thru the door.

"Yes, Miss Boniface," piped up Sophie and Lara together.

They had in truth been ready for some time, but had been investigating the windows for possible breaches in security. They were only ten yet they could certainly detect the stench of putative danger in the air, in the rancid rooms and in the demeanors of the only two adults that they had so far come into contact with. The girls had left no stone unturned in trying to find a method of escape.

"Come on then," the woman called out, clanking the rusty key in the lock and holding the door open for her charges to pass under her thin, outstretched arm. "You know Father Dupree will be angry if we're late for Matins."

"Miss Boniface," Lara mooted in a small, frightened voice. "When can we go home?"

"Let's have none of that nonsense, my child," she returned swiftly. "You know that's impossible at the moment. Until then, Father Dupree has been charitable enough to give you girls a safe place to stay. You should thank God he was there for you. Such a kind, holy man he is, our Father Dupree."

"But why can't we go home?" asked Sophie, taking her sister's cue, looking up with huge, pleading eyes at Miss Boniface.

The wizened housekeeper for a second was flustered. They had asked this question already at least a dozen times each and each time it were posed to her she averted her eyes and shuffled on the spot. It was an easy question to answer, but one which she knew she could not with any verisimilitude – not to these beautiful, pure ten-year-olds (even with all her years of experience of running Father Dupree's household), not with those two pairs of innocent eyes staring up at her, with all the vulnerability of utter virtue. This was by far the hardest task she had encountered, that she had had foisted upon her, in all her years of loyal service at St. Cuthbert's.

A willing accomplice, yes; she had always strived to do her best for the Father – be it cooking, laundry, cleaning or the other thing which stalked these musty corridors, the thing which dared not speak its name but which imparted its impure imprimatur upon the very air they all breathed.

The priest himself made no apologies for it, for in his mindset it was a part of his priestly duties, the enigmatic, yet sacred corollary to his chasteness – the thing which, in his own warped mind, had long been tacitly preordained as permissible for the higher ecclesiastical echelons; tolerated by the Church for nigh on a millennium, his unsullied conscience told him, since the vows of celibacy were first inculcated under the Second Lateran Council of 1139.

"Now, Sophie, you know why. Let's hurry or you'll make Father Dupree angry," she replied acidly, looking above the twins' heads at the phalanx of students making their way along the corridor which ran perpendicular to theirs.

This part of the building was set away from the living quarters of the students. It was, but for the fact that they had to pass the end of the girls' corridor to reach the chapel, all but hermetically sealed off from prying eyes.

The girls followed Miss Boniface downheartedly and a minute later they were all three settled in the rear pews. Thoughts of their lovely home, their loving mother and father, had inevitably squatted their minds and expelled all thoughts of the moment. Each heard Father Dupree's 'Bon Matin' addressed to the assembly but only dimly on the horizon of their respective consciousnesses, so ensconced were they in their individual yet parallel reveries.

"……Espiritu Sanctu, ipsi Domine ……"

The commencement of the service barely entered the orbit of the girls' perception and it was not until the portly priest fixed his beady eye on first Sophie and then Lara that they realized that everyone had turned around and were looking at them expectantly.

"Come on, my children. Don't be bashful," the priest encouraged with a sharp circular motion of his left hand.

"Go on, dears. Father Dupree wants you to step up to the altar for his special blessing," Miss Boniface urged, putting her hand on Sophie's back. "Go on," she went on. "It's a great honor."

The priest smiled at the twins benignly as they began inching anxiously up the aisle. He waited until they were on the second step prior to holding out his hands to each of them.

"O Lord, may you make the sun shine on Sophie and Lara during their time of need. He gives them the strength to overcome their sorrow and grief. May He grant them the courage to become a credit to the memory of their parents, whom God, in his infinite wisdom, has split asunder from them.

"As long as you girls are staying with us I want us all to be your new family. We know we can never replace the one which has been cruelly taken, but we want you to know that we are all here for you, my blessed children."

He took a book from a pocket in his satin surplice and went to a dog-eared bookmark. Latin verses peeled out thru the cozy chapel, his authoritative voice at once tuneful and yet brimming with charismatic power:

"Tibi fatémur crimina admissa:
contrito corde pándimus occúlta:
tua, Redémptor, pietas ignóscat.

Atténde.

"Innocens captus, nec repúgnans ductus,
téstibus falsis pro impiis damnátus:
quos redemisti, tu consérva, Christe.

Atténde."

Father Dupree finished the liturgy then kissed both Sophie and Lara delicately on the forehead. They returned to their seats, their watery eyes a mixture of confusion and grief.

Until this point, Miss Boniface had refrained from answering their questions directly. Now she forlornly watched their eyes fill as they assumed their positions next to her. She did not know what she could do other than place a sympathetic hand on their shoulders. As a spinster woman who had lived her whole life in the company of single men, it was too much for her to bear. She was, if not emotionally barren – then certainly inarticulate in the language of feelings.

"What did Father Dupree mean?" asked the elder girl, still weeping.

"Yes, Miss Boniface, are our mum and dad dead or something?" followed up Lara, usually the less forthright of the two.

"What I have to tell you is not easy. You must be brave, my dears... It does seem that your parents perished last Tuesday in the New York disaster. I spoke to the principal of your school yesterday and it seems that no one has come forward with any new information so far. We must assume the very worst, dears. I'm extremely sorry. I can't possibly tell you how much, girls."

The housekeeper effected a purse-lipped façade, the better to denote sympathy, and stroked Lara's hair in a slow act of condolence.

"What happened last Tuesday, Miss Boniface?" Sophie enquired, wiping her eyes with the back of her hand.

"A really terrible thing, my dear – some very bad men flew two airplanes into the World Trade Center. Many, many people were killed as the Twin Towers collapsed."

"Oh my God!!" screamed Lara, turning on her heels and taking flight.

"Dad… Our dad worked in one of those towers," said Sophie simply, her little face blank with shock. "I'll go after Lara."

"Yes, you do that, dear," agreed the housekeeper meekly – that woman who had lacked the moral courage to do as she had been instructed by Father Dupree, to inform the girls of their true plight, of the events of Tuesday last.

Day by day she had put it off and then this Sunday morning service, which she could have had no inkling would serve up the intelligence, had been upon her.

The priest, thus far in their stay, had had little to do with the girls. He had presumed that by now they knew why they were here, that his loyal and trusted right-hand woman had long since broken the terrible news to them.

The service carried on amidst raised eyebrows and curious looks, whilst Miss Boniface excused herself quietly and followed the girls upstairs. Although she regretted the way in which they had found out the truth, she now had to concentrate on her primary duty of care to both the twins and Father Dupree – safety and security. She looked thru the bedroom doorway at Lara splayed out on her bed, sobbing uncontrollably into the old-fashioned eiderdown. Sophie, who suddenly seemed not merely a twin but a so much more mature sibling, was consoling her, her arms wrapped around Lara's waist, head nuzzling her shoulder blade.

Miss Boniface closed the door silently and locked it. She did not return to the chapel but instead walked to a long, thin leaded window in the corridor. It was a window that she often came to in order to meditate, to reflect on things whilst looking out over the urban countryside which lay between the old seminary and the city – that huge, phantasmagorical metropolis which, from her favorite aperture, seemed like one huge castellated palace floating free in the clouds.

Manhattan has always exerted its sophisticated and magical influence over the inhabitants of the semi-industrial wasteland between New York and Newark. The two are forever separated by a distance of only a few miles, but in demographic and cultural terms it may as well be on another continent.

She had dedicated her life to the place in which she had been given succor all those years before. It had been the only refuge in those days for a woman like her. It had never been her destiny to be anything other than one of life's menials. Maybe it was the harelip that had militated against her from childhood and made her excessively grateful for any acceptance by any other person or institution. Perhaps it had been the rejection by her mother that had seen her imbued with a lifelong emptiness where normally love would linger and be allowed to gestate. It could have been none of these things of course. She could have been mentally scarred in a multitude of different ways and yet still framed a moral courage in the face of adversity, in the presence of others' sin. However this had not happened at any time in her life. Surely she thought, as she took in the grandiose scene, watched the tumbleweed roll between the forecourt and the used car lot, it was too late for her now in her mid-fifties to assume a new persona, to stand up for what she believed to be right.

Miss Boniface watched as the sun came up, throwing its light on the brown fields and the abandoned automobiles and gas cylinders. Her self-absorption was however punctured by a terrible, pained scream from inside the girls' room. Quickly she took out the key and stepped across the corridor.

"Just a second. I'm coming in," she called out, nervously.

"Miss Boniface, we're okay. Thanks for your concern, but go down to the kitchen and make us some of your excellent malt-loaf, if you don't mind."

The priest's rich baritone voice rang out thru the paneled door.

The housekeeper halted mid-turn of the key. Shamefaced, she retracted it and went on about her Sunday chores. Instead of feeling demeaned by her acquiescence in Father Dupree's games, she in fact felt stupid for not realizing straight away what had been going on – all that she had now achieved was to embarrass both of them. She went down to the kitchen and took the whole meal flour out of the pantry. Her ruminations seemed, all of a sudden, a veritable light-year away.

Her collusion in Dupree's nefarious activities had now been ratcheted up a notch. She had forgotten about the back stairs leading to the other door to the room. She had wondered why he had asked specifically for the houseguests to be accommodated there. Now she knew the reason. He had a key to that door. The access would be even more discreet thru there than thru the one in the corridor.

Miss Boniface took the sieve and the white ceramic bowl and adjudged that she was now once again an accessory after the fact.

A student, the one with the gargantuan appetite that was seemingly never sated, entered the kitchen.

"Can I get a bowl of cornflakes, Miss Boniface?" he asked.

"Sure, help yourself," she said, waving her hand in the direction of the cupboard. "Breakfast will be in half an hour. I'm afraid I'm a bit behind this morning," she explained distractedly.

"Don't worry. The boys won't be down for a while yet. It's just that I'm a bit peckish."

"That's all right. I like to see a young man with an appetite," cracked Miss Boniface, her mind clearly on other things.

The student took his bowl and went into the adjoining dining room, sitting down at the long refectory table. The housekeeper continued with her bread making. It was still only six fifty-five. There was something in her that needed to know what exactly was going on. She had been a party to the perverted goings-on for so long in her long tenure of service to Dupree that she had absorbed the knowledge of his activities, purely as if by osmosis, over the years. Now she had an overarching desire to see once and for all exactly how disreputable, how reprehensible he actually was. She left her cooking and baking and went to the key cabinet in the alcove. She felt tingly with fear and apprehension as she went quietly and slowly up the flights of stairs to the attic room on the fourth floor.

It was with trepidation that she went into this room that had always been designated as utterly out of bounds by Father Dupree. She somehow knew deep in her bones, in the very center of her chakras, that if she were caught it would be the end for her. The clergy are, by definition, creatures of their faith and she had always been somehow aware of the priest's tacit contention over all these years that he would dispose of her without a second thought should she ever trespass into this penthouse theatre of unknown sin. She did not doubt that this was how it would be – should she be discovered.

Into the room she stepped. Immediately she discerned some low whimpering and sobbing coming from the other side of the attic. Carefully, she shut the door behind her and then went to the table whence the sound was emanating. There was a computer monitor there showing a scene of such complete and visceral heinousness that Miss Boniface retched automatically as her eyes met the screen. She could see the girls, she could see Dupree, she could see her own long-time guilt by association writ large in sickening pixels.

She picked up a book from the table in front of her. It was an address book but then entries were e-mail not geographic. Besides each one was also a credit card number and an expiry date. She picked up a merchandiser's receipt form from the top of a spike on the desk: it was for six thousand dollars. The payee was the St. Cuthbert's Orphaned Children Appeal. It was the first time that Miss Boniface, with all her intimate knowledge of the affairs of the seminary, had ever heard of this charity. She fingered thru the other receipts and found that they were all for the same amount. This was serious money. The clients all seemed to be companies or associations, their names, to a one, suitably mundane and conventional, as if designed to protect the individuals' identities, to throw anyone stumbling upon this treasure trove of vice off the scent.

Miss Boniface cupped her hand to her mouth as another high-pitched cry of terror peeled out. Looking around she noticed a Mercator map of the world stuck on a pin board. There were colored drawing pins stuck all over it, every continent represented bar Antarctica. She saw that there must be at least fifty or so credit card invoices and therefore perhaps fifty pairs of sordid eyes watching this selfsame scene on their own PCs around the world.

Finally she realized the extent of her priestly superior's extra-curricular activities. Until two minutes before she, in her naiveté, had been disingenuously vague about what Dupree had been up to all these years, save for his obvious and inappropriate predilection for young flesh. Somehow she had always turned a blind eye, yet had given, a multitude of times, her unspoken assent to what was occurring. Even sometimes she had done his bidding, albeit subtly intimated, and procured victims for him. Abruptly, she felt sick again at her own part, both mentally and physically. She went to the window and opened it, leaning out and letting herself throw up into the courtyard below.

She did not need to glance at the screen to know what was occurring in the bedroom. She could hear the cries, the incessant aching sobs, the desperate pleading for a cessation of this evil being perpetrated by the perverted instincts of a depraved mind which was, even now, deconstructing the normal childhoods of two innocent young girls.

For them, for the rest of their lives there would always be one great defining divide – 'before' that terrible day and 'after'.

The housekeeper now wanted to get as far away from this vile and God-forsaken bedchamber as possible. She stole out of the attic, locked the door and hurried down the stairs. She knew now that she must do something to abate the evil, to at long last atone for her quarter century of connivance by default – and for all the times she had been an explicit accomplice too.

Dupree was a highly charismatic man. A dominant part of her submissive personality had, for as long as she had worked there, been in thrall to his powerful and manipulative persona. Perhaps she was even more than a little in love with this extremely dangerous and Machiavellian pedophile.

There could be no excuses however for her putrescent complicity – only explanation.

Moreover, if a whole nation can become mesmerized by a forceful yet fatally flawed leader, then what real defense could the singularly weak-minded Miss Boniface have against Dupree?

Still, just as modern Germany has now left the nightmare years behind her, this simple housekeeper had seen the scales fall from her eyes and now wished to make her own restitution.

It may well prove too little too late but it was surely better late than never.

Be merciful to me, Lord
For I am in trouble;
My eyes are tired from so much crying;
I am completely worn out.
I am exhausted by sorrow,
And weeping has shortened my life.

(Psalm 31)

Chapter XXII

"I need to get on this flight. It's very important," said the smartly suited man to the Delta Airlines employee.

She arched her eyebrows and told him that there were no available seats on Flight 3756 to JFK.

"But I've told you it's absolutely crucial I get on this flight. There must be a way."

"Sir, there is no possibility I can get you on this flight. It is fully booked."

She smiled wearily at this ultra-confident man whom she vaguely recollected from somewhere – whether it be the airport, the newspapers or perhaps the television, she was not sure.

"Here's my business card, just in case you have any no-shows," he said, proffering a hundred-dollar bill along with the laminated card.

"I'll do my best, sir. You can rely on me," she replied, tucking the note into her sleeve as if a stray Kleenex and smiling now.

"I'd appreciate that. I'll go get a coffee. You can page me, right," he said, already looking around for the nearest Starbucks.

"Certainly, Mr. Paradiso," she responded.

She now knew where she had seen him before. She had watched him a hundred times or more on the local news. It was yet another minor celebrity to add to her expanding list. Not the biggest fish by far, but a very profitable one.

Customer services at the airport was an unenviable job at the best of times but after the 9/11 shutdown it was one continual headache as too many people were now chasing too few seats.

Marcus Paradiso realized that he was not going to be able to get to the East Coast as easily as he had first imagined.

An hour ago he had been making himself a leisurely breakfast at his apartment when his eye had been caught by the name Montifort scrolling along the bottom of his TV. His first thought was to call Desdemona at her friend's place and see whether she had heard yet – no one was picking up, however. His next thought was to go over and see her, but then he realized that he did not know for certain if this Trip Montifort was indeed her husband or not. It was not a common surname but he had to be sure before getting up her hopes. If he went there and asked her for her husband's first name, she would likely as not clam up. After what she had been thru she would hardly be in the mood for small talk with a reporter.

He had gone onto the Internet and entered 'Trip Montifort + Berkeley Brothers Stock Brokers. He knew by now that this company had occupied the entirety of the eleventh and twelfth floors of the second tower. Within seconds, he had, to his growing sense of professional jubilation, confirmed that it was very unlikely that it could

236

be anyone other than Desdemona's husband who was lying comatose in that hospital bed in Manhattan. There were no other Montiforts working for the company. His razor-sharp journalistic instincts had scented a fantastic news story prior to this, but now…this really could be mega. He did not know how it was to pan out but he knew that if ever he had seen one then this was it – a coast-to-coast story that could play for weeks in Poughkeepsie.

He had dressed hurriedly and gone around to the waitress's apartment. Nobody was answering though, however many times he rang the bell. Paradiso supposed that they must have gone for a walk by the lake or perhaps even to church. He knew what these small town women were like – it didn't matter what the state of the world or even their own life, if there was a church to give thanks in then they would be first in line.

He decided there and then that he would go east right away. Time and tide wait for no man, especially one in hot pursuit of an exclusive.

The BMW turned around with a screech of tires and within two hours he was at the airport.

<<"Paging Mr. Paradiso. Paging Mr. Paradiso. Could Mr. Marcus Paradiso please go to the Delta Airlines customer service desk?">>

The words on the airport PA system knocked him out of his self-absorption. He had been thinking that he would be lucky to get to New York before Monday night. Now he hastened over to the lady whom he had been talking to two lattes ago.

"Mr. Paradiso, we have just had a late cancellation on the next flight," she announced. "I can get you on it, if you want?"

237

Paradiso was a man used to getting what he desired. He smiled at the woman and nodded. If he had time, he might even have tried to chat the woman up – she was certainly his type (blue eyes, slim figure, luxuriant blonde hair) – but he was now a man on a mission. Nothing could stop him. He would be in the Big Apple by nightfall.

Paradiso paid his fare and then called the TV studio to book him a hotel. The flight would ETA at 19:38 AST He could be at the hospital first thing; when following a hot story one had to be in the right place at the right time. He possessed this knack that he hoped would one day propel him to the stratospheric heights of news anchorman on a major network. If he failed, it would not be because he lacked motivation. Failure was, to Paradiso, the preserve of those who played by the rules. He himself was a Master of the Universe in his own eyes. He would not fail. He could not fail.

The plane taxied to a halt at JFK and Paradiso disembarked and made his way thru the terminal. It was nearly eight twenty p.m. He took a taxi to the hotel and registered. Having slept fitfully on the flight he was now wide-awake. The change in time zones meant that he was good for another few hours of work before he turned in. He set up his laptop on the bed and began doing some further research into these incredible lives that had so suddenly brushed up against his own.

His first internet port of call was the hospital website. On it he saw at once the headline that had instigated his journey. *'Comatose Twin Tower Survivor ID'd'*. There was a pen picture about the neurologist who had been treating him and also an article that expounded the tale of how a firefighter had heroically carried the patient down eleven apocalyptic flights of emergency stairs. Anyone who knew Trip was asked to get in touch with the hospital. To date there was no news on whether anybody had come forward.

Paradiso wrote down the names in his notebook and then moved onto checking the CNN website. This was more or less a reprise of everything that he had just read. He went to the regional TV networks' websites and again found nothing earth shatteringly new.

It seemed that no one had yet made the connection between this most unfortunate victim of a terrible crime in the North West with that of her husband, the victim of an exponentially worse crime on the East Coast.

He fell asleep at about three in the morning. By this time he believed that he knew Dr. Milsom better than his own brother. As for Trip Montifort – he knew what his company did, but nothing much about the individual, the private man.

Paradiso dreamt of skyscrapers and swish offices, desert firebrands and fire engines and then it was time to wake up.

* * * * * *

The hospital looked austere in the weak September sunlight, all concrete and dull, gray glass. People went in and out of the main entrance, some in uniform starting their shift, others visiting loved ones on the way in to work.

"Can I help you, sir?" asked the matronly nurse as the reporter hesitated in the foyer.

"Well, I hope so. I've come to find out how your Mr. Trip Montifort is doing today."

"Are you family or friend?" Nurse Roberts enquired, suspiciously.

Since his name had been revealed almost every nut in the New York metropolitan area had been by, wanting to say hello to Trip, claiming that they were cousins or work colleagues or even, on one occasion, the janitor in his block.

It was weird the way they came crawling out of the woodwork only when his name was discovered and not before, but that was the way that it was. Perhaps the much damaged people who had come forward, imposters to the last, needed a name to cleave to, a real person to relate to. Whilst a purely anonymous patient, he was worse off in his twilight world than they were in theirs, but once he had acquired an identity, and by extension a family, a role in life, the place in the world that they so sorely felt the lack of, he became someone to whom they were attracted, who might provide them with a reason to live or feel good about themselves by association at least for a little while.

"I'm a work colleague. Trip and I both worked on the twelfth floor. Fortunately I had a day off last Tuesday. I saw the newsflash yesterday that he was your mystery man. How is he?" Paradiso dissembled shamelessly.

He had taken the route of least resistance as he had so often done before when working on important stories. Sometimes one had to be scurrilously impartial to the truth in order to win people over and by so doing fulfill the bigger truth, the story itself.

The nurse relaxed. She could see that he was not the usual type of pond life whom she had been sending away with the standard form of words – 'that unfortunately Mr. Montifort was still in a coma and would not be receiving visitors for quite a while yet'. In fact he looked like a respectable yuppie type and so she felt on safe ground by letting him gently into the hospital's confidence, especially since Dr. Milsom's memorandum about the importance that family and friends can often play in recovery.

"If you follow me, sir. I'll take you up to see Davey Bo… I'm sorry, I mean Mr. Montifort," she stammered, blushing at her guileless faux pas.

"Did you say 'Davey Boy'?" Paradiso asked her straight back, as they made for the elevator.

He was not about to miss out on any tidbit that might fuel the appetite of the American media. He could already see syndication rights nationwide. As long as his ruse succeeded, he was going to milk it for all it was worth. He had heard something of this Davey Boy on the news but it had not registered with him that he and Trip Montifort were one and the same. From the news value perspective this was another shot in the arm for the story.

"That was the nickname that the fire officer gave him – the one who rescued him."

"Yes, of course," said the reporter. "I should have connected …"

They entered the mirrored elevator.

"You mean Rosario?" went on Paradiso, glad that he had done his homework.

"Yeah. How did you know that?" she answered, looking slightly beetle-browed at him.

"I found out Trip was here only yesterday when the news about his identity came out. I immediately looked up the hospital's website to find the address. The story about Rosario was there."

241

"I see," she said, scarcely mollified. "But you live in the city?"

"Sure," he averred, sensing that he had said the wrong thing and only hoping that it was not a deal breaker.

What New Yorker would not know how to get to Cedar Plains without recourse to a map?

They arrived at the fifth floor and alighted.

As they turned into the corridor, Paradiso wondered if he would be allowed to see the patient. He even harbored hopes of using his Pentax that he had brought out East. He consoled himself that he was to be given a second chance. Whilst the nurse did not appear the sharpest tool in the medical bag; he realized that he must watch what he said more carefully, however.

"Well, I'm sure Dr. Milsom would like to see you. I'll just ask you to wait here, M…"

"…Smithson," he replied, having just read an article in the on-flight magazine on the Smithsonian Institute. He mentally prepared a line in case he was asked for ID.

"Well, I won't be long, Mr. Smithson."

He watched her retreat into the ward.

It was nine-forty a.m. He looked around him and saw a coffee machine. He needed his morning caffeine intake. He settled back down with what passed for a cappuccino and looked at the cheap and cheerfully framed Impressionist prints on the clinical white walls.

Fifteen minutes went by and he was just starting to get agitated when he heard the approach of the nurse.

"Hello, I understand you're a work colleague of Trip Montifort's," Milsom stated baldly.

He had already been on three of these expeditions yesterday, dealing with those hoaxers whom had evaded the nursing staff's filter, and was becoming increasingly disenchanted with the amount of time that this was taking away from his work.

"Yes, Carl Smithson's the name. I'm a stock broker like Trip. We had adjoining offices."

Paradiso held out his hand, whilst the nurse looked on. It seemed to Paradiso that she was still suspicious of him and held back from carrying on with her other duties in the hope of seeing him exposed for the fraud that, judging from her expression, she undoubtedly believed that he was.

"Dr. Milsom. I'm the consultant in charge of Trip's case," he said, a half-smile playing on drawn features, his eyes betraying however, his naked lip service to the conventions.

He held out his hand and clasped the visitor's coldly. The nurse waited for the finale of the scene, narrowed eyes boring into Paradiso.

"Glad to meet you, Dr. Milsom," said the visitor, effusively, as if to make up for the lack of warmth in his medical co-protagonist.

"Now without appearing to be rude or ungracious to you for responding to our appeal for friends of Mr. Montifort to get in touch with the hospital, there are however a few preliminary formalities which we do have to go thru. I hope you understand, Mr. Smithson."

Milsom sized up the man standing before him. He did not seem to be either a wacko or an inadequate. Far from it, he was smart and articulate – like a stockbroker would be. There was something about him however that made him uneasy and it was not just what Nurse Roberts had told him about his not knowing the whereabouts of the hospital. Nevertheless he could not quite put his finger on it.

"I understand completely," Paradiso answered smoothly, his face the open book of a man concerned to look as co-operative as humanly possible.

"If you don't mind, we'll go to my office."

The doctor started walking and Paradiso followed, whilst the nurse pushed the button for the elevator. He was obviously thru the first hurdle. His hold on the exclusive was still extant if perhaps slightly more tenuous, whilst behind his veneer of slick charm pumped the accelerated cardio-vascular system of the undercover reporter.

"We've had many frauds to contend with since we made Trip's identity public. It seems every nut in New York has called to say they're bosom buddies or even his wife."

"I can assure you, Dr. Milsom, that I'm perfectly genuine. I do understand however your need to be certain before I can see Trip. How is he anyway, doctor?"

"No offence, Mr. Smithson, but you're not family, are you? However, I hope that you may be able to help us to find his loved ones, if you know Trip at all well."

"I'm with you now," Paradiso announced, covering up his disappointment.

He would have to rethink exactly what his next step was. It was always going to be a long shot, getting in to see the patient and firing off a few heart-tugging pictures for the one O'clock news. He rued the security ethos of the hospital, however, as he was sure that those snaps alone could have bought him a gleaming new sports car.

They entered the office.

"Please, do sit down," Milsom invited his guest.

The neurologist offered him a coffee and whilst he poured it asked the question about proof of identification which his interlocutor had been dreading.

The reporter made a big show of searching thru his jacket pockets. He looked around the office briefly yet effectively as he did so, took in the shelves of books and the pot plant on the windowsill. His eye reverted to the books – most were medical but others were, it seemed, anthologies of twentieth century poetry.

"I'm afraid, Dr. Milsom that I came on the subway…so I haven't got my driver's license on me."

"Credit card, business card?" the professor enquired tetchily.

It seemed almost unbelievable, in this day and age, for a man of Smithson's obvious status not to have any of the accoutrements of modern life about him.

"I only take them out when I'm going shopping, doctor. And as for my business cards, really…my place of work is lying under a million tons of rubble, so please, doctor."

Milsom took this in and swallowed. Nevertheless he remained unconvinced.

"Okay, well let's leave all that to one side for the moment," Milsom pronounced, handing him a cup and saucer. "What can you tell me about Trip, Mr. Smithson?"

"Well, for one thing…"

Milsom interrupted with a diplomatic cough.

"Sorry…firstly could you tell me why you've only just come forward now, Mr. …Smithson? I'm curious. We put his picture in the papers, on the TV, right from the day after he was admitted."

"I've been so traumatized about the whole thing; I didn't really want to see the news. Yesterday was the first time since... before, you know... that I've put the news program on deliberately."

"I see," said the doctor, thoughtfully.

He had not actually contemplated the severe psychological impact that Tuesday's events may have had on this man sitting before him with all the obvious intelligence and presentation of a Wall Street whiz kid, the epitome of a man about town thirty-something. He cursed his own failure to even consider the ongoing effects on Smithson, the individual, the survivor – he who would have lost so many colleagues, so many friends and, for all he knew, his very livelihood as well. He, Dr. Milsom, the eminent neurologist, so-called master of the human mind in all its complexity, had been so fixated on the protocol of security that he had temporarily mislaid his own Hippocratic Oath.

"What can you tell me about our mutual friend? Is he married? Has he got children? What were... I mean, are... his main interests? Especially music. Do you know his taste in music? That could be very important."

Milsom took his seat. He had a sudden sense of déjà vu. A mental picture of Rosario sitting where Smithson was now ensconced came unbidden into his mind.

"Trip is married. His wife went on a camping vacation in the North West a couple of weeks ago and probably doesn't know about Trip being here. She's probably still under the impression that he's dead."

"I see," said the specialist, thinking that this would explain her non-appearance quite neatly.

On the other hand, an obviously intelligent man like Smithson would be quite capable of inventing something if he indeed was an impostor.

"As for children, no. To the best of my knowledge they have no kids."

"What?" Milsom exclaimed. "You don't know for sure? But you work together?"

"Doc, we stock brokers work hard. We're all hyper-competitive and Trip and I never were that close. We had what you might call water cooler moments. On the other hand he was always very pleasant."

"I'm sorry. I do appreciate your candor. What about parents, brothers, sisters?"

"As I said, we never socialized. I do know however that he liked classical music, especially Mozart, and now I come to think of it, he always had a book of poetry on his desk – T.S. Eliot" he elaborated, throwing into the ring a completely false yet eminently plausible concoction without jeopardizing his short-term credibility, even possibly enhancing it, knowing, as he did, that the good doctor liked verse.

Trip's father or a sibling could indeed walk in at any moment to contradict him, yet after all this time that was increasingly unlikely.

"I think it's time we let you in to see Trip. Just for five minutes, if you wish. It might just help, might just register somewhere deep down in his subconscious mind."

The doctor pondered his own statement, opened his desk drawer and took out a slim, elegantly bound volume.

"Would you mind reading to him," Milsom enquired, handing his treasured copy of T. S. Eliot's *The Waste Land* across the mahogany desk. "He may just recognize your voice. You never know."

Paradiso received the book, feeling the beautiful leather, seeing the tooled silver letters on the cover. He was in. He felt a sense of jubilation mixed with relief.

Sometimes in this business a reporter lucks out.

He felt his camera in his inside jacket pocket. All he required was ten seconds alone by the bedside. He was on the inside track at last.

"I would be delighted," Paradiso replied, a suitably Byronic look coming into his eye.

It was not however the thought of the epic verses which caused this, rather the mental image he had suddenly acquired of a new red BMW coupe.

Then the earth trembled and shook;
The foundations of the mountains rocked and quivered,
Because God was angry.
Smoke poured out of his nostrils,
A consuming flame and burning coals from his mouth.

(Psalm 18)

Chapter XXIII

Mr. Albie Sholtz looked at his reflection. He had not shaved in days, not since the news had first come out. He felt better now that his chin was clean, his stubble recalcitrantly smeared now around the basin and not his jaw line.

His wife had taken it far worse, however. She had even stopped watching her soaps and now sat, staring into space, for hour upon hour.

He did not know what he could do for her. He was thinking about seeking clinical help, but he did not quite know how to bring the subject up without offending her.

The couple fell into that unhappy bracket of people deemed too well off for Welfare but not sufficiently so as to be able to afford private medical insurance. He had to view her sink more into the quagmire of squalid dementia each day until she was only even dressing if he forcibly insisted.

"Why don't you come out with me for a walk?" he asked in a tone that implied that it was a merely rhetorical gambit.

He knew that she would not leave the apartment today.

"It looks like a sunny morning. We can walk to the railroad if you like. You know you've always liked seeing the trains."

He thought a fleeting interest in the idea crossed her eyes and then the opaque fog of melancholia clouded in.

She was sitting on the edge of the bed fidgeting with an old black and white photograph of her son. Albie so much wanted there to be something that he could do to ease her pain but he was at a complete loss.

She turned the picture over in her hands time and again, sometimes kissing it, sometimes clutching it to her heart. Suddenly he thought of the reporter who had called. Maybe if she could go to the funeral it would ease her pain. It was impossible to imagine for a man as proud as him but he had realized that they just did not have the money for her to go to the funeral of their only son. If however this journalist could arrange and pay for Alice to fly out West for the ceremony then maybe he should permit it; perhaps by attending she might get a little closure – that thing they were always spouting on about on Oprah, on Springer and the other 'goddamnawful' programs (his typical phrase of disparagement when he came into the kitchen to make himself a sandwich and those trailer-trash freak shows were on).

"Alice, darling," he began, taking her hand in his and sitting on the bed alongside her. "Would you be up to going to the funeral?"

She carried on playing with the photo in the fingers of her other hand, like some strange monochromatic St. Vitus's dance. There was only silence, however.

"Why don't you come into the kitchen, dear? You can watch your program."

He tried another tack. Still there was no response.

He made to go, exasperated. It had been like this since Saturday.

"Can I really go say goodbye to Robert?" she exclaimed, the question at once poignant yet testament also to the prevailing power discrepancy in the household.

Her husband spun around at her voice – it was the first time in forty-eight hours that she had uttered a word. Retaking his seat next to his wife, he looked into her sad eyes, scanning for signs of her normal intelligence.

He wished that he could go with her but he knew that he could not. It was not just the money. He had relinquished his son years previously and although he naturally wanted to support his wife in her present fragility he could psychologically no more attend the funeral than cut off his own arm. It would be like an admission that his son had been normal, ordinary when he had patently been anything but. If he would not be able to take her to the crematorium then there was no point in him acting as dutiful chaperone on the rest of the trip. It would be emotionally cheapening not only as to his decision but somehow might also implicitly undermine Alice's own emotionally affirmative action. It was hard to explain but whatever the reasons they were his reasons, and he was as convinced that he was doing the right thing for himself as he was that she believed that she was – for herself. He did not want to impose his values on her – not anymore, not after the hell of the last two days. All he now wanted was a quiet life.

"If you want to go you'll have to go on your own. I won't...legitimize his life by flying to Seattle – even for you, darling. If you want to go, then go – but I won't be able to escort you. You'll be all right, I'm sure – you know, with the TV people; they'll want to interview you, of course."

He looked at her – this frail woman whom he had spent nearly fifty years with. He had loved her so very much at the beginning. Their lives had only later been blighted by the product of their union. He would, however, always love her.

"Be careful what you say to that reporter though, won't you."

He took her in his arms and kissed her.

"Thank you," she said, when his lips came away.

He was nonplussed for a second.

"Will you go? You'll go to Robert's... funeral?" he asked, touched beyond measure by her words, relieved that he had finally got thru, that she was still the woman he knew and loved. "Have you got the number of that TV guy?"

"Here it is," she whispered, taking a ragged slip of paper out of her nightgown pocket.

A mentally reinvigorated Albie Sholtz took it and read aloud the name and cell phone number inscribed in his wife's fair handwriting.

"I'll call the fella right now," he said.

* * * * * *

"...... Trams and dusty trees.
Highbury bore me. Richmond and Kew

Undid me. By Richmond I raised my knees

Supine on the floor of a narrow canoe.'

252

'My feet are at Moorgate, and my heart

Under my feet. After the event

He wept. He promised a new start.

I made no comment. What should I resent?' ......"

Paradiso finished reading the passage from the Waste Land. The allusions within held no great moment for him. Culturally, he was more of a Schwarzenegger movie type of guy who could not see the point of so-called great literature and certainly not this verse about a far-off place he faintly recognized as being London.

There had not been a flicker of activity on the electroencephalograph connected to Trip Montifort during the fifteen minutes in which he had been allowed to sit with the patient. When in most timely fashion – doesn't fortune so often favor the brave? – Nurse Sheryl Baker had been called to an adjoining private suite, he had taken the opportunity of firing off approximately a dozen headshots of the comatose man with his Pentax.

Dr. Milsom had come in unannounced at the tail end of his photographic activities. It had been all the reporter could do to retake his seat swiftly and hide the camera lest the good doctor discover his nefarious alternate agenda.

He excused himself, shaking hands with the unsuspecting professor and left the bedside. As he retreated into the corridor leaving Milsom examining the paper output from the hi-tech apparatus, and talking about ordering an MRI scan, he felt his cell phone vibrate. Eager to quit the building now and pursue a string of illicit sales pitches to numerous East Coast press agencies, he was abrupt in answering.

"Yes, Paradiso here," he shouted into the mouthpiece.

"Yes, is that Mr. Paradiso?" the rasping voice asked down the line.

"Yes," he responded impatiently. "What can I do for you?"

"My name, Mr. Paradiso, is Mr. Albie Sholtz and I believe you spoke to my wife on Saturday…"

"Oh yes, Mr. Sholtz, I am very sorry about your son….."

"Well, yes, that is why I'm calling. My wife, Alice, has been very upset and although I was, at the beginning, totally against her going to the funeral, she really does want to go. I understand, Mr. Paradiso, that your TV station is prepared to finance my wife's journey to Seattle, or possibly Helena, and that you will look after her while she is there. She is very… fragile at the moment and I am not asking you this lightly, but anything which will help her to come to terms with our son's death must be worthwhile."

Paradiso was out of the hospital now; the voice of his interlocutor straining to be heard above the din of the Manhattan traffic. All Paradiso really wanted to do in all of this was to use the story to advance his bank balance and his career. If he was ever to achieve the giddy heights of anchorman on the 10 O' clock NBC News he would, however, on occasion, have to subsume his naked ambition beneath a fluttery veil of human warmth and concern.

"Yes, Mr. Sholtz, would you yourself want to go to the funeral? You could look after your wife…" Paradiso ventured with as much empathy as he could muster.

"No. It will just be my wife going west. I washed my hands of my son years ago, Mr. Paradiso, and my wife understands that I cannot go with her."

"OK," he responded. "Have you any objection to meeting up as soon as possible so that I can ask you some simple background questions for the story I am writing?"

This was the moment of truth as far as having an angle on the whole Sholtz side of the exclusive. There was a slight hesitation, only perceptible to Paradiso because of his heightened journalistic senses and then Albie averred.

"Yes, that's all right, Mr. Paradiso," he agreed. "All I ask is that you take good care of Alice – she's all I have left. Have you any children Mr. Paradiso?"

"No, Mr. Sholtz, I've not had that pleasure in life as yet… But I would sure like to think that I will have a son one day to play one on one with."

"Well, Mr. Paradiso…"

"Please, call me Marcus…" he smarmed, shamelessly.

"OK, Marcus, don't make the same mistake I did – if you do have a son one day, as I hope you will, don't let him fall under the influence of anyone else but you and your wife. Robert had always been a good boy until Father Dupree arrived on the…"

He trailed off.

The two men agreed on a time – the logical and most convenient place to meet for the reporter was at the hospital. They would make all the arrangements at two O'clock and Paradiso would get a few ounces of his pound of back-story flesh.

As Paradiso hailed a cab to go back to his hotel for a shave and something to eat, Mr. Sholtz, conversationally, asked the TV man what business he had at the hospital.

"Oh, you don't know, do you? I'm not altogether sure I ought to tell you…" he prevaricated.

Albie interjected that if it was private then he was sorry for being so intrusive; he only hoped that whatever it was it was not too serious.

"No, you misunderstand," he replied at length. "It's not my health which has brought me to the Big Apple, Mr. Sholtz – it's nothing like that."

He slammed the door of the taxi and even still considered whether he should opt out of telling him. As the car drove off and he reflected that it would all be out soon enough anyway, he decided to take the bull by the horns. The journalist was not surprised that the bereaved father had not heard the announcement of Trip Montifort's name on the news and put two and two together. He could not begin to imagine what hell he and Alice had been going thru for years and years – having had the genetic misfortune to have combined to produce a mongrel son like Robert Sholtz.

"Look," the reporter started, aware of the emotions that this intelligence might unleash in this unsophisticated yet seemingly decent man. "There is a man lying in the hospital who is the husband of the woman who Robert raped in that log cabin…one of the women who… killed… your son. His name is Trip Montifort and he's been in a coma for a week. He was in the second of the skyscrapers."

He wished that there were a cell phone that guided one on the etiquette of breaking important, traumatic news – one that popped up specific advice on the screen at every difficult juncture of the conversation. That this had not been invented, as yet, was as tellingly indicative of the difficulties of a third party, even a gee-whiz computer, second-guessing each individual situation, as of the leap in technology required.

There was a long period of silence. Paradiso was able to hear the sound of water running in the background down the line. He almost regretted saying it; he did not know what to say next – to somehow ameliorate the blow without sounding like an idiot backtracking, apologizing for telling the truth unvarnished.

He had entered the hotel in this hiatus. Now, still unsure what to say, and even checking his phone was still connected – it was – he strode thru the lobby to the front desk. Ten seconds or so had elapsed yet it seemed to Paradiso like at least double that.

"Marcus, thanks for telling me. I heard about that guy on the news yesterday," the old man said in a soft voice choked with suppressed tears. "Please can I ask you one thing?" he went on.

He was surprisingly calm given the drama of the information just imparted to him.

"Sure, Albie," answered the reporter, multi-tasking, flashing his driver's license and taking the proffered key card from the smiling hotel receptionist. "Anything I can do to oblige."

"This may be all too much for Alice. She's at the end of her tether already. Can you not mention this to her – not for now anyway? I'll hope that she doesn't connect the two things if she hears about it on the news. I didn't. Otherwise it could be the final straw."

He finished his emotional plea and then Paradiso agreed most amenably to his request. The elevator arrived and the conversation was abruptly, but only slightly prematurely, concluded as the signal gave out on the ascent. Paradiso silently said a prayer of thanks to Otis for not yet having gotten around to solving this technical glitch. He had become bored with the old man.

Paradiso was a past master at appearing transparently honest when the situation required it. If he were not a newsman, he would have made either a successful snake oil salesman or a politician. He was a true believer in Marx – not the dialectical Karl, but the diametrically funnier Groucho, who once extruded the aphorism: 'If you can feign sincerity, you've got it made'.

He caught a glimpse of his chiseled features in the mirror and realized that for all his honest sounding empathy he was the slyest bastard he knew. Soon this news story made in heaven – or should that be hell? – would be all over the world. If he had his way it would be humanly impossible for the lamentable Mrs. S to avoid it. He smiled knowingly to himself and practiced his best presenter voice in the privacy of the rising cubicle:

'And now, without further ado, we go over to our Washington D.C. correspondent for some breaking news from the White House.'

Soon the whiff of NBC's executive washroom could be competing with the stench of his own tawdry business ethics. It was definitely game on.

And he, Marcus Paradiso, had the inside track.

He was definitely in Starting Gate One.

If they do not change their ways,
God will sharpen his sword.
He bends his bow and makes it ready;
He takes up his deadly weapons
And aims his burning arrows.

(Psalm 7)

Chapter XXIV

Miss Boniface felt the chill, fin de siècle wind of New Jersey upon her hawk-like features and her crimson-flushed cheek. It had been a few hours only since she had seen the evil epicenter of Dupree's perverted tendencies and now, as she hung the priest's designer label silk shorts on the line in the drying breeze, she felt even more tiny and insignificant by her own lack of moral courage.

She stared at the haunting outline of Manhattan, framed ethereally by the gray watery sky beyond the sweep of the railroad track, and agitated inwardly at the degree of her own complicity in the abuse of minors.

For all her insular world-view and bereftness of social confidence that had seen her confine her life to this backwater and to domestic servitude, she knew from the base of her soul that she had to now stand up and be counted.

She remembered the Mother Superior, Sister Mary-Therese, who had taken her in from the Chicago City orphan's home when she was unwanted by anyone. She remembered her saintly pale face in the glow of the chapel at Evensong and she remembered her sermons on the devil and on the hellfire and damnation that followed in the hereafter to those who strayed off the righteous way and

259

took up with Lucifer in his Den of Iniquity. It had been ripe language for an impressionable young girl. Somehow now maybe the penny had finally dropped, almost fifty years on.

She realized that Father Dupree had taken up with him – the Devil. She had seen with her own eyes and heard with her own ears the scale of wickedness that went on in his secret lair. Sophie and Lara's darling faces streaked like mental meteors thru her gray matter, reinforcing as if by some form of psychic influence, her sense of what had to come next.

For the first time in her life, on a major fork in the road, she knew with certainty what she must do. It was a damascene moment in her life – all urges towards the selfish, calm cover-up and the self-preservation of the status quo were banished with newfound fortitude. Thoughts of her own safety blew away during those three minutes of hanging washing, along with the Russian Thistle and the torn chip packet in the quadrant. She would finally make Sister Mary-Therese proud of her, she told herself, picking up the empty plastic basket and walking back to the scullery.

* * * * * *

Meanwhile, at the hospital, Albie Sholtz had just arrived in the main foyer, having walked the six blocks from Penn Station. He stood to one side of the hustle, feeling every one of his years beside the scurrying young nurses, his pale and careworn face tearful as he contemplated the gilt-framed photo that he held.

He was slightly early for his meeting with the reporter, a fact which he did not ascribe any undue significance to – he was always early, ever since he had been a young man in a hurry, rushing about town trying to make a buck, chasing girls, frenetically enjoying his youth in this metropolis of dreams.

He had never intended his life to go like this, had long since stopped regretting the fact that it had – yet he had never for one second stopped loving Alice – even though his life might have been so very different had he not been so bowled over by her kooky charm during that far-off, rainy hour in Blezinki's back in '55.

He had been working on the Lower East Side and, after popping into the shop for a salt beef sandwich, he had watched her sitting up at the counter, transfixed and entirely entranced by the picture of prettiness before him. It had not been so very long in the grand scheme of things before he had proposed and not so long after that that a baby boy had arrived to make them as happy as any couple could be.

Now, forty-five years hence, he clutched to his bosom the black and white likeness of their son as innocent altar boy and raged savagely inside at the bleak randomness of life – but mostly at his own in particular.

"Hello, Mr. Sholtz."

He did not hear the man at his elbow, so immersed was he in those golden memories and philosophical musings. The slick journo, unfazed, tried again.

"Mr. Sholtz, I presume. How're you doing?"

Albie slowly raised his eyes and allowed the words to permeate his consciousness.

"Hello, I didn't see you there," he said, quickly regaining his composure and smiling weakly at Paradiso. "Please remember, call me Albie."

"Okay, Albie. What say we go for a coffee to discuss things?"

"Fine by me," the older man replied, placing the picture in a zipped document case.

"What's that?" Paradiso asked, ever the inquisitor.

"Oh nothing, Mr. Para… Marcus. It's just a photo of Robert when he was a boy."

"I'd like to see that, if I may," he asked politely. "I'd like to get a whole overview on his…Robert's life, including when he was a child."

"He was a good boy, always a good boy, back then…"

The grieving father paused and the tears that had surfaced were replaced by a stern yet calm expression in the eye.

"There's no need to dance around me, Marcus. I'm not my wife. I know what it is that he became. You don't need to refer to him by name to spare my feelings. He was a goddamn murdering son of a bit…"

He stopped himself just in the nick of time from his unfortunate choice of phrase. He handed Paradiso the photograph.

They started walking to the hospital cafeteria that was located on the first floor.

The reporter studied the image: a common or garden picture of a boy in church dressed up in his white collar and gown, well-scrubbed smiley features, pudding basin style dark hair.

How mundane is the origin of evil, Paradiso reflected. What makes it take over? Was there a decisive turning point in its gestation? A critical mass of bad thoughts? Was it a voluntary thing, that he woke up one morning and decided – just like that – to make himself evil or was it all in the genes, in the upbringing? Was it indeed, possibly, as attributable to the seemingly nice old man who now walked besides him as it was to Sholtz's own freewill?

"You mentioned a priest on the phone, a Father Dupree?" the reporter enquired, handing back the photo. "I got the impression that you were not overly impressed by him, that perhaps he held some …"

He searched his mental RAM for the right word.

"…pernicious… influence over young Robert? Am I on the right track here? You seemed very upset..."

"I can't prove anything, but there were always rumors back then. He was our priest though. I always thought it was wrong to believe gossip, especially since Father Dupree was generally so well respected in the community. All I can tell you is that when Robbie was fourteen he became withdrawn, sullen. He wouldn't talk about it, wouldn't talk to his ma or to me. He changed…"

"Like a lot of adolescents, a lot of teenagers. That's totally par for the course," Paradiso interjected.

They took their coffees to a corner table where they would not be overheard.

"At the time I thought that, we both did. Of course! We're not stupid people. It's only later when I looked back searching for a reason, for an explanation for …for his becoming like he was, that I realized that there was more to it than that."

He stopped, his head bowed now over the steaming cup.

The TV man waited. This was all good stuff. He had put his Dictaphone on 'voice activated' when he had first spotted Sholtz Snr. in the lobby.

At length, after a few sips, the bereaved, though hardly bereft, father continued.

"He completely changed after his confirmation. It was as if he became a different person. He was such a good boy. Oh, he gotten himself into pranks like all kids but he was a real good lad. He loved nature, loved going for walks with his old man, loved fishing for sticklebacks with the other neighborhood kids. That all stopped."

"Kids grow out of things, Albie. It's totally natural..." Paradiso remarked, beginning to think perhaps that he was on to a red herring with this priest thing — that it was nothing more than the ill-founded ramblings of a distressed old man, desperately looking to pin the blame on someone... anyone for the way his son's life had turned out.

Albie drew a deep breath and then spoke again, slowly and deliberately, so that there should be no misunderstanding.

"No. There was more to it. There's one thing that I'd never thought anything about at the time but that years later I remembered."

"What?" asked Paradiso in a low delivery designed to elicit the goods without risk of disrupting the mood.

"It was a little thing. One night I went into Bobby's room to say 'good night' and there he was with scissors in his hand cutting up a photo of himself. It was one from his confirmation, one of a number of him being congratulated by Father Dupree. I asked him what he was doing and he said that he didn't like the picture of himself so he was cutting it up. Years later, long after Robert had left home, I found the half of the picture with Dupree's face on it. It was in Robbie's scrapbook. It was cut into thirteen pieces and stuck down with glue. His face was smeared with blood and traces of what at first I thought was chocolate. Only when I looked closer did I realize what it actually was…"

Paradiso gagged and spluttered on his coffee.

"That sure is weird."

"Yeah, I burned it. Didn't want the damn thing in the house! I never mentioned it to Robert…or to Alice. There was no point in dredging it all up again."

"So you think this Dupree had been …" He swallowed hard. "You don't mean abuse, child abuse? That's a very serious allegation, you know."

"I don't think it. I know it. Know it in my bones. He ruined my boy, my lovely son…ruined him, made him into what he became as sure as if he'd …"

Albie Sholtz's voice fizzled out in seeking the correct analogy, yet there was none – not in this singular case, not really in any case, because each case comprised different human beings with different motivations, different latent proclivities. There could never be an apt analogy because there could be a million and there could be none. It was yet both impossible to pry apart the thicket of cause and effect and yet all too easy also to see a correlation.

* * * * * *

"Miss Boniface, let's be having one of your special cherry pies, if you don't mind?" the priest asked, coming into the kitchen. "And I'll have a cup of tea with it, merci beaucoup."

"Right you are, Father," she replied, flicking the switch on the red electric kettle. She did not meet the priest's eye, could not, but she could see that his face was almost the hue of the simmering utensil.

Dupree coughed and sat down at the kitchen table – a scene they had played out together thousands of times down the years, he having a slice of pie and a refuel of tea, she going about ministering to him, whilst preparing lunch.

This time though there was a definite edge in the air – a mutually strained atmosphere.

"Will you take the girls a slice as well and maybe a glass of milk?" he asked as if everything was normal, as if he were playing now with the concept of paternal benevolence.

She realized with a sudden pang of conscience that normal it probably was. She had probably brought cherry pie to many traumatized victims over the years, too many to contemplate and yet all the time, at some level, she had known – had unconsciously blotted out her sentient feelings, her humanity, in a haze of loyalty and service and meekness.

"Will you be wanting whipped cream on that, Father?" she asked, as she always did.

There was almost something sexually significant in his abiding love for this combination – something Freudian perhaps?

"Look, Miss Boniface, about before, you know...Yes, I'll have a dollop...You do spoil me so, Miss Boniface, and I thank you for it, but my waistline disagrees, of course. I'd just gone into the girls' room to comfort them, you know.

After all they've lost their mummy and daddy in that terrible tragedy. God save the souls of all those poor, poor, innocent people."

"That's as maybe, Father, but I do wish you'd told me, then I wouldn't have worried when I heard them crying," she found herself saying, realizing as she said it the profound irony inherent in the statement. "I never knew you had a key to the other door either, Father," she added.

"Oh, that. Funny thing… I only found it the other day. Been lost for years, has it not? My, this pie is excellent, Miss Boniface. You are the tops when it comes to looking after old Dupree aren't you, my dear Miss Boniface," he schmoozed, tucking in greedily.

She blushed scarlet at the over-effusion and poured the boiling water onto the three tea bags in the teapot – one for each, one for the pot, just as she had learnt at convent school.

"You'll be having one as well, Miss Boniface? Come, have a sit down. You know – you work too hard, my dear."

He watched her thin frame as she filled up the kettle and switched it on.

"No, I've got eight lunches to do, Father. I haven't got time for sitting around eating pie."

"You know, if I didn't know you any better, my dear, I'd think you were having a little dig at me there. I work hard too, you know, Miss Boniface."

He looked at her with scanning eyes as if seeing her afresh, a new woman, minted in a trice after a lifetime of being congenitally unable to say boo to a goose.

She ambled casually into the scullery which doubled as a store for the gardener.

She picked up the petrol-driven chain saw that she had seen the man use time and time again to hard prune the plum and apple trees and calmly walked back into the kitchen. Only occasionally did he, of necessity, require its full power. Nevertheless it was autumn and she had seen him lubricate it, fill it and test it for another season only a couple of days previously.

"Miss Boniface, what are you doing with that thing, for Christ's sake?" Dupree exclaimed. "Edith, dear," he hurried on, using her Christian name for the first time in living memory.

"I've been thinking for a while now that perhaps you should have a little vacation. You've heartily earned it with all the work you put in around here. Edith, dear…I'll make some enquiries and see if I can't arrange a few days in New England for you, so you can be seeing all those lovely leaves turning gold and red…You'd like…"

There was a sudden whirring and the excruciating sound of metal on bone as Miss Boniface brought the tool into action over his cranium. The machine was only on for twenty seconds in all, the rich vermilion yet corrupt blood of Dupree mingling sickly with the cream on the top of his half-finished cherry pie.

Students came running at the horrific screams and were, to a young man, blanching and retching at the indescribable sight that greeted them. There was no appetite for administering the Last Rites, nor would there have been the opportunity, even if they were capable physically of so doing.

His reign of heinous terror was at an end.

One vertical cut thru the crown of his head, made diagonal thru an instinctive final, agonized move to evade his fate, had dispatched him.

Miss Boniface had thoughts only for the children in the aftermath of her deed. She collapsed into the opposite chair, staring at the gory tableau before her. She summoned a seminarian who was vomiting and in tears in the doorway, to go free the girls from their containment and to call 911.

She sat staring ahead. There were no tears from her eyes – only peace at last. From her housecoat pocket she took an old faded photograph and kissed it tenderly. She would still be kissing it when the homicide team arrived hotfoot, eleven minutes later.

Whether Mother Superior Mary-Therese would have been proud of her was entirely another matter.

* * * * * *

Paradiso and Sholtz had dealt with the negotiations for the TV documentary and for Mrs. Sholtz's trip west. A modest fee was decided upon for their time and insights and the network would underwrite the tab for the flights and accommodation.

Paradiso had to work quite hard to get Albie to agree to be interviewed on camera, but agree he did, in the end. It was not the usual platitudinous media-speak which won him over – not the usual line about 'you owe it to yourself to explain so people know it was nothing to do with you' or 'you surely owe it to society to demonstrate how this can happen in any family, so others can be even more aware to prevent it from happening'. No, these fell wide of the mark.

What really convinced Mr. Albie Sholtz to appear on film and tell his story was the idea that he could say on film things which he had never said before to his wife. He would be able to express his deepest feelings for Alice and what she had meant to him all these decades and to let her know also, finally and fully, the real depth of his grief for their son.

It was sometimes easier to tell a third party how one felt than one's own wife, so bound up in the usual rigmaroles of our distracted and compartmentalized lives are we. Rarely do we get the opportunity to step outside the banal and embrace the emotional lurking unspoken within us. This was often the case, especially with men of a certain generation – men who had been brought up with John Wayne and Gary Cooper, men who preened themselves not on their feminine side like some metrosexual males of the twenty-first century, but on their stoicism, their discipline, their strength of character.

"So it's all arranged," the TV man stated, starting to get up and proffering his outstretched hand formally across the chrome and glass table.

They shook on it.

Suddenly there was a commotion behind them. Paradiso had been with Albie for an hour and a quarter. In that time he had not listened to the radio nor checked in with his office, nor viewed the news updates on his cell.

In short he had not heard the news that had now brought twenty or so media hacks to the hospital in such a hurry. A positive stampede of them came rushing into the cafeteria. They looked somehow as if they would have preferred to be attending an electric chair execution than to be here. A story hard and certain and black – not a good-news story, but a good news story, at least in their hard-bitten terms. Even the women reporters looked like they were scornful of the common man and of his common morality-that they essentially despised the unwashed masses that they provided with their daily inane quota of the sensational and prurient.

A friendly and upbeat female voice came over the PA system:

<< WILL ALL MEDIA PERSONS HERE FOR THE PRESS CONFERENCE PLEASE CONGREGATE IN THE HOSPITAL CAFETERIA. DR. MILSOM WILL ARRIVE SHORTLY >>

Paradiso asked one of the herd what was going.

"It's that coma guy. He's finally come round. Didn't you hear the news? It was on CNN two hours ago – the jerks. They always seem to be first with everything."

Paradiso realized that he had been so taken up with everything he had neglected to keep informed about Montifort's progress. He thought of the lovely Desdemona and wondered if she was already in the building. He had called her apartment not two hours previously from the hotel but there had been no answer.

Now he bade his farewell to Albie Sholtz. There was more to this story than him and his deviant son. Paradiso had been most negligent in not keeping his eye on the main chance. Trip Montifort was undoubtedly the mainspring of the story now – everything else was just background – colorful background – but still only the hors d'oeuvres to the big bucks entrée.

"I'm glad he's going to be okay, Marcus. At least he'll be there for his wife," Albie said, nodding his head, as if this was one less thing on his family's extended conscience.

"We'll have to wait and see what the doc says," replied Paradiso vaguely, his eyes focused on an attractive journalist with flowing blonde locks.

He shook Mr. Sholtz's hand.

"I'll be in touch," he said simply. "The station will arrange the flights for Alice and a female escort to accompany her." He added rather offhandedly, "Goodbye, Mr. Sholtz."

He already had his mind on the impending press conference, on the whereabouts of Desi, on the exclusive story that suddenly did not quite seem so exclusive.

The use of the surname alerted the blonde. Another reporter's ears pricked up as well.

She ventured forward and smiled radiantly at the Seattle-based reporter.

"Sholtz – that's not exactly a common name, is it? Is that man any relation to Robert Sholtz, the mass murderer who went on a killing spree last week in Montana?"

"It's a not unusual name in New York, Miss...?" Paradiso stonewalled.

"Taylor, Karen Taylor. New York Independent News Channel. And you are?"

"I'm nobody. We're just two private people who met in the hotel restaurant and had a pleasant conversation over a doughnut and coffee."

The other correspondent raised his eyebrows quizzically.

"I think the reporter doth protest too much," Miss Taylor asserted.

"No, I'm not a reporter," he replied agitatedly, just as Dr. Milsom walked into the room.

"Aren't you that guy with the Sholtz story from Montana TV?" submitted the other man, but Paradiso was already on his way out.

He heard Karen Taylor say a self-congratulatory "I knew it" as he beat a hasty retreat thru the throng.

It was not the end of the world if he missed the press conference, he reassured himself. In fact he had no choice, lest he betray his profession to the good professor of neurology. Later, he may well want to perpetuate his ruse to elicit information or even to gain admittance to Trip himself. However, it was now obvious that his syndicated feature had made his face recognizable in the city.

He made a mental note to check how much the worldwide rights for the pics had sold for. It was obvious now that this was a huge story across the world. He could decipher Japanese, French and Australian accents among the journos. He had never doubted that it would play big with Middle America and beyond – but this was huge – truly international.

Who was he trying to kid? His face was too well known to pursue another opportunity to visit Trip again.

Within barely an hour he would see developments in the saga that even he could not ever have envisaged.

Idly, he wondered if his stentorian rendition of the Waste Land had contributed to Trip's regaining of consciousness. Somehow, he liked to think that it had.

He sneaked out of the cafeteria unseen by Milsom. He would hear the minutiae of Trip Montifort's miraculous recovery soon enough. What was important was that he find Desdemona and sign her up for an interview before the other jackals got to her first.

He took out his cell phone and tried her apartment. There was still no answer. He did a quick mental calculation in his head. The news had been out for a couple of hours the reporter had said. A couple of hours to get dressed, to call the hospital, to call God knows who and to get a cab. He was sure that she must be on her way to the hospital. She would surely have heard the news by now. He went out of the building and lit a cigarette. He would wait for her to show up.

It was only a matter of time. He had only ever seen her in the immediate aftermath of the siege. It had been dark and he had been kept well behind the police cordon, but even from a distance and under the stars of the Montana night, only artificially illuminated by the police headlights, he had recognized a stunner when he saw one. He had heard her voice, a throaty, sexy voice with a hint of latent danger and he had wanted her. He was a man who always got his woman, professionally speaking and otherwise, and this one would be no exception, he told himself grittily, drawing up his overcoat lapels against the biting wind blowing in from the Hudson.

Firstly though he had business to conduct and she of course had to play her starring role in the unfolding drama. Forget Albie and Alice Sholtz, forget their mutantly chromosomed son (if that was what he was?), forget even Trip Montifort himself – if this was to be the story of his career that would turbo-blast him to a life of fame and fortune there had to be glamour and sex appeal and Mrs. M had that in spades.

Moreover, she was at the very heart of the story and only he knew what she looked like. His profession was not rocket science but when it all came together it was a brilliant buzz.

He lit another cigarette and waited.

A street vendor came by and made his regular mid-afternoon dive into the hospital selling the evening paper.

"Murder in Seminary. Vicious Murder of Priest. Get all the news here," he called out. "Only a buck."

As he paid his dollar, a yellow taxi hoved into view thru the main gate.

Paradiso just had time to see the name 'Miss Edith Boniface' and the phrase 'chain saw killing' before he rolled up his paper in anticipation of the main protagonist's arrival.

He watched as an elegant, black-stockinged leg stretched itself out of the cab. He could feel his mouth go dry as he approached. Back in her metropolitan milieu, and with access once more to the secrets of her personal boudoir and the time to apply them, she was more jaw-droppingly beautiful than he could ever have imagined that terrible night in the wilds.

She would look fantastic on a standard 32-inch screen – tears of joy an optional extra.

Sin speaks to the wicked deep in their hearts;
They reject God and have no reverence for him.
Because they think so highly of themselves,
They think that God will not discover their sin and condemn it.
(Psalm 36)

Chapter XXV

Albie arrived home and sought out Alice in the kitchen to tell her his news. The television was blaring, her eyes trenchantly engaged on the screen. She was watching a news channel. He regarded her and the TV with a curious rising of his brow and wondered why it was not displaying its usual soap or reality show. Something must be up, he told himself apprehensively. He sat down next to her and watched as a certain Lieutenant Paul Meyerson was being interviewed outside a large gray nineteenth century building.

<<At this time, we are not looking for anyone else in connection with this crime,>> he muttered quite casually at the blonde reporter.

The subtitle continuously rolled: 'Karen Taylor, Serious Crime Correspondent, reporting from the New Jersey seminary where the homicide of Father Thomas Dupree occurred earlier today'.

Albie recognized the woman as the one at the hospital. His ears pricked up.

<<Is it true that the alleged perpetrator, a certain Miss Edith Boniface, was found by the arresting officers with a photo of the notorious mass murderer, Robert Sholtz, as a young altar boy?>>

She held the microphone under the officer's nose.

<<I am unable to make any comment on this at this time,>> Meyerson replied, deadpan.

<<Is it not true that the housekeeper, Miss Boniface – the female perp arrested for Father Dupree's shocking murder – was holding the photo when she was captured? And also, Lieutenant Meyerson, can you possibly comment on the fact that Sholtz had once been a member of Dupree's congregation when a boy?>>

<<I'm sorry, but our investigations are ongoing in that direction among others and I'm unable to comment on that at this time.>>

<<Is it true, Lieutenant, that Father Dupree was being investigated by the NYPD Child Protection Unit for pedophile activities at the time of his murder and, if so, do you believe that there could be a link here with these activities and his being chain sawed to death by his hitherto loyal housekeeper of thirty years service?>>

<<As I've said before, Miss. Taylor, the investigation is in its infancy at present and we will be examining all possible theories on motivation. Now, if you don't mind, Miss. Taylor, we'll be having a press conference tomorrow at 3p.m. at Newark Central Precinct. Thank you.>>

<<Thank you, Lieutenant Paul Meyerson of Newark P.D. Can you just confirm one final thing, Lieutenant, before I let you go?...Is it true that the two ten-year-old girls that you found locked up in the seminary are the daughters of Trip Montifort, the Twin Towers victim, who only hours ago regained consciousness in a Manhattan hospital?

<<Can you possibly throw any light on this absolutely extraordinary scenario and the reason that they were being held here?>>

<<No. I can make no comment on that at this time. Thank you.>>

The detective turned his back on the reporter and on the half million TV viewers and was seen walking to his unmarked automobile. Karen Taylor improvised a closing peroration for the segment and handed back to the studio with professional aplomb and a dazzling yet still somehow somber half-smile.

She said a silent thank you to the indiscreet journalist from the sticks of Montana for unintentionally giving her the best break of her career. Whilst all the other journos were intent on chasing after the easy glory of a man reawakening from his brush with death, she had, uniquely amongst them, realized the significance of the link with events out West.

'What a story it is!' she thought to herself as she, the cameraman and sound recordist returned to her silver Toyota.

She had put two and two together and quickly made four. She had guessed that there was a link between Montifort and Sholtz when she had heard the latter name mentioned and then recognized Paradiso in the hospital. It had taken her no more a few minutes on her laptop in a close by coffee house to determine that indeed Desdemona Montifort was married to Trip. She had thanked heaven for Wi-Fi.

When one of her police contacts had then called her with news of the murderess's possession of a photograph of a young Robert Sholtz everything had started to slot together. She had raced to Jersey and found an even more mind-blowing story than ever she could have imagined.

She very definitely had the exclusive, had first run on the colleagues whom she had left at the hospital, Paradiso included. It was, however, with tears in her eyes that she started driving to the TV station, thinking all the while of those poor, poor young girls. It was all barely credible and yet she had it on good authority from her best police source that it was so.

It was like a giant labyrinth, this story, she mused – a beastly entity with seemingly its own mind and its own dizzying momentum which turned back on itself and that gorged on itself and was thus self-perpetuating – and it was her story now.

"Karen, this could be a real shot in the arm to your career," the cameraman said amiably. "You do realize that, don't you?"

"Sorry, Brad, I can't think about that right now," she said softly, hardly audible above the noise of the engine. "This is such a sad story... sorry, no that doesn't even begin to do it justice – it's a terrible, awful story."

The soundman could not resist chiming in with his own superfluous verbiage. "It's incredible that there are so many links back to Sholtz and to the woman who killed him – this Desdemona woman. It's almost as if it's the plot of a Hollywood B-movie."

Karen Taylor did not respond.

It was as if she did not care anymore about her scoop. This was too disturbing a story to be thrilled at it's uncovering. She pulled over to the side of an old disused gas station, hurled herself out of the Japanese import and sprinted in high heels, hand over mouth, towards some undergrowth.

As she returned to the driver's seat and took a swig from her habitual bottle of mineral water to cleanse herself, she realized that she had never before been so physically affected by a story. She had not even, as yet, set eyes on the two little girls but somehow the blonde twins had inhabited her mind's eye in toto since arriving at the crime scene. Somehow, they reminded her of why she had always wanted, even as a little girl herself, to become a reporter.

She was gender-inhibited from being Superman and Wonder Woman was and always would be Lynda Carter and no other. Anyway, she lacked the upholstery for that ambition, she had realized with disappointment on hitting thirteen. No, to emulate Clark Kent's love interest became her ultimate dream as she entered adolescence – to set the world to rights like Lois Lane!

It was not about career or money or power. It had always been about idealistically making people sit up and take notice at all the bad things that happen in the world – so that they could be made better.

She had recently felt that she had somehow let these priorities slip down the agenda over the years. It had taken the cruel heartache and pain of two little girls, whom she had not even met, to restore her to her original and admirable modus vivendi.

Ms. Taylor took another refreshing drink.

She would long remember this day that she had finally gotten her professional integrity back. She somehow felt cleaner now, as she drove on, even with the sweet, cloying smell of sick in her nostrils, than she had when she had set out.

Albie had watched the interview with the homicide detective in silence. Now he put his arms around Alice and hugged her close.

"Is there no end in sight?" he wailed inwardly.

Alice responded by changing the channel with the clicker. An episode of Frasier sprang into life. She was seeking solace now in the familiarity of the known, the routine. She was but a simple person for whom this new situation involving her son came as not so much a shock as a sensory volcano in the midst of her already mournful and broken state. The further intelligence about Trip Montifort's connection to her firstborn had not yet reached her ears in so far as Albie was aware. He had been determined to protect her as much as humanly possible from the distressing knowledge that when this man came round his first thought would be for the welfare of his wife – this woman whom their son had raped, this woman who had taken part in the killing of her beloved Robert. Someone would have to inform the poor man, after his own singularly terrible trial, of what their benighted son had done. Now he realized with a jolt that the high profile of any news with a connection to Robert meant that it would be impossible to keep anything under wraps. It would be surely far better, in her fragile mental condition, that she finds out from her own husband.

He determined to tell her as soon as the episode had come to its 'Tossed Salad and Scrambled Eggs' closing credits.

'Lord knows, she could do with a little light relief for half an hour,' he told himself, poring over her blank face, trying to figure out what degree of anguish she was going thru.

It was different for a mother, he told himself. Though he too was severely perturbed by recent developments, he was able to a greater degree to compartmentalize his feelings, to appreciate that though these things were abhorrent to behold, there was nothing much he could do, nor could have done about them, nor could reasonably be held responsible for. Notwithstanding the fact that Robert was also the fruit of his loins, he had never felt responsible for his son's evil, no nook or cranny of his conscience had ever been remotely troubled in that sphere. A mother, on the other hand, felt an almost umbilical bond with her son which might on some deep, dark psychological level, make her want to bear some of his burden of guilt, almost as a genetic imperative – in some strange way the better to absolve her progeny from the full weight of personal responsibility for his crimes. He knew not where these ideas came from, nor even their level of soundness, but he knew instinctively that Alice had taken the news of their son's demise into first psychosis, then murder, rape, and now death itself far worse than himself – of this, as he searched her distant, disengaged irises for the minutest, reassuring spark of normalcy, he was quite sure.

For himself, his initial response to the news item was confirmation that whatever the faults inherent in their son's DNA and in their own parental inadequacies, somehow it was a release to find some new confirmation of his long-held suspicions that Dupree was seemingly also responsible for the warping of Robert's pubescent character. There was now, however, in some core part of him, a sense of paternal feeling welling up, a fossilized relic of a father's long-latent love for his son – for this tortured and torturing offspring whose life had been so traumatized and misshapen by the counterfeit holy man with whom they had entrusted their so-adored boy.

The fact of his facing the abuse alone, for years maybe, unable to say anything, wary, fearful of the reaction – for who would believe an adolescent youth above a priest? – was a haunting image and one to which the corollary was this unexpected upswell of love for the sweet, loving son whom they had effectively lost, thirty years previously.

He was certain that a lot more news would come out about Dupree, but equally that behind his killing lay a web of incredible evil which had proved contagious – for it had permeated, infected and fatally diseased his son's very soul.

He could remember too Miss Boniface as a young woman. She had been pleasant and self-effacing. Robert and she had, as far as he could recollect, a perfectly ordinary relationship for their respective positions and ages. It was, however, even at the time, obvious that she had a soft spot for Robert in an entirely innocent way.

What possible ripple effect of this had traveled thru the intervening years to finally cause the woman to snap? Had she followed his megalomaniacal career with an increasing feeling of personal guilt for not stepping in at the time and saving him?

It was all conjecture of course, but it was not necessary to be a genius to guess at the catalyst for Miss Boniface's loss of control nor also her reason for harboring a photograph of the young Robert for so many years.

To Albie it seemed that the recent media coverage must have brought those days vividly back to her and raised her levels of guilt to tipping point. Perhaps she clung to the photo to persuade herself that the reality of his destructive crusade thru others' lives had not actually happened – that he was still the sweet, angelic choirboy who had been her favorite.

It was a psychiatric line of enquiry that, it was not difficult, even for a layman, to pick the bones out of. It would indeed become a cause celebre in the annals of psychoanalysis for years into the future.

Albie did not presume to know all the answers, only that he owed a debt of gratitude to the woman now being held in custody. Not only had she had the courage to kill Dupree and avenge in part the wrongs done to Robert, but moreover she had by her actions re-awoken in him that part of him that had once been a father, the part of him which he had always felt completed his life.

Now he had that feeling again because of her... and he was grateful for the memories of his son being returned to him, perhaps feelings in aspic from when Bobby was a young boy, but more than that some real sense that Bobby was not alone guilty for his sins; that he had been unable to do anything but those things once the malevolence of the clergyman had insinuated its sylphlike wickedness into his mind and body and so destabilized his psyche.

Although neither a philosopher nor a determinist by intuition, it was a comforting theory right now and one that he would cleave to for the remainder of his days.

He turned the television set off as the familiar refrain sang out and the comedy finished.

He had been so consumed with hate for his son for so very long that it had been contaminating him from within, suffocating his own happiness like one vast, mental melanoma.

Now, however, perhaps by some telepathic prod from the fictional psychiatrist, Mr. Frasier Crane, he felt his heart brimming with unadulterated love for his departed son – mass murderer or not – he had still been his son.

He put his arms around his wife and wept at last for *his* Bobby – not, as a priori, for himself, for Alice or for the multitude of victims.

"I loved him, darling. I really did. He was my son, my only child," he sobbed. "Surely… surely, Alice, you always knew that."

"Yes, dear," she muttered, briefly, almost automatically and with that she picked up the remote and changed channels.

Montel was on Channel 9.

She sought refuge from her own pain in that of strangers.

You make springs flow in the valleys,
And rivers run between the hills.
They provide water for the wild animals;
There the wild donkeys quench their thirst.
In the trees near by,
The birds make their nests and sing.

(Psalm 104)

Chapter XXVI

Dr. Milsom ushered Mrs. Montifort into his office. "Please sit down." He spoke courteously. "Coffee?"

"I'm very anxious to see my husband," she non-replied.

After all she had been thru, to arrive at the hospital only to be accosted by the selfsame reporter, whom she thought she had evaded out West, had been most nerve-racking. Dr. Milsom had rescued her. He had already apprehended that Paradiso had played him for a dope, when he had caught sight of the smarm ball on the TV news in his office.

The other reporters had left the press conference and one had overheard Desi introduce herself and ask which floor her husband's room was on.

All of a sudden there had been a flash flood of halogen lights and a volley of quickfire questions. It had been the furthest thing from her mind that she would have to run the media gauntlet, when all that she wanted was to see her husband. Trip was the love of her life, the man whom she thought she had lost and yet now had been returned to her.

Dr. Milsom was sure that she was genuine. She was dressed in a Hermes pink and cream plaid coat over a russet, silk two-piece that oozed class. Her hair was in a chignon with corkscrew bangs, effortlessly caressing her temples. She wafted Chanel No.5 subtly and her make-up, from the kohl eyeliner to the cerise lip-gloss was impeccably applied and in perfect taste. She had to be the real McCoy, Dr. Milsom reasoned, otherwise the standard dress code for crank visitors had suddenly risen a thousand fold. Nevertheless, he had to make absolutely certain – the hospital could not allow any more cranks or reporters to gain admittance to its celebrity patient. They would all be laughing stocks.

As they went up to the fifth floor in the elevator, she explained that she had been in the bath when she had heard the news, that she had only just flown back into town. She explained that she had thought at first that she was imagining it, imparting her own subconscious desire into the voice of the radio newsreader, in the haze of her own rememberancing and jet-lag induced drowsiness. Then she had switched channels and had heard the news repeated. It had been like a dream – a miracle.

Having ordered a cab, she had then dressed carefully in Trip's favorite outfit and teased her hair into his preferred soignée style. She had been in a daze most of the time since hearing the broadcast. It was unimaginable, unbelievable – all that she wanted now was to see her husband and hold him. She had dressed up for Trip, wanted him to see that she had made a special effort to be beautiful for him – though in truth, of course, it was no effort at all to please the man that she loved.

"I would like to see my husband, please," she insisted, standing up.

"Yes, of course," answered Dr. Milsom. "I just have to validate your ID and then I'll take you up to see your husband, Mrs. Montifort."

"I don't understand. If you think I may be a weirdo, an impostor – God knows for what reason, but anyway – why don't you take me straight there? You'll see that I'm his wife immediately by his reaction."

"I believe you are Mrs. Montifort," he conceded.

He smiled, unsure whether he should pour a coffee or not. "But we have to go thru these checks – purely as a formality, you understand."

"I don't know anything anymore, Dr. Milsom. The only thing I know is that I thought my husband was dead and then two hours ago I found out that he's alive. I need to see my husband right away, doctor and you've got no right to stop me."

"I…um…have heard about your…recent troubles, Mrs. Montifort," he said softly. "Please, accept that I understand that this is very difficult…"

Milsom had, by now, seen the syndicated TV reports from Montana and, besides feeling aggrieved as he had realized that he had been hoodwinked by Paradiso, a shiver had ran down his spine as he had heard the name Montifort.

"Difficult?' You say 'difficult'. You don't know what I've been thru these last few days. I've been to hell and back."

"I do… sympathize, Mrs. Montifort."

Even as he uttered the word he realized how inadequate it sounded.

"Now, please allow me to see some identification and I will take you to see Trip right away?"

"Identification, identification. This is my I.D..." she stammered, her eyes streaming suddenly with long-suppressed hot tears, her mascara running down her cheeks.

She held out her wrists, sore and bruised still from being hurt by Sholtz.

Dr. Milsom took a sharp intake of breath.

"I do believe I read about it in the newspaper, but it said that you had lost your husband in the Twin Towers. At that time we hadn't yet ID'ed Trip so when I read your name, of course, it didn't mean anything to me. Now, of course, I can understand why you may have thought that your husband was..."

"I called him – the office, his cell phone... I assumed that he was dead and then the siege..."

She blurted this out, her tears relentless now, her shoulders quaking with the raw recollection of that most terrible night and with the incredible relief that she had suddenly felt rush over her, a couple of hours previously – that her loving husband, the man she had traveled over two thousand miles to get away from and then whom she had found once again, out there in the Montana wilderness, was still alive.

She dried her eyes.

"Come on, Mrs. Montifort. It's time to see Trip. He's already asking for you."

She finished dabbing her face with a Kleenex and gave herself a cursory inspection with a make-up mirror. It was not so crucial what she looked like, she admonished herself, thru panda-eyes and smeared lip-liner. Trip was waiting.

"How long has he been out of the coma?" Desi asked, as they walked to the elevator.

"Three hours...and he was asking for you and the twins from the very first," Milsom answered, giving himself a metaphorical pat on the back for having deduced from the Johansson Signatures that it would be approximately lunchtime when his patient came round.

"Twins? What are you talking about? What twins?" she exclaimed between floors, the force of her vocal ejaculation catching Milsom by surprise.

He went white.

The shiny steel doors opened; they were barely one minute's walk from Trip's room.

It was incredible, Milsom thought, the way in which Trip had seemingly returned to normal so quickly. It was as if he had just stepped out of a commercial for Medicare — all pressed pj's and beaming smile. The doctor would run the usual MRI scans the next day, but, on a superficial level at least, it seemed as if Trip Montifort had made a full mental recovery. Milsom, at one stage, had idly imagined that Trip might well break into a song, so happy and refreshed did he seem, especially when asking about his family and being reassured that all would be well.

For three hours now he had been attended full-time by Nurse Sheryl Baker and the word on the wards was that he was sitting up and making jokes with her and the other nurses who invariably popped in to see their famous patient on some pretext or other. It was only after two hours, with still no impending sign of his wife or family, that he had started getting suspicious that he was being kept in the dark about events pertaining to him and his nearest and dearest.

"Trip's looking forward to seeing you and the twins," Milsom repeated at length.

He had stopped moving now, was looking deep into her smudged eyes, searching for a legitimacy that he did not now expect would be forthcoming and one which would preclude the need for him to call security. There were just so many wackos in this town. It was impossible to take anyone at face value anymore.

"I don't know what you're talking about. I really don't. I'm here to see my husband. We have no *chi*ldren."

She stressed the first syllable of the last word as if the doctor should be left in no doubt that she abhorred the whole concept of maternity.

"But your 'husband' said that you have twin ten-year-old girls," he re-stated.

He could feel the situation rapidly becoming surreal.

She could not be Mrs. Trip Montifort; either that or the man awaiting her arrival was no more Trip Montifort than he, himself – and if he was not, then who the hell was he?

"Please, in light of this, I have to insist upon seeing some positive ID," he said with all the stentorian gravity that he could muster.

He was ready to call security; yet still, as from the moment that he first met her, the primary instinct that he could not help but want, even now, to cling to, was that she was genuine.

His legs, however, had turned to Jell-O. He had been looking forward to the case raising his profile among the medical fraternity, to Melissa looking at him once again with that proud, admiring look of old. Now he could suddenly envisage the hospital governors hauling him over the coals because of his rash biometric identification, his neurological peers writing him off as a joke, as yesterday's man.

All bets were off, and yet, in no small part, his expertise and experience had been responsible for a man's almost miraculous recovery in only six days. Possibly, he thought, he would now never receive any credit for this, overshadowed, as it was, by all the negative connotations of the case.

"Doctor, I came here to see my husband. I did not think I would have to present identification papers. Or do we live in a police state now?"

"I can't let you in – not without you having some proof that you are who you say you are," he rejoindered.

He called after a nurse who had just walked past.

"Nurse, please call security, if you don't mind. Tell them to meet me here."

She nodded and skipped down the corridor to find a phone.

"Who are you?" he said unguardedly. "Are you another weirdo like all the rest?"

"I'm Mrs. Desdemona Montifort," she said, calmly now.

She had been thru so much that she was somehow inured now to the trivial inefficiencies of ordinary life. Sholtz had forever cauterized the nerve-endings of her sensitivity to minor inconvenience.

"And Trip is my husband; I swear on my daughters' lives, so help…"

She halted mid-sentence, clasping her forehead with her elegant fingers.

Milsom stared at her and remembered the stomach-churning newspaper story that he had skim-read only that morning over an orange juice and muffin.

The security guard arrived in the elevator.

"What can I do for you, doc?" he asked.

"Nothing right now," Milsom said.

She had turned ashen gray. He took her by the hand and gently led her along the corridor and into the ward.

"Nurse, I need a chair – PDQ!" he said sternly, almost having to hold her up now. "This lady is feeling faint."

The young nurse retrieved a stray seat from another room and returned. She assisted Dr. Milsom in lowering the woman.

"Thank you, nurse. Now could you get a glass of water for the lady?"

Desi was by now seated with her eyes closed and her head tilted back at an acute angle; both hands were supporting her lovely head, rosebud lips pressed together in an approximation of an air kiss.

"What's wrong with her?" the nurse asked quietly, giving Milsom the glass. "She looks kinda funny, doctor."

"She's been thru a nightmare, actually two nightmares. She's suffering from post-traumatic amnesia."

"Who is she?" the nurse asked, looking on curiously at the woman hyperventilating.

"You'll find out soon enough, nurse," he responded, enigmatically. "Get me a pillowcase. Quickly, if you please."

She went to an empty bed and swiftly returned. He held it over Desi's mouth.

A few seconds later, a man in a hospital dressing gown came rushing into the ward.

"What's happening, Desi, darling? What's wrong with her, doc?"

"Trip, she'll be fine. She's just hyperventilating. She'll be fine in a minute," Milsom answered, without stopping attending to his new patient. "You go back to bed. You need every ounce of rest you can get at the moment."

"I'm fine, doc. I feel great," he said with feeling, looking all the while at his beautiful wife, inhaling and exhaling into a pink pillowslip. "I knew Desi was here. I was lying there and all of a sudden I just kinda knew she was here... I just knew it! Tell me the truth doc, what's going on?"

"Please return to bed, Trip. You don't want a relapse, do you? Everything's under control here. She'll come and see you just as soon as she's breathing normally. Go on, Trip."

Milsom chided him to return to his bed, but to no avail. He was, in fact, so relieved that there was to be a happy ending that he could not bring himself to be too clinically officious. He was also, not that this amounted to a hill of beans in the context of his euphoria, personally off the hook. His mired career would be shot into the fame-game stratosphere after all — mostly though he was just jubilant to be present at this touching and unusual reunion, the culmination of all of his skill, his tendering, his prayers.

"Desi, my beautiful Desdemona, I'm here. I'm all right," Trip stuttered unsurely into the obscured face of his wife. "I love you, darling. I'll love you forever. I'm okay! I'll never let you leave my side again. Thank God you've come back to me safe and sound, darling."

The nurse, still on standby with the water, knew now what she was witnessing; she too had devoured the newspapers for the story, watched the TV news with almost too salacious   an appetite.

She coughed, involuntarily, as she realized with a start the irony of his last sentence – he did not know what had happened to her. He had only been back in the land of the living for a few short hours – he did not know. They would not have told him so soon; perhaps it was not their place to intervene at all? Let them enjoy their being reunited – let her find the words to tell him in her own good time.

"Darling, what happened to you? Is it the shock of my waking up? Did you leave the girls with Madeleine?"

He loved her more than life itself – knew that he would be completely without compass without her. He had had that awareness reinforced these last newly minted waking hours when joy had turned to frustration and frustration to suspicion.

If Desi was not at his side, then his prosperous life was transformed into mere subsistence. She was the sine qua non of his happiness and she always would be – she and the girls, those beautiful daughters whom they both doted on and who had made their happiness finally replete beyond all imagining. Until she had wanted more…that something extra in her life that he could not comprehend and which, he was not even certain, Desi, for all her angst, did either.

He hadn't yet seen his wife's lovely face unshaded or unanimated by heavy breathing but his memory of her exquisite features was as vivid and fresh as his recall of those last seconds of consciousness in the WTC.

Slowly, gradually, Desi's breathing became stabilized and her head came forward, her mussed eyes straining to meet those of the man whom had just professed such undying love for her, the man whom she had come to see and to help repair – the man whom she loved more than anything else in the world ...besides her children, of course – children that even now she could not quite place in the overall scheme of her life, not quite remember what their sure-to-be chocolate box pretty little faces looked like.

Her head was oscillating still, even as it leveled up and as she seized eye contact with the man in front of her, this good-looking man who loved her beyond reason. Suddenly there was havoc at the double doors entrance to the ward and everyone turned to see what was happening.

"Sorry, doc, I couldn't hold them," shouted the security guard.

"What's going down, Professor?" screamed Marcus Paradiso.

A ragbag of journalists, all pushing and shoving to enter the ward, closely followed the man from Seattle. Milsom recognized the majority of faces from the press conference but many others, drawn to the hospital by the links with the Dupree development, now in the public domain, had swelled their numbers.

Reporters rely not only on CNN or Reuters or the likes of Karen Taylor for their information but on their own internal grapevine and nose for a story; it was thus here. No one wanted to let her rest on her laurels, for all that she had enjoyed a substantial head start. This saga had everything and no news organization wished to be playing catch-up, no self-respecting newsman or woman wanted to be left out in the cold.

As elbows flayed and cameras fizzed in the chaos that was now the fifth floor, all vying for pole position as they were, there was a cacophony of different voices and accents that effectively prevented any single one from being distinguished by the strange little group: a beautiful yet apparently neurotic woman, a pretty young nurse, a central-casting doctor in a white coat and last but not least a handsome man in pajamas and a purple robe, his head swathed in bandages.

As if in answer to the tacit prayers and frenzied pleas of the media fraternity Trip Montifort took Desi in his arms and kissed her full on the lips for a number of seconds. She reciprocated with passion and then their congress, which concluded almost three weeks of separation that had taken its indescribably cruel and heavy toll, trailed off into a lengthy hug which made their marriage somehow real and true and pure once more.

"I love you, Trip, darling," she whispered confidentially into his ear, then kissed him demurely on the neck.

Furry boon mikes from all angles strained to pick up the words which would soon seal ten thousand news broadcasts around the world and determine a million prevaricating couples to take the plunge forthwith, so perfectly romantic was the moment, so effective was it as an advertisement for love and the institution of marriage.

The hardened hacks looked on mesmerized and in total silence. Each was thinking that they wished Desi and Trip Montifort well after all that they had been thru – each however knew very well that the commercial diktats of their profession meant that it would, likely as not, be the unwavering media attention over the ensuing weeks which would indubitably pose the most potent foe to their happiness.

Although each knew, by now, enough of the Montiforts' stories to write a feature piece or record a five minute segment to camera, there were still a lot of loose ends which needed tidying up. None of the reporters present wished to break ranks at this juncture by assuming that the husband knew anything about his wife's trials out West.

Often reporters are pilloried for their incursions into people's personal lives; less often do we praise them for the dull self-editing and integrity that often runs tandem with the worst excesses of invasive journalism.

This was a story that seemed to be in a constant state of fluidity and none of them wished to pre-empt the next step in the couple's refamiliarization process and thereby become a resented part of the story itself. A good reporter should not engineer a story for the sake of copy, but wait and honestly report the next quantum shift in developments when it happens. By doing anything else they would be devaluing the news. Eventually people would come to lose all respect for it and they would stop watching, reading, listening. This was the conventional wisdom and for once the line held.

In this scenario they all knew that it was only a matter of time before Trip found out about events in Montana. It ill-behoved any one of them however to jump the gun and raise the specter of Sholtz at this juncture. The story, as it was, was so good that tinkering with people's lives was not only unjustifiable ethically but really, simply not necessary, commercially. Even as things stood, nobody present could tear themselves away from watching the reunion.

"Darling, how are you? You must have been so worried?"

"I honestly thought I'd lost you, Trip."

"You look fantastic."

"I look terrible. I know I do. But thanks."

They came together once again in a heartstring-tugging clinch.

"Where are Sophie and Lara? I can't wait to see them, darling."

On this cue as Desi's mouth opened for a moment and then shut, like a beautiful guppy, and her forehead was creased by an uncomprehending frown, Dr. Milsom grabbed Trip's arm and took him to one side.

"Please give us a moment and some privacy please," he said in a brusque timbre to the assembled throng – a tone that brooked no contradiction.

Trip looked back at his wife with pathos in his eyes as he saw for the first time that she was not fully compos mentis. Her watched her sit on the chair again as if the names of her daughters had affected her sense of balance – in fact the mere mention by Trip of the twins' names had knocked her literally off her stiletto heels and one could almost perceive a million confused synapses fire off in her befuddled cortex.

Trip looked at the doctor once they had withdrawn to a confidential distance, his eyes, just now bright and full of hope and love, now however hinting at a suddenly contracted dark desperation of the soul.

"Doctor, what's up with the kids? Tell me what it is? Tell me, doc?"

He pulled the doctor's lapels.

He towered over him, if not cerebrally then certainly physique-wise.

"Is that why Desi's been hyperventilating, doc?" he shouted.

Thirty-six pencils started scribbling into notebooks; flashguns started up again. Milsom looked down with calm equanimity at the burly hands firmly fixed on his clinician's jacket. He called over to the security guard who had long since given up the fight to keep the news teams out and had been watching with rapt fascination along with everybody else.

"Call reinforcements, man. This is a hospital for Christ's sake. Get some of your damn colleagues up here to clear the ward."

The security guard got on his radio and muttered something to the control room.

Milsom turned his attention to Mr. Montifort.

"Look, Trip, there's something you should realize…"

"What? What is it, doc? You've gotta tell me…"

"It's your wife."

"What, what is it?" he stammered.

"Tell me – did you notice your wife looks a bit… how should I put this… diplomatically? …A little disengaged?"

"You mean 'a bit spaced out' doc? Sure I noticed. After what she's been thru this last week, it's hardly surprising, is it, doc? She must have been to hell and back worrying about me."

"It's not just that, Trip. She's suffering from post-traumatic amnesia. I noticed before, when I asked her about the twins. I didn't know what to make of her at that point but then I saw that she had all the classic symptoms."

"You mean the hyperventilating…"

300

"Yes, indeed. That – and dilation of the pupils; feeling faint. More seriously though, long-term memory loss is evident… You see, Trip, she's going to need all your support and the proper professional care over the next few months in order that she can make a full recovery."

"Is that why she never mentioned the kids straight off? I thought that was strange…"

"Actually, Trip, she claimed that you never had any children…"

"Christ, no wonder she came over all faint when I mentioned the twins. Will she be all right, doc?"

"With understanding from her family and the right clinical expertise, she should be fine," Dr. Milsom assured him, utilizing his best bedside manner.

"Oh my God! Where the hell are the kids, then, doc?"

"Are you feeling strong, Trip?" Milsom enquired. "I don't so much mean physically as mentally."

"Sure, I feel A1, doc!" he replied without thinking.

"I can't stress enough, Trip – you're going to have to be there for Desdemona. She's been thru a helluva lot. Something happened to her in Montana while you were comatose. I'll let her tell you, herself, but Desi will require lots of patience and sensitivity. It's not going to be easy. Here's my card. Feel free, Trip, to call me at any time for advice… or even if you just wish to talk."

"I've had all I can take of this, Milsom. I'm her husband for God's sake. Why can't you tell me what happened to her out West?"

"It's not my place to tell you, Mr. Montifort and you're not exactly in a fit mental state at the moment to be told, anyway. You've only just come out of a six-day coma

301

yourself. I'm sorry. I'm sure that Desi would want to explain to you, herself, in her own time."

"For crying out loud, just tell me where my kids are, Dr. Milsom?"

"They're safe, Trip, and for today that's surely all that matters."

Milsom had heard the news from the seminary. He had read the newspaper and had turned on the television in his office and caught Karen Taylor's dispatch. It was the talk of the hospital. Indeed, of those present, only Trip and Desdemona were completely unaware of what had occurred.

Three other security guards had by now been pressed into duty. They were busily taken up with forcibly shooing the press out of the ward and into the elevator. The paunchy middle-aged guards were however heavily outnumbered and therefore reliant on the goodwill of the people whom they were trying to evict. They went about their business in a style rather more akin to well-fed sheepdogs than lean, mean doormen.

Paradiso entered the elevator as part of the first tranche. He was going to make his way over to the seminary building to see what he could discover. It seemed that the sassy female TV reporter had got first run on him. All of his colleagues were talking about her recent newscast. He cursed his preoccupation with Sholtz Senior which had meant he had missed the new developments, but more so the professional savvy of Ms. Taylor which had degraded him from Leader of the Pack to also-ran.

Notwithstanding all this, however, the story had suddenly got a whole lot juicier and so it was with some optimism that he could turn around his fortunes that he alighted at the first floor.

As he called his producer to see if she could arrange a broadcast team to meet him at the seminary, he saw a policeman and two pretty young blonde girls approach reception.

"What floor is Trip Montifort on?" Lieutenant Meyerson asked.

"Fifth, sir. Can I help you?"

"No, I've just got something from Lost and Found for him. May we go on up?"

"I'm sure that will be all right, officer," the receptionist replied, smiling confidentially at the two girls who did not reciprocate but stared back hollow-eyed.

She had seen the news on the TV. She recognized Meyerson and it did not take a genius to therefore deduce that the twins were Trip's.

She crossed herself. The receptionist felt light-headed with the drama of the day already and now hopefully there was going to be a no doubt tearful but happy ending to that poor family's uniquely unhappy week.

'Unhappy' – that was surely the grossest understatement of her life, she reflected, forlornly. This case had touched her beyond measure – had touched the whole city, country, world. She looked at the gaunt faces of the girls, their eyes dead and inexpressive. She wondered at what indignities they had been put thru, whether they would ever be able to be just normal little girls again. Her eyes misted with tears for this family that she did not know. She hoped and prayed that they would be all right – at the end of this week, when from behind her all too unhermetically sealed desk, she had seen so much misery, so much human pain.

"God bless you, girls!" she shouted after them, as the elevator doors closed.

She discerned a heartbreakingly slight flicker of distant recognition in one of the girls' faces and was rewarded by a slight half-smile in the other's.

"Thank you," Meyerson replied in his strong Queens accent.

Paradiso stared at the steel elevator doors. If he could double-back then maybe he could possibly rectify things by witnessing the touching reunion and at least shoot off a frame or two – maybe even snatch a word with Trip or even one of the tragic daughters.

"Don't even think about it, fella," a behemoth of a security guard told him firmly in a gruff voice. "You're not going no place but out," he added with an open-handed gesticulation towards the main exit.

There was no doubt at all now.

It was definitely not his day.

Happy are those who obey the Lord,
Your work will provide for your needs;
You will be happy and prosperous.
Your wife will be like a fruitful vine in your home,
And your children will be like young olive trees round
Your table who live by his commands.

(Psalm 128)

Chapter XXVII

It was the fall of 2002. The rich tapestry of life had inexorably moved on. Afghanistan was no longer the lair of Osama Bin Laden. Saddam Hussein was solidly fixed in the crosshairs of Rumsfeld and Cheney.

The bronze and gold patination of the trees in the New England livery yard spoke of a world one remove from international tensions in a nation come to terms with self again, a reimbued sense of the United States' historical destiny stalking this great land.

One year on from the avalanche of newsprint, the tsunami of VT and CD and DVD chronicling the Montifort family across all of its debilitating victimization by fate, the world had at last had its fill of their singular plight. Their's had been a story which had awakened in Americans a poignant sense of sympathy and at the same time had, it seemed, held up a mirror to society of what insanities can and do take place under the aegis of the leading democracy on Earth.

It had been a year – an extremely tortuous year for this beleaguered family – during which they had each been strained to the outermost limits of mental fortitude and familial cohesion. They had however fought their personal battles, even the children – in a less self-aware way than their parents, perhaps – day-by-day, week-by-week. Progress back to normality was incremental; three out of the four had seemingly seen off the potential for long term psychological harm and had been able to consign the memory files of that catastrophic week to their mental recycle bins.

For Desi, however, it had been a year in which her interred hurt had been ever-increasingly revealed, ever more painful for her husband and daughters to have to witness. The memory loss which had seen all knowledge of her beautiful twin daughters excised, as if by scalpel from her frontal lobe, had been the major trial for her family – especially Sophie and Lara for whom the effective loss of their mother's natural feeling was almost harder to bear than their own recurring flashbacks to the nightmare of Dupree and his perverted proclivities.

When in the hospital the children had suddenly appeared, Lieutenant Meyerson at their side, Trip had yelled with unrestrained joy, sprinting to embrace them, kissing each adoringly and then picking each up in turn and hugging them as if his very life depended on it. Tears of relief had flooded down his face.

Cameras had whirred and flashed, reporters had raced into lyrical notation. The emotion was almost tangible in the air, smiles endemic, tears the norm – even amongst the hardened hacks that had had to repulse the best intentions of the security staff to enable them to capture the scene for posterity.

Milsom could not contain himself and stood watching the moving reunion with a handkerchief pressed against the bridge of his nose. After a minute Trip had ushered a beaming Sophie and Lara over to the still, fragile figure of his wife who had been watching the scene with apparent detachment in her eyes.

She had scooped the girls up together in her arms and kissed them one after the other on the cheek. Nevertheless it was obvious to all spectators, all of the professional voyeurs, that there was no depth of feeling conveyed, no dammed-up maternal outpouring evident in her demeanor. It was as if she was doing by rote what she knew was expected of her – for the sake of her kith and kin, the assembled media, the millions watching the telecast live. The cameras did not capture the inimitable lustrous purity of a mother. Desi's face was not the radiant, emotionally charged epitome of love and happiness that Mr. and Mrs. America demanded. She had valiantly gone thru the motions, knowing with every particle of her being that she had mislaid a whole promontory of memory, of life, of feelings – and there was damn all she could do other than try to carry off the pretence, the white lie – for Sophie, for Lara, for Trip himself. In the event her acting was consummate – all things considered – but she could not bring to her part the subtle nuances that ensured complete suspension of disbelief.

* * * * * *

Dr. Milsom arrived in his new Mercedes Coupe, wheels crunching satisfyingly on the gravel drive. He walked over to the paddock and saw Trip and the girls standing by the white rail.

"Hi, Trip," he said, smiling, clapping him on the back.

"Hey, doc!" he returned, putting out his right hand in greeting.

"Hello, girls! How are you doing?" Milsom continued, foraging in his briefcase and pulling out two identically wrapped presents.

"We're all right, sir," Lara responded hesitantly, looking up with wide saucer eyes at this man whom she could not quite remember.

"Girls, this is Dr. Milsom. I told you he was coming to see us, didn't I? Say 'hello' to the doctor, Lara."

"Hello, Dr. Milsom," Lara said, putting out her hand for him to shake.

He bent slightly and handed her one of the dolls.

"This is for you, Lara," he said.

"Thank you very much."

"Sophie?" Trip said the name of his eldest with a rising intonation.

"Nice to meet you again, Dr. Milsom," she told him self-consciously.

They shook hands. He proffered the other package – she accepted it with a wonderful smile.

"Thank you very much, Dr. Milsom."

"You're both very welcome," he said, smiling, looking around – enjoying the Indian summer sunshine, the fact that they all looked so very well.

A striking white horse was being ridden on a long lead in the enclosure. He raised his hand and waved.

The rider momentarily took her left hand off the reins and returned the compliment. The instructor rebuked her mildly.

"Don't get too casual up there, Desi. You'll be riding bareback next!"

He was rewarded with a radiant smile. The instructor knew that she was the best pupil he had ever had. She was a natural horsewoman. She also looked magnificent up there, chestnut locks glinting in the autumnal light in free-flowing contrast to the darker mane of the beautiful Arabian mare.

She had made great strides in confidence around the horses since Dr. Milsom had recommended equine therapy as a way of rebuilding her sense of self-identity. It was a form of cognitive behavior therapy that seemed to work on a deeper level and was often highly effective.

The horse is a very sensitive creature which seems to be able to sense the emotional temperature of every human who comes into its orbit and by his or her behavior seems to be able to transmit empathy to those suffering inside. Whatever the psychiatric rationale, the course seemed to be working excellently for Mrs. Desdemona Montifort. She had a regular three-hour session with the horses and from the start her whole spirit, which had seemed so negated by the black clouds of depression in the weeks and months of the aftermath, had seemed to lift markedly. Gradually, so the theory went, as she became more centered psychologically, then so her long-term memory should begin to return. That which had been blotted out by the mind as a defense mechanism, in order all the more to concentrate on its own precarious situation, would, in the window of opportunity afforded by this newfound sense of well-being, start coming back.

"Okay, we'll call it a day then," the instructor shouted.

Desi brought the horse to a gentle halt and dismounted elegantly. She patted the mare on the neck and the beautiful animal nuzzled into her, braying amiably. The instructor took the reins from Desi and she jogged, beaming, over to Trip and the girls, kissing each in turn.

"Looks like you're enjoying yourself with the horses," Dr. Milsom commented.

"I absolutely love it, doctor," she replied, throwing her arms around him in a hug which spoke eloquently of her gratitude for all that he had done for her family, for herself.

"And your memory? Trip says things are a lot better now..." the neurologist asked quietly as they disengaged.

"Every day it gets better. I even remembered the girls' teacher's name from last year. Thank you, doctor, for... everything."

"Don't mention it. I'm just glad to see you all looking so great. By the way, Trip, I've got a little surprise for you in the Merc."

"Oh yeah, doc. I'm intrigued," he responded, grinning.

"Let's all walk over to the car, shall we," he prompted, directing the little party with a flourish of his palm.

When they rounded the corner of the stables a figure emerged from the front passenger seat.

Trip's face instantly lit up and the two figures ran to each other and embraced, looked at each other, tears instantaneously rising up in both men, and clasped each other once again.

"How ya doing, Davey Boy?" the man said, an involuntary and affecting vibrato in his voice.

"It's been too long, Rosario. It's great to see you – you're looking fine," Trip gushed, an emotional catch in his tone as well, as he addressed this man who had rescued him from the apocalypse.

The remainder of the family group and Dr. Milsom looked on contentedly as the two men, forever bonded by the intertwining of their two so separate, so different lives at that one point in time, renewed acquaintance.

As the sun skulked behind the serried ranks of alto-cumulus cloud and the watery light made the sandstone outbuildings resonate with an almost ethereal pink glow, Desdemona's cell phone rang its latest electronic jingle.

"Hello," she answered casually.

"Hello, Mrs. Desdemona Montifort?" the caller enquired formally.

"Yes it is," Desi replied, raising her crescent eyebrows at her husband in an expression of bemused curiosity – as one is inclined to do when the caller is unknown.

"Please wait a second, Mrs. Montifort...I have the President of the United States on another line. I'll just transfer you..."

"Who is this?...Hello?...Hello?...This is not funny...I'm going to hang up..."

"Please don't do that, Mrs. Montifort. I've had three people do that already today and one of them was the President of France. Sorry – I didn't say 'hello'. Hello, this is George W. Bush for real, Mrs. Montifort. How 're you doing?"

Desi waved her free hand in a pulsating motion to Trip. Her eyes became wide with pleasure and her mouth gaped open. Everyone looked at her in consternation. Her glossy lips pursed and opened as if to formulate a word, then closed, unbidden, again. She had recognized the President's Texan drawl at once and now nerves had got the better of her vocal cords. The roof of her mouth was suddenly as dry as the dirt that she stood on. Desi swallowed hard and her forehead creased into a frown of concentration – it was a full five seconds before she regained her composure and could speak.

"Yes, Mr. President...I'm doing okay. Thank you for taking the trouble to enquire..."

Everybody present, excepting the twins, clapped their hands to their mouth or their chin in theatrical astonishment. Sophie and Lara looked up for a moment but then continued playing happily with their new Barbies.

"Well I'm very pleased to hear that, very pleased indeed...and Trip...how is he? And your lovely daughters, of course, Mrs. Montifort?"

"Yes, Mr. President, they're all doing great...we all are, thanks. Thanks for calling. I...I...I sure do appreciate it, Mr. President."

By now the three men had closed around her, heads cocked at uncomfortable angles, each straining to hear even a smidgen of the presidential voice thru the earpiece.

"Mrs. Montifort, Laura and I would like to invite you and your family to the White House for Thanksgiving dinner. It won't be a big affair – just your family and mine. I wonder, would that be all right with you or have you made any prior arrangements?"

"Mr. President," Desi began at length, a sudden self-assured light in her eyes like she had not had in over twelve months. "I'm sorry but we have made plans actually for Thanksgiving...but please thank the First Lady and of course yourself for wishing to invite us. Thank you very much, Mr. President."

Trip, Dr. Milsom and Rosario all looked totally dumbfounded at her negative response.

"Not at all. Well you all look after yourselves, won't you, Mrs. Montifort. The whole country wishes you and your family well. All Americans' best wishes will always be with you and your heroic family."

"Thank you, Mr. President. Thank you."

"Goodbye then, Mrs. Montifort."

"Goodbye, Mr. President."

Desi replaced the cell in her purse and called out, "Sophie, Lara."

Then she sank into Trip's arms and their beautiful twins wrapped themselves around their parents' waists – it was as if they did not have to be told that a watershed in their mother's emotional life had just been reached and passed. That somehow things would work out and they would be all right once again – would become once more a normal happy family and the traumas of the past year would be as naught compared to their courage in facing their bright futures.

After a while Lara spoke up in a soprano voice vibrant with the innocence of unsullied childhood and replete with simple love.

"Mummy, why can't we have Thanksgiving at the White House?" she trilled.

Desi looked at her daughters and then at Rosario and at Dr. Milsom.

"That's because, Lara darling, we're inviting Rosario and his family and Dr. Milsom and his family for Thanksgiving this year," she replied with an expansive wave in their direction.

The two men's visages instantly glowed their happy assent to the plan whilst Lara and Sophie's eyes lit up in unison.

"Cool!" they announced cheerily as they went back to playing with their dolls and everyone – but everyone – laughed.

* * * * * *

In the Oval Office, the President was naturally disappointed. On the other hand he could understand that his family who had endured so much may just want a quiet Thanksgiving at home. He could not begin to imagine the traumas that that family had been thru this last year.

There were many families across the world who likewise had suffered much in the last year – many families which had been bereaved. The Bali bomb had just taken the lives of many young people. Al-Qaeda had been behind that too. It was a miserable world sometimes and yet it was also fantastic and rich and good.

Could he, in all conscience, take the sons and daughters of America to war again, he asked himself? What about the children of Iraq? – Iraq, the cradle of civilization! – Iraq, the Babylon of yore, a cultural and scientific powerhouse a thousand years before Alexander the Great!

These thoughts weighed heavily on his mind. And what if he did nothing…? That would surely be giving Saddam carte blanche to continue with his belligerence and his international mischief-making? Where would that all end, especially if he continued to stockpile biological and chemical weapons? Sometimes one has to take a stand.

He picked up his bible and turned to page 557. He began to silently read his favorite psalm, Psalm 23:

About the author: Johnny Richards is 41. He lives in Hove, East Sussex. This is his first novel.

The author would love to receive any comments from his readers on this book. Please email Johnny@damagerendered.wanadoo.co.uk